CONSTABLE THROUGH THE MEADOW

A perfect feel-good read from one of
Britain's best-loved authors

Constable Nick Mystery Book 8

NICHOLAS RHEA

JOFFE BOOKS

Revised edition 2020
Joffe Books, London
www.joffebooks.com

© Nicholas Rhea
First published in Great Britain 1988

This book is a work of fiction. Names, characters, businesses, organisations, places and events are either the product of the author's imagination or are used fictitiously. Any resemblance to actual persons, living or dead, events or locales is entirely coincidental. The spelling used is British English except where fidelity to the author's rendering of accent or dialect supersedes this. The right of Nicholas Rhea to be identified as author of this work has been asserted by him in accordance with the Copyright, Designs and Patents Act 1988.

Cover credit: Colin Williamson
www.colinwilliamsonprints.com

ISBN 978-1-78931-415-1

CHAPTER 1

> Meadows trim with daisies pied,
> Shallow brooks and rivers wide.
> *L'Allegro,* JOHN MILTON, 1608—74

For the rural police constable going about his daily routine, this is more than a poetic image; sights of this kind are a pleasant part of country life and the constable's patrols take him through a whole galaxy of meadows, sometimes along major roads, sometimes along narrow lanes and occasionally by little-used bridleways, green lanes or tortuous footpaths with centuries of history beneath them.

On the edge of the moors where I used to patrol, some of the fields are divided by rippling brooks which we call becks or gills, other boundaries are marked by the sturdy drystone walls of the region, and some make use of hedgerows or even timber-and-wire fencing. There are spacious flat fields used for the growth of cereals or the nourishment of herds of milk-producing cows, and tiny patches of grass which have the appearance of being artificially created from the heather or bracken of a wild moorland hillside.

Some of the meadows adjacent to the moorland are almost too small to be considered fields or meadows, perhaps being better described as paddocks. One local name is intake because they have been cultivated after being securely walled from the wilderness of pervading heather, but they continue to provide a refuge for a few hens or moorland sheep, even a cow or horse.

Those on the edge of the moors usually contain a patch of smooth, short grass with very few flowers because the black-faced sheep of this region continually nibble at it until they produce a surface which is as smooth as a prize lawn. In the dales below, however, the meadows are more lush; on the fertile earth, they thrive upon the natural goodness which has accumulated over the years. They feature as parts of a beautiful green carpet decorated with profuse and colourful vegetation; in the spring and summer they are a delight, and in the winter they sleep unmolested.

There were times when I patrolled beside meadows filled with butterflies and bees busily exploring a bewildering range of blossoming wild flowers. Clovers and vetches patterned the greenery with tiny dots of colour and in the changing seasons I noted celandines, red poppies, sorrel, a variety of thistles, pretty red campions, cow parsley, buttercups, daisies and more besides, sometimes with a charming border of wild roses or honeysuckle along the carefully trimmed hedgerows.

In the late spring or early summer, before haytime, the meadows are rich with a multitude of pretty grasses and I learned there are about a hundred and fifty varieties in this country, our farmers knowing which will produce the best nourishment for their grazing livestock, or which are most suited for transformation into hay and silage. I discovered that after the grass has been cut for haymaking, the coarse grass which follows is called fog by some Yorkshire farmers.

'By yon fog's leeaking well,' a moorland farmer noted one morning. I looked for the familiar wispy clouds in the valley and wondered why he had made this comment on a clear sunny morning, but was later to learn he was speaking of the grass in a recently mown hayfield. I believe there was an old Scandinavian word 'fogg' meaning a limp type of grass.

In addition to this form of fog, there is a variety of grass called Yorkshire Fog which is most attractive and very widespread throughout Britain and Europe. Growing up to two feet in height, it has a soft green/grey stem and when it flowers in the summer, it produces a most delightful pink and white hue which turns to purple as the long days of summer edge towards another autumn.

Whatever their functions, these meadows and the highways and byways that knit them together like a huge patchwork quilt are an echo of history. Many of the fields which today support livestock or produce crops have been fulfilling this role for centuries, altering their functions and appearance to keep pace with the requirements of good husbandry. The changing techniques of farming and the increasing use of large agricultural machines mean that the size, shape and uses of our fields must alter to keep pace.

Some of us grumble about the removal of hedges with all the consequent upheaval among the wild life that depends upon them, but we may not appreciate that this results from the desperate need to feed the expanding human race by making the best use of modern machinery.

We grumble about the disappearance of footpaths or the use of chemicals, the removal of small copses or the way new roads and buildings encroach upon the natural landscape. We may not like these changes, but they are part of the moving pattern of the landscape which has been occurring since man first cultivated the land and made the countryside his home.

History has noted the fields existed more than 3,500 years ago; there were fields in medieval times, fields born from the enclosures of the eighteenth and nineteenth centuries, and the extensive but controversial fields of modern times.

Throughout history, the countryman has loved the fields which surround his home, so much so that they have been given names. For the village policeman going about his daily business, it was necessary to know these names because they cropped up in his work. They were just as important as other place-names in and around the village and I was soon familiar with names like Hundred Acre, Highside, Beckside, Rough Edge, Stoney Heights, Back Lane, Maypole Hill, The Bottoms, Low Leys, Croft End, The Carrs, Hagg End, Manor Intake, Hob Hole, Castle Lands, Hawthorn Leys, Lucy Ings and others.

Some of these names are self-explanatory, and others are widely used to describe the nature of a field. For example, a carr or The Carrs refers to an area of heavy, rough marshy ground which is not close to the moors, often being used in connection with a low-lying area.

Ings is another word for a pasture with these features — many local ings are covered with water and there is a fine example at Fairburn Ings, a modern haven for wildlife close to the Al near Ferrybridge in West Yorkshire. A ley is a rich arable field which has been put down to grass, while an intake of the kind mentioned earlier is generally a patch of land which has been re-claimed from the moor. In our local dialect the word is often abbreviated to intak. Of some curiosity interest is the prefix Lucy, as in Lucy Ings mentioned above. This word is spoken and written in different ways such as Lousey Lane, Lowsey Ings, Lucy Field and so forth. It is nothing to do with a girl called Lucy nor does it mean lousy (as in awful); it comes from an old word meaning pigsty, one derivation of which is loosey. So Lousey Lane, Lowsey Ings or Lucy Field refer to places where pigs were once kept.

Another interesting word is neuk; it means the corner or angle of a field and is perhaps more widely known as nook, as in nooks and crannies. This also appears in some locations such as Cocquet Nook or Blew Neuk, both being place-names on the North York Moors.

During my patrols, I was frequently traversing the heights of the moors from which magnificent vantage points were available. Time and time again, it was possible to park my police motorcycle and sit astride it as I gazed across the panoramic landscape below.

The fields and meadows decorated the countryside in a manner which has become so much a part of the English country scene, and from these lofty positions I could only wonder at the range of colours, shapes and locations. From a distance and from a height, those meadows were truly a gigantic patchwork quilt, but in the course of their history, they had witnessed a thousand stories, ancient and modern. They had seen more changes and innovations than we might hope to recall, and many of them remained stubbornly silent about their experiences. Some, however, did contain relics of earthworks, old tumuli, bygone settlements and even Roman remains, and from these sources the history of our district could be told.

Sometimes, at the crack of dawn, I would sit upon my police motorcycle and gaze in wonder at the illusion of history before me and, later, I came to realise that my own duty was somehow reflected by changing circumstances of those meadows. Just as they appeared in many shapes and sizes, so did the duties I was bound to perform. Large tasks and little tasks, major incidents and minor jobs all came my way, and just as the meadows changed during the year, so did my work. It was altering all the time, with constant innovations forcing changes upon the entire police service, changes which eventually filtered down to my level. In a lifetime, those meadows would evolve beyond all present recognition but in spite of that, they would remain English meadows.

My work would be transformed too, but an underlying feature was that it would always be police work, albeit of a very special kind. Whatever variations were wrought upon society and upon the police service, the vital ground-level work of the constable would continue. With an air of permanence that can be under-estimated, those meadows and the British police constable will modify and be modified to accommodate society's needs.

I had arrived at Aidensfield just as the era of the pedal-cycling village constable was ending; I enjoyed the swift transportation offered by a little Francis Barnett two-stroke motorcycle, even if that transportation was tainted with the need to cater for the British climate. To perform a patrol, however short, I had to smother myself in oily waterproofs and if I visited anyone's house, I had to stand outside lest the oil from the bike or water from the road caused damage to the home. Carrying papers and documents was fraught with danger and there were immense difficulties in conducting a roadside interview in pouring rain.

But, in many ways, I did enjoy my motorcycle patrols. The power of freedom and the rush of fresh air combined to give a tremendous feeling of elation and I like to think this open-air life kept me healthy and free from colds. But change was on the horizon.

One day in early summer, I was informed that I was to be issued with a mini-van.

It would replace the motorcycle I used for my patrol work and at first I welcomed the news. A four-wheeled vehicle with a roof and comfortable seats would be so much better for my duties; I'd be able to carry equipment, forms and circulars and it would in all respects be a great improvement upon the motorbike. But there was one snag. I had to share the van with the constable on the neighbouring beat whose house was seven miles away. If the authorities could not appreciate the problems this would create, then I could. The chief snag would be the possibility that the little van would be miles away when I required it urgently. I might be marooned with no official transport. When a constable lives on official premises as I did, he must be expected to cope with any emergency that occurs, even during off-duty periods. And there would be complications in making the change-over at the end or the beginning of each shift whether it was then in my possession or the possession of a colleague. On paper, it seemed a feasible idea; in practice, I knew it would generate problems. But the police service, always a Cinderella when it comes to local authority expenditure, could not afford to supply every rural constable with a van.

Its arrival, however, signalled another change in the methods of patrolling a policeman's rural patch. Instead of being on duty twenty-four hours a day, the village bobby would now work in shifts of eight hours, sharing his beat with other constables and performing duties away from his own beat.

It meant that I must now patrol an expanded area, albeit for only eight hours a day, but my work would thus become more formalised and regimented. I would have to work shifts to accommodate the changing work pattern because, in order to ensure a full twenty-four hour cover every day of the year, the system requires about five officers. Three are needed every day to span the twenty-four hours in eight-hour shifts; to cater for days off, sickness, courses, holidays, court appearances and other absences, expected or unexpected, extra officers must be available. And so, with the stroke of a pen and the gift of a van, the policing of Aidensfield changed. I would be expected to patrol other parts of the district, while constables from afar would be invading my patch.

I did not welcome this; I would far rather have been fully responsible for the Aidensfield beat for twenty-four hours a day, and allowed to work at my own discretion. But it was not to be; progress had arrived and it could not be halted.

On the day the van was to be issued, I had to drive my little motorcycle over the hills to Police Headquarters. This was its last trip as a police motorcycle and it was rather sad; quite unexpectedly, I felt a twinge of sorrow at its departure and was tempted to try and buy it. But official wheels had already started to turn, and the Francis Barnett was to be sold, along with other redundant motorcycles, to the dealer who had won the contract to supply the vans. The outdated bikes were therefore part-exchanged for up-to-date transport in the shape of little grey vans.

Having said a rather emotional farewell to my bike, I relinquished my protective clothing, crash helmet and gauntlets and handed over the bike's log-book to the admin department of our Road Traffic Division. Thus I severed all links with my motorcycle. I was shown to my new van which stood among rows of others awaiting their drivers; each was gleaming in the morning sunshine and they were all alike. There seemed to be hundreds of them, all in symmetrical rows with their bonnets facing east, but there were probably about fifty! Each was a brand-new Morris mini-van clad in a pleasing grey livery; this surprised me. I had expected black or navy blue, but it seemed the service was moving away from its past stereotype colours. Furthermore, none of the vans bore police signs, the only visible link with the service being the blue lamp perched in the centre of each roof. Inside the cab, however, there was a police radio set plus an official log-book for recording dates, times and distances of journeys, petrol issues, oil consumption and the name of each driver. There was a tool kit, a spare wheel and nothing else.

The rear of each little van was completely bare and empty; the ridged metal floor had no covering and there were no shelves or compartments for storage or for conveying the paraphernalia of constabulary duty. In truth, that empty rear compartment was of very limited value; no one (except a child) could sit there although I did note the huge battery strapped down near one of the rear-wheel arches.

This had replaced the original car battery because of the additional power required for the radio which would be functioning virtually round the clock, and for activating the flashing blue light should it ever be required. After a short course of instruction about operating the mini-van, the radio and the blue light, and a lecture about the need to regularly clean the vehicle inside and out, to rigidly abide by servicing dates and oil changes, to enter details in the log immediately upon completion of each journey and to report any fault however minor, I was allowed to leave.

It was at this point that another problem faced me and countless other constables. It was a simple problem — police officers are among the largest of people and mini-vans are among the smallest of motor vehicles. Getting some officers into those driving-seats was rather like a size 6 foot being squeezed into a size four-and-a-half shoe. Not being as tall or as broad as some, I found that I could get into the driving seat and, with the seat pushed back to its maximum, I could operate the foot pedals and hand controls. But I could not wear a cap while driving. Even though we wore peaked caps and not helmets, I now knew the purpose of that empty rear part — it was to carry the caps of constables at the wheel, even if they were liable to rattle around in that empty bare area. Once inside, however, I started the engine, listened to the crackle of the tiny exhaust and switched on the official radio. Having booked on the air, I found first gear, noted the fuel tank was full and set a course for Aidensfield.

On the journey home, I gained impressions of my cap bouncing around in the rear, of me bouncing around in the front and the little van *et al* bouncing across the moors. I was later to learn that passengers in mini cars are nervously aware of this bouncing motion because their rumps hover dangerously near to the road surface while the suspension of the vehicle gives the overall feeling of riding in a high-speed motorised trampoline. But we made it.

During that half-hour trip, I learned to drive with my head slightly bowed to avoid crowning myself on the roof, and managed to manipulate the miniature pedals by judicious use of my police boots. Sometimes, however, the expanse which formed the soles of my boots made me strike two pedals at the same time, but protests from the mini rapidly corrected that fault. The simultaneous operation of a brake, clutch or accelerator is enough to confuse the cleverest of transmission systems and the mini had the sense to protest loudly and actively at this abuse.

Once at home, the children were delighted. Tiny as they were, they thought it was my personal van and so I let them sit in the back; for them, the experience was wonderful and they squeaked with delight as they tumbled and rolled about the bare metal floor. Lots of little faces peered out of the rear windows like miniature prisoners in a miniature Black Maria, and more squeals of delight occurred when one of them tweaked the switch of the rotating blue light which flashed and reflected brightly in the windows of the house.

They spent a few minutes playing in the van, sometimes listening to the burble of voices that muttered eternally from the official radio and sometimes pretending to drive it to an accompaniment of suitable brum-brums and pip-pips. It was a moment of fun in a vehicle that had a very official function to perform. After a coffee, I rang Sergeant Blaketon to announce my return to Aidensfield with the van and he ordered me to drive to Ashfordly Police Station so that he could formally inspect this newest of acquisitions. Before leaving, I made sure the children hadn't left anything in the van, because Oscar Blaketon was not the sort of person to appreciate a child's desperate need to play 'going to Nanna's' in Daddy's new police car.

I parked it outside the square brick-built police station at Ashfordly and entered; Sergeant Blaketon was writing something at the front desk and actually smiled at my arrival.

'All correct, Rhea?' he asked; this was his way of saying 'Hello.'

'All correct, Sergeant,' I chanted the ritual response.

'The section's new vehicle functioning all right, is it?' he continued. 'No breakdowns, mechanical defects, malfunctioning of equipment, unnecessary rattles, squeaks or groans? Damage or wear and tear? Punctures or oil leaks?'

'No, it seems to go very well,' I said. 'Good acceleration, the braking seems OK and it corners very well. I didn't hit anything on the way here either,' I added.

'You're to share it with other beat men, Rhea,' his face never cracked at my veiled sarcasm, for his smile was now stored away for use at a future time. 'That van does not belong to Aidensfield beat, you appreciate?'

'Yes, I know that, Sergeant.' I was now behind the counter and had removed my cap. I had some report writing to complete, and this seemed the ideal opportunity to do it on the office typewriter. 'You wanted to see the van?'

It is imperative that this instruction is obeyed. Failure will be considered a disciplinary offence.

'Members will, repeat will, ensure that the vehicle is driven courteously at all times and that drivers set an example to the public by the high standard of their driving.

'Members will not, repeat not, consume food or drink within the vehicle.

'Members will, repeat will, at all times be correctly dressed when using the vehicle. Caps will, repeat will, be worn, tunics will be fastened correctly and ties will be knotted. When meeting a senior officer of or above the rank of inspector, members will emerge from the vehicle before saluting.

'Members will not, repeat not, carry unauthorised members of the public, friends or family in the vehicle, unless their presence is necessary in the performance of their duty, e.g., upon arrest or other emergency.

'Members will, repeat will, ensure that ashtrays are emptied regularly and that the vehicle is thoroughly cleansed inside and out at the conclusion of every tour of duty, unless the exigencies of the service prevent otherwise. In these circumstances, a report will be submitted to explain those exigencies'.

Having written out his instructions, he handed them to me and as I began transferring them to paper, he went outside to examine the van. He spent some minutes and I saw him stooping to examine the tyres and to seek evidence of any damage, however minor, that might be present. He looked inside, checked the radio for its effectiveness and the ashtray for residue, looking into the log-book and then lifted the bonnet. He dipped the oil and spent some minutes tugging at plug leads and checking internal engine matters. Next he tested all the lights, the flashing indicators, the windscreen wipers and washers and even the interior light.

Then he took it for a brief drive around the block, and, satisfied that it was absolutely correct, took out his own pocket-book and made a note to that effect. Woe betide an officer who might suggest the vehicle had been delivered with a fault.

'In a moment, Rhea. I'm busy compiling a set of instructions right now,' he said, 'You'll have to familiarise yourself with them, so you might as well type them out for me. Copies to all users of the van, copy for the office notice-board, copy for Divisional HQ, and a copy to be stuck inside the van's log-book. All to note and sign as having read and digested the said instructions.'

I knew Blaketon's obsession for detail and his practice of committing his orders to writing; I could visualise the contents of his order. I was not disappointed when he presented his neat handwritten work for me to type. After identifying the vehicle by its registration number and the call sign of the radio set, he listed a host of 'dos' and 'don'ts.'

These included the following:

'Members will, repeat will, maintain the vehicle in a roadworthy condition. Under no circumstances will road traffic laws and regulations be infringed. Members will therefore inspect the van before and after each journey.

'Members will, repeat will, inspect for defects such as faulty lights, worn tyres, defective windscreen wipers, brakes and steering, and any other fault, mechanical or otherwise, which might infringe either the Road Traffic Acts or the Construction and Use Regulations. The van will not, repeat not, be driven upon a road if it is in such a condition that statutory provisions are infringed.

'It will be the responsibility of drivers to thoroughly check the roadworthiness of the van; responsibility will be deemed to devolve upon the person driving it when such a fault develops. It will therefore be in the interests of all members to check the vehicle meticulously before taking it on the road. Any defects or damage then discovered will, repeat will, be reported immediately.

'Members will, repeat will, ensure that the vehicle is filled with petrol at the conclusion of every tour of duty, and that the oil, water and tyre pressures are checked, and if necessary, replenished. Details will, repeat will, be entered in the log-book, and in the pocket books of the officers concerned.

Blaketon's record showed that it was in perfect order upon arrival, therefore any faults which developed would be the responsibility of the driver at the time. I knew that we must all treat the van as if it were our very own and I also knew that some officers, upon damaging an official vehicle (even accidentally) would not mention the matter, hoping that a subsequent driver would be careless enough not to check the vehicle before taking it out. Thus blame or responsibility could be avoided and the unwary innocent saddled with another's sins. We all knew the value of being ultra-cautious in such matters.

I completed Blaketon's piece of typing and made no comment as I passed it to him for signature. By the time I had finished my own work, copies had been signed and one was prominent upon the office notice-board.

'So the van's yours for today and tomorrow, Rhea?' he said.

'Yes, Sergeant.' After studying the duty sheets, I understood the arrangements.

'So when you knock off duty tomorrow night, at ten, you will deliver it to Falconbridge beat?'

'Yes, Sergeant.'

'Make sure it's filled with petrol,' he said. I nodded.

'Shall I book off duty late then, or will PC Clough come on duty early?' I asked.

'I don't follow your logic, Rhea.'

Knowing his attitude for precise timing, I said, 'If I arrive at PC Clough's house at 10pm to hand over the van, and he then drives me home, I will not be able to book off duty until 10.20pm or thereabouts. I will be in uniform, in an official vehicle, with an officer who is on duty. So I will be on duty, won't I? And this will happen every time the van is handed over. One of us will have to work extra time either before our shift or after it. Shall we all claim overtime for the hand-overs, Sergeant?'

He looked at me steadily, his dark eyes never showing any emotion . . . . .

'Rhea,' he said, 'a constable is never off duty.'

'So if the van is involved in a traffic accident as I am being taken home, and I am injured, will I be able to claim that I was injured on duty? It makes a huge difference if there is a question of compensation or an entitlement to an ill-health pension, Sergeant.'

He knew I was right, and I guessed this aspect had never occurred to him, or to those who had dreamt up the system of change-overs in this way. He was thinking rapidly, mentally assessing the enormous legal complications which could accrue from any incident which might happen within those disputed few minutes.

'I will ask the Superintendent to authorise half an hour's extra duty for at least one of the officers involved in every change-over,' he said. 'I will ask for it to be included on your overtime card and to be taken off when duty commitments allow.'

'Thank you, Sergeant,' he knew, and I knew, that this matter had to be determined right from the outset; minor though it appeared on the surface, there could be immense ramifications which might affect the officer or his family if something went wrong during those contentious few minutes. For an officer to be killed or injured when on duty differed hugely from one killed or injured when off duty.

The next problem, unforeseen by Sergeant Blaketon, occurred when the Superintendent visited me at the beginning of one of my tours of duty. The little van was parked on the hard-standing in front of my police house and the Superintendent parked behind it, awaiting my emergence from the house. He did not come to the office which adjoined but preferred to wait outside to see if I was late on duty; that's how some senior officers operated. But I had seen the arrival of his black car and went outside prompt on the stroke of two o'clock. I was to perform an afternoon shift from 2pm until 10pm and had custody of the van because PC Clough of Falconbridge was enjoying a rest-day.

As I emerged, therefore, I slung up a smart salute and smiled as the Superintendent clambered from his car.

'Now, Rhea,' he said. 'Anything to report?'

I updated him on events which had occurred on my beat over the past few days and he nodded approval at the way I had dealt with them. Then he turned his attention to the mini-van and asked my opinion upon its suitability.

I enthused over it but refrained from mentioning the handover complications. Sergeant Blaketon would have seen to that — it was a matter of internal politics.

Then the Superintendent began, 'I came past your house last night, Rhea, around midnight.'

'I finished at ten last night, sir. Same hours as today.'

'Yes, I know. And when I drove past, I saw the van standing there, on the hard-standing.'

'Yes, sir.'

'It was not in the garage, Rhea. There is a garage at your police house, and I would have expected you to garage the van there, for security and safety.'

'It's a private garage, sir, my car's using it.'

'The official motorcycle used it, Rhea.'

'There was plenty of room for both, sir, I could park the bike alongside the car. That garage was added to the house long before official cars and motorbikes were issued. Garages adjoining rural-beat houses have always been used for the officer's private car.'

'Then I feel the practice must cease, Rhea. Now that you have the official use of a van, the van must surely take precedence over your private vehicle.'

I noticed that he did not directly order me to garage the van nor was I ordered to remove my car. I felt there was scope for manoeuvre which in turn suggested there was some official doubt about the rights of the occupants of police houses. After all, the police house was my home but unlike some civilian tenancies, there was no rental agreement. A police officer simply moved in and out when instructed and obeyed orders if there was a dispute. I knew of no order which dealt with the current matter and the only condition of occupancy that came to mind was that I could not take in lodgers without permission!

As I pondered the Superintendent's remarks, I realised that if I was unreasonable in my attitude, he might post me to a less-than-pleasant urban area, and I felt sure there was scope for discussion or flexibility.

'You are responsible for the care of the van while it is in your possession,' he reminded me. 'It is a police vehicle and it does contain valuable police equipment, such as a radio. The van and contents are your responsibility, Rhea.'

'Yes, sir,' was all I said. I understood the import of his remarks.

'It will not be resting at your house every night,' he reasoned and I saw a twinkle in his eye. 'Others will be making regular use of it and it will be used for night shifts, so I think a little common sense will sort out this dilemma, don't you, Rhea?'

'Yes, sir,' I agreed.

And so it was. My private car continued to occupy the garage at my police house, and from time to time, I would give the mini a treat by placing it inside for the night. Then I discovered that if I parked the mini on the front lawn, it was obscured from the road by the privet hedge. Neither the Superintendent nor Sergeant Blaketon was in the habit of coming into the house or office, preferring to wait outside at the other side of that tall, thick hedge. And if they could not see into my garden, then neither could potential breakers-in of police vans . . .

Common sense did prevail and no one grumbled about the van's open-air life.

The van, its other drivers and I soon settled into a trouble-free working routine and we had no problems; indeed, the little vehicle proved its worth over and over again. Its tiny engine and small size coped with the large constables it had to carry, and the steep hills of this dramatic part of Yorkshire. It was most useful for carrying assorted objects and for protecting us from the English weather, thus enabling constabulary duties to be performed with far greater ease than hitherto. But on one occasion when I was surreptitiously carrying a load of rather doubtful legality, I found myself face to face with the redoubtable Sergeant Blaketon.

It happened around 10 o'clock one Wednesday morning.

I was working a day shift from 9am until 5pm, a rare treat. Such routines are few in a police officer's life and I was looking forward to the evening off. At 9am, therefore, I began work in the office which adjoined the house and by 9.45am was ready to begin my patrol.

Just as I was leaving, my wife, Mary, rushed in.

'Oh, thank heaven I caught you!' she panted. 'The car won't start.'

An immediate problem was presented, for it was Mary's turn to convey seven or eight children to the village playschool. Elizabeth, our eldest, had started playschool and thoroughly enjoyed it, and the mums worked on a rota system, each taking their turn to tour the nearby farms and cottages to collect pre-school-age youngsters. It was an important part of village life, a bonus for the children and a welcome tonic for the mums.

I had a quick look at our car and decided the battery was flat; it had been causing problems in recent weeks and I had never got around to replacing it. Now I had no choice and would obtain a battery today, but first, we had pressing commitments to keep. Those youngsters and their mums would be awaiting collection at farm gates, isolated spots and remote cottages.

'I'm going out on patrol,' I said. 'I'll collect them. Give me a list.'

And so, armed with a list of children's names and addresses, I set about this mission. Most of the mums saw nothing odd in their local constable collecting their offspring in a police van, while the children thought it was marvellous. Squatting on the cold, hard metal floor, they pretended they were chasing robbers as they listened to the dour voice from the police radio. They blew the horn and Elizabeth showed them how to flash the blue light, as a result of which we flashed the light at every halt to announce our arrival. By the time I returned to Aidensfield, the rear of the van, and the front passenger seat, were full of small, noisy but excited children. I had lost count of the number on board, but they seemed so happy at this change in their routine.

They babbled and chattered, made police siren noises, caught robbers, arrested thieves, chased speeders, battered my brain with questions, and generally created something of a party atmosphere in the back of the little van. The bouncing didn't seem to bother them, for in their minds, they were keen police officers engaged upon a matter of grave importance. I've no idea how many villains we arrested on that trip, but I reckon each child caught several and tonight they would recount their experiences to their dads. As a public relations exercise it was marvellous and as a means of getting those children to school it was a success.

But the noise they generated within the confines of the van was colossal and I was pleased I was not a playschool teacher having to tolerate it for longer periods. On the last lap, I turned into Aidensfield and was about to drive down the lane to the house which hosted the school, when I saw the tall, severe figure of Sergeant Blaketon standing on the corner of the road. My heart sank. Of all the people to meet this morning of all mornings . . . I thought of his instructions about using the van, about unauthorised passengers, about disciplinary proceedings, about the law on overloading, about insecure loads . . .

I had probably broken several laws on my goodwill mission.

I could not avoid him. I eased to a halt before him, flushing furiously as I anticipated his wrath. I switched off the engine and climbed out, my mind full of excuses, reasons, apologies . . .

'It was urgent . . .' I began.

But he ignored me and thrust his head inside the van and I heard him say, 'Now then, what's going on in there?'

There was an instant babble of juvenile response; I heard tiny voices shouting at him about catching robbers and poachers and making people drive better and then, after asking more questions and generally joining in the chit-chat, he emerged.

'Is this the village bus service, Rhea?' he asked me.

'Er, no, Sergeant, you see . . . well . . . they're going to playschool . . . er . . . the car taking them wouldn't start, you see, so they were stuck . . . I . . . well . . .'

'Got a Public Service Vehicle operator's licence, have you?' was his next question. 'Know about seating requirements in vehicles, do you? Safety of passengers?'

'Er, well, Sergeant,' I started. 'It was an emergency

'So all you lot have been arrested, have you?' he poked his head inside again.

'Ye . . . e . . . e . . . s . . .' came the sing-song response. He emerged, smiling with joy.

'Nice one, Rhea. Creating goodwill with the public and making the kids happy, eh? All right, carry on.'

And so I did.

I learned afterwards that the playschool teacher had asked them to draw a police van and, without exception, they had included Sergeant's Blaketon's big smiling face.

CHAPTER 2

> Our deeds still travel with us from afar.
> And what we have been makes us what we are.
> GEORGE ELIOT, 1819—80

Patrolling in the warmth and comfort of the mini-van was heavenly after the inconvenience of the motorcycle and I think it is fair to say that one adverse effect was to make us rather lazy. When using the motorcycle, particularly during chilly weather, it was sensible to walk as much as possible, if only to keep warm. But that exercise was unnecessary with the mini-van. We were cosseted in an all-embracing warmth from which, especially in the chill of a long night, we were unwilling to emerge. This tended to make us drive where we should have walked; we took the van around all manner of unlikely places, roaming behind buildings, through factory premises, into farmyards, along narrow alleys and over fields, all of which were the kind of places we should have walked in our efforts to prevent and detect crime.

Our supervisory officers and our own consciences told us it was not a good thing to spend so much time sitting in a van, that exercise was necessary for continuing good health and that foot patrols were a vital part of the constable's crime-preventing and public relations repertoire. Each of us appreciated such precepts and although we began our patrols with those aims uppermost in our minds, they soon evaporated once we settled into the cosy routine of heated and motorised patrolling.

We learned, for example, the best places to park in order to shine either the van's headlights or our own torch beams upon vulnerable windows and doors; we located places in which the van could be concealed for a short nap, a tasty but forbidden sandwich or sip of coffee from a flask. We knew where to hide from Sergeant Blaketon or which unmapped track offered the best short-cut through the lush and scented meadows of Ryedale.

It was a bout of idleness of this kind which led me into a spot of bother one night. It happened like this. Tucked in the centre of my beat, well away from urban civilisation, was a derelict airfield. The nearest village was Stovensby, a tiny collection of pretty stone houses on a gently rising street, and everyone knew this patch of cracked concrete and unsightly old huts as Stovensby Airfield even though no aircraft had used it since the end of World War II. Leading from the village into one corner of the airfield was a narrow, unmade lane, across which someone had, years ago, erected a gate.

As time passed, however, that gate had fallen into disrepair which meant that courting couples, trespassers and all manner of other inquisitive folk ventured on to the airfield from time to time, perhaps to steal bits and pieces from the derelict buildings or perhaps to conceal themselves in the old ruins so that their love-making was kept a secret from prying eyes, as well as from suspicious husbands, wives and neighbours.

Squatters, tramps, down-and-outs and persons on the run from life, from HM Forces, from the police or from their families would sometimes hide here too.

The area covered by the old airfield was huge; remnants of the Air Traffic Control Tower remained, as did buildings which had been station headquarters, squadron offices, hangars, sleeping accommodation, etc. Many of them were windowless, some were roofless and none had been officially occupied or used for almost a quarter of a century. In the broad light of day, the airfield reeked of dereliction and decay, although the old runways themselves were in fairly good order. They were like huge modern highways which crossed and re-crossed this patch of Ryedale and they had survived surprisingly well without any formal maintenance. The area between them comprised overgrown grass, weeds and scrubland, although some of the fertile areas had been leased to a local farmer who managed to grow wheat there.

No one seemed quite sure who owned the airfield; perhaps the Air Ministry had forgotten it was there, perhaps someone had purchased it years ago and had no idea what to do with it . . . I never knew. What I did know, however, was that the deserted runways were regularly used by learner drivers, by young men who fancied themselves as racing motorists, by teenage motorcyclists who roared about the place doing crazy things with their moving machines such as wheelies or headstands on the saddles, and even by pedal-cyclists who organised time trials and races around the perimeter track.

The old notices saying 'Trespassers will be Prosecuted' or 'Air Ministry Property — Keep Off' had fallen down and although there could have been a question of illegal use, it was not the job of the civilian police to enforce any such rules. We knew that the public, rightly or wrongly, made use of the old airfield and we did not raise any formal objection because we knew where many of the youngsters got to. They were safe here, far better using this enclosed area for racing or showing off than attempting their doubtful skills on the open road.

So we closed our 'official' eyes to the many trespassers although, at night, we did make routine patrols through the airfield, checking for possible lawbreakers who might dump stolen cars here, steal bits from the buildings, cause damage or perform a host of other illegal acts. Children on the run from school or home were another aspect of our searches, as were depressed folks who wanted to be left alone with their thoughts, or even to commit suicide.

One night in early May, I was performing an all-night duty, having started at 10pm. I booked myself on duty from home by ringing Eltering Police Station at 10pm and asked for any routine messages. I was given a list of unsolved crimes committed locally during the day, plus details of a car which had been stolen from Scarborough. It was a Ford Consul, five years old and a dark green colour, and it had been stolen from outside the Spa before eight that evening.

According to the police at Eltering, a villager from Stovensby had telephoned at quarter to ten to report a car with blazing lights repeatedly circling the old airfield at high speed. There was just a possibility that it was the missing vehicle in the hands of joy-riders, as other cars stolen from the coast had been found abandoned here.

I was therefore asked to check out this report.

It was a foul night with pouring rain and lingering mist as I arrived in Stovensby village. The time would be around 10.20pm and the late spring dusk had matured into a heavy darkness due to the weather. I drove the little van down to the fallen gate which marked the entrance to the airfield, the windscreen wipers having trouble coping with the teeming rain. I extinguished the van lights as I peered through the gloom, hoping to catch sight of roving car lights somewhere in that vast expanse of misery and darkness. I saw none, so maybe my own approaching lights had alerted the thieves? Perhaps they'd gone? Perhaps it was just a local lad having a fling around the place in his own car? Maybe it was thieves who had run for shelter and were hiding in one of the many disused buildings? The lights could have been anything or anyone, harmless or potentially harmful.

I waited for five or ten minutes; there was no sign of activity on that airfield, not a hint, not a light. But if a car had been seen earlier — and not all that much earlier — then a full search would have to be made.

To make a proper search, I should really walk; I should take a torch although, strictly speaking, I should make a search in complete darkness so as to surprise the villains in possession of the stolen property. In the darkness, I could creep up on them . . . But, I reasoned, if they were in a car, they could escape simply by driving off and I would be marooned in the middle of the airfield with no car, no radio and no chance of catching them. I reckoned that if I circled the airfield in the mini-van, shining my lights into and behind all the old buildings, I might flush out the thieves. Then I could give chase, and my radio would allow me to summon any necessary aid. That seemed a far better idea.

So I switched on my lights, crossed through that tumbledown gate and found myself driving along the glistening wet concrete of an old wartime runway. The rain, the mist and the darkness made driving very difficult, and without a detailed knowledge of the layout of the airfield, I really had no idea where I was heading. My only hope was to pick out the buildings one by one and then scan them in my headlights. If I did detect anything or anyone suspicious, then a more detailed search could follow.

With the excitement of the chase making my heart pound just a little faster, I located the first of the buildings and drove towards it; it was an old hangar, vast and empty in the darkness so I drove right inside, did a sweeping turn in the mini and watched as the beams explored every corner.

Old oil drums littered the floor, a few rats scuttled off at my intrusion and there was an old settee against the far wall, but it was otherwise deserted. I moved to the next location, another hangar similarly deserted. As I searched each building, the radio in the van burbled into life and I recognised my own call sign.

'Echo Seven,' it said. 'Location please.'

Every half-hour, our Control Room sought our location in this manner, then plotted our movements on a map so the most conveniently-positioned vehicle could be directed to any incident. It was also a means of checking our individual safety; if we failed to respond, we might be in trouble.

'Echo Seven' I spoke into the mouthpiece. 'Stovensby Airfield.'

'Received. Echo Nine?' the next car was requested.

As locations were sought from every mobile on duty, I continued my search. Sometimes, I walked in the light of those headlamps, sometimes I drove around a block or behind the more remote buildings, but I did make sure that every possible hiding place was examined. As I progressed, I found it was becoming more difficult to see the buildings ahead; the rain and mist obscured them and so I found myself having to drive at a crawling pace in the gloom. From time to time I'd leave the van with its engine running and lights blazing as I fought my way through the thickening mist to a building with a difficult access.

I must have searched every conceivable nook and cranny without finding anything remotely suspicious, by which time I had decided that no stolen car was hidden there. There was nothing and no one lurking on that deserted airfield. Of that, I was positive.

I radioed Control. 'Echo Seven,' I announced. 'Have completed search of Stovensby Airfield for reported stolen vehicle from Scarborough. No trace. Am resuming patrol. Over.'

'Received Echo 7. Control out.'

With the windscreen wipers assailing the tumbling rain, and the dense fog now blanketing the entire airfield, I screwed my eyes against the white screen outside. While I had been busily searching the buildings, the fog had dramatically intensified and now I could barely see the runway ahead of me. I could not determine the edges of the concrete . . . I moved to one side, swerving to catch a glimpse of the runway's extremities. I failed. The twin beams cut into the fog like two long shafts of solid light, but they did not penetrate it. The light simply reflected back at me. I was moving at less than walking pace now, my head out of the window hoping to see where I was heading . . .

But I was hopelessly lost. I'd lost all contact with the buildings which had, to some extent, broken the fog's density and I was encircled by a thick white blanket of dripping clinging mist. I was somewhere inside a dark fog-bound wilderness and had lost all sense of direction.

I found myself fighting the onset of panic; I knew that I was only a few miles from home and from civilisation, but at the same time, could not find the route which led off this old airfield. It was almost like being trapped, like driving through a black, unlit tunnel and into a massive blockade of cotton wool; the mist was so thick that it had become a wall of brilliant white through which nothing could apparently pass. Although I was still driving, I had no impression of movement or distance for I could see nothing but the reflected glow of my headlights. I was upon a featureless plain and the headlights would not even pick out the surface of the runway. I had no idea whether I was in the middle, on the edge, doing a circuit of the perimeter track or simply driving around in circles on an expanse of featureless concrete. I have never been so helpless. It was like one of those nightmarish dreams that childhood worries can cause and there seemed no immediate relief.

I knew it would become easier in daylight, but dawn was hours away, and I felt such an idiot. I was lost within such a small patch of England . . . but I could not stay here all night. I had to find a way off, and so I kept moving. Once or twice, I ran off the edge of the runway, but fortunately the ground was solid enough to carry the weight of the mini-van, and after each mishap I managed to regain the solid surface. I had no idea how long I'd been looking for the exit until my call sign sounded from the radio.

'Echo Seven, location please,' asked the voice.

I must have been chugging around for nearly half an hour! I did a rapid mental calculation. If I failed to reply to this request, Control would think I was missing or injured, and a search would be established. And in this fog, more officers could get lost as they hunted for me! Furthermore, at the last 'locations' I'd already said that I was resuming patrol and if I now announced that I was lost in the airfield, I'd look a real idiot in the eyes of our Control Room staff.

Surely I would soon find the exit? I'd been going round in circles for ages, and must have covered miles, however slowly I'd been driving.

'Echo Seven, not receiving. Echo Seven, location please,' repeated the voice.

'Echo Seven,' I decided to pretend I was patrolling normally and made a guess about where I might have been if I'd emerged from the airfield. 'Echo Seven. A170, travelling east and approaching Brantsford. Over.'

'Received, Echo Seven. Echo Nine, your location please,' all cars were now being asked this question.

As the half-hourly ritual continued, I renewed my efforts to drive off the runway. Travelling at less than walking speed in the darkness, often with my head out of the window for better vision, I continued to search. But it was hopeless. By the time of the next 'locations' call, I was still on the airfield. But I daren't admit it.

When Control Room next asked Echo Seven for its location, I said, 'Echo Seven. Eltering towards Cattleby.'

'Received Echo Seven,' responded the voice. 'Echo Nine?'

And so it continued. I daren't halt the vehicle for any length of time in the fog to search on foot in case the battery could not cope with the demands upon it from the combined effects of the heater, radio and the lights; I did not feel inclined to switch off the lights in this ghastly silent world. So I continued to drive around; in any case, I wanted to find my way out! For each half-hour, therefore, I provided a fictitious location when asked, and when the time came for my refreshment break at 2am, I took a gamble.

We were supposed to take our refreshment breaks at police stations and not in our vehicles; I knew Ashfordly was unmanned at night and hoped no one would attempt to contact me there by telephone. So, when I would normally have broken my tour of duty for refreshments, I radioed to Control 'Echo Seven, refreshments Ashfordly. Over.'

'Received, Echo Seven.'

I halted in the gloom and had my break at the wheel, in contravention of Sergeant Blaketon's rule about not eating or drinking in the mini-van. I kept the engine running and the equipment and lights operating, for I needed light and heat, and then, after enjoying my sandwiches and flask of coffee, I decided to risk a brief exploration on foot. I'd leave the lights on and the engine running so that I could retrace the van. Perhaps this would help me find the exit?

With my hand torch, I tried to determine my whereabouts but failed. In whatever direction I walked, I found nothing but more featureless expanse of runway and the thickest fog I'd ever encountered. I daren't stray too far from the car either, in case I failed to re-locate it. And so, at 2.45am at the official termination of my break, I had no alternative but to recommence my circuits of the airfield.

'Echo Seven,' I introduced myself. 'Resuming patrol at Ashfordly, towards Gelderslack.'

'Received, Echo Seven,' acknowledged Control.

And so the second half of my shift began. The rain had ceased now, but the fog had not lifted and the darkness was just as intense, but I knew that before my knocking-off time at six o'clock, daylight would arrive. This would help me find a route off this awful place.

For the next two and a half hours or so, I continued to provide fictitious locations, listing places I would have visited during a normal night patrol. Happily, it was a very quiet night and I was never directed to any incident. And then, soon after I'd given my final location at 5.30am, the fog lifted. A gently breeze had risen as dawn was pushing the darkness aside, and I saw the distinct movement of the thick fog. Wisps began to float away and then, with remarkable speed, it began to disperse. In the daylight, I could now see the outline of some buildings and hazy roofs of the village on the edge of the airfield.

And I was less than a hundred yards from the exit!

I need hardly express the cheer that I felt as I drove out of that old gate, and with considerable relief, I made for home. According to the log-book which I had to complete, I had covered nearly forty miles around that airfield, a useful distance for a night patrol. My eyes were red-rimmed and sore with the strain of staring into that wall of fog, and I was mentally shattered.

I arrived home at six o'clock to find Sergeant Blaketon and PC Clough waiting for me. They were in Sergeant Blaketon's official car. Clough was to take the van out from 6am until 2pm, and on this occasion, Sergeant Blaketon had decided upon an early visit to both Ken Clough and myself. And he had undertaken to ferry my colleague to Aidensfield Police House to collect the van.

'Morning Rhea,' he said as I emerged, bleary-eyed and very anxious to get some sleep. 'All correct?'

'All correct, Sergeant,' I managed to say.

'The duty chap at Eltering said something about you searching for a stolen car on the old airfield?'

'Yes, Sergeant. I searched for it just after commencing my shift. It wasn't there.'

'You sure?'

'Yes, Sergeant!' I snapped the answer. 'I searched every possible place. The airfield was deserted.'

'Good, I thought you'd have done a thorough job.'

'Is there a problem?' I asked.

'It's just that Eltering Police Station got one or two calls during the night from residents at Stovensby. They reckoned cars were running round the airfield all night. They reported seeing lights and hearing engines in the fog. Eltering's sending a car to have a look in daylight — apparently, a road-traffic car attempted to investigate last night but turned back because of dense fog.'

'I've just come from there, Sergeant,' I decided to tell him. 'I did a final search myself, in daylight with the fog thinning. I saw nothing — that was only half an hour ago.'

'They must have imagined it, Rhea. So, nothing else to report, eh?'

'No, Sergeant,' I said with determination.

'Good, then sleep well,' and they left me.

It was a long, long time before I returned to Stovensby Airfield and I never ventured there during a fog!

Mind, there were times when I wondered how those wartime pilots had coped with these Stovensby pea-soupers. Perhaps they had never become airborne, pretending instead to fly upon long circuitous missions into enemy territory?

* * *

There was another occasion when a duty trip in the little van caused something of a headache, and again it involved a journey which would certainly have caused Sergeant Blaketon to consult his book of rules. Happily, he never learned of this particular mishap.

Like so many memorable incidents, this one happened through a chance conversation. I was on patrol in the mini-van with instructions to deliver a package to a member of the Police Committee who lived on the edge of my beat. The package had come from the Chief Constable via our internal mail system and I was the final courier in this postal routine. I think it contained a selection of local statistics and pamphlets required for a crime prevention seminar in which she was to be involved. She was out when I arrived, but I spotted a gardener at work in the grounds of her spacious home and he told me to leave the mail in the conservatory. She'd find it there, he assured me. He pointed me towards the door and then, eager for a moment's respite, asked me how my family and I were settling in. I did not know the man but saw this as yet another example of how the public knows the affairs of their village constable!

As I'd been at Aidensfield for a year or two by this time, I was able to say we were very happy and enjoying both the area and the work.

'Got the garden straight, have you?' he asked with real interest, and perhaps a little professional curiosity.

'Not really,' I had to admit. I love a well-tended garden which comprises vegetables, flowers and shrubs, but I never seemed to have the time to create the garden of my dreams. Mary, however, in spite of coping with four tiny children and a hectic domestic routine, did manage to spend some time tending the garden.

I told him all this and he smiled.

'Tell her not to be frightened to ask if she needs owt,' he offered. 'Cuttings, seeds, bedding plants, that sort o' thing.'

'Thanks, it's good of you,' I responded.

'Well, we've often a lot o' spare stuff and t'missus is happy to give bits and pieces to t'locals.' By 't'missus' he meant his employer. 'You've only to ask.'

It was at this point that I remembered Mary asking me to keep an eye open for horse manure during my patrols; she'd mentioned it some days ago and it had slipped my mind until now.

'That reminds me,' I said half apologetically, 'she did ask me to look out for some horse manure. That was ages ago.'

'Ah, we don't have any o' that,' he said. 'But there's plenty at Keldhead Stables. They can't get rid of it fast enough. It's free to take away. Just go along and help yourself.'

'They're the racing stables, aren't they?' I asked.

'Aye, they get some good winners from there if you're a betting man. Grand National, Cheltenham, Lincoln, Derby — they've won some big races. You can't go far wrong if you follow them — they've often winners at Stockton, Thirsk, Ripon, Beverley and Wetherby an' all. I don't mind admitting I've won a bob or two on 'em.'

'So their manure should make our rambling roses gallop along, eh?' I laughed. 'Thanks, if I'm ever out that way, I'll pop in.'

We chatted about other trivia then I moved on. Keldhead Stables was off my beat in another section and it was highly unlikely that I would be able to pop in during a duty patrol, so I made a mental note to tell Mary. Perhaps we'd make a special trip there on my day off.

Then, through one of those flukes of circumstance, I was directed there within a week of learning about their manure offer. It was a Saturday evening in late May and I was making a patrol from 5pm until 1am, being responsible for the entire section in my little van. Shortly after 7pm, I received instructions over my radio to proceed immediately to Keldhead Stables where a prowler had been sighted — by chance, I was the nearest mobile.

This was not uncommon — people did trespass upon the stables' premises, sometimes just out of curiosity or to see a famous winning horse in its home surrounds. The motives of some, however, were a little more suspect because, at some other stables, there had been attempts to dope horses which were favourites to win. Scares of this kind had led to increased security at all racing stables (and many existed in our area), consequently reports of such trespassers were fairly frequent.

I rushed towards Keldhead and drove into the stable yard. Waiting for me was J.J. Stern, the noted trainer, and his face bore clear signs of relief at my arrival. After a very brief chat, he pointed towards the stable block and said a lad had seen a man creeping furtively about. By now, something around half an hour had passed and I felt sure any visitor would have left, but I made a thorough initial search of the premises. Stern had already examined his horses without finding a fault and nothing appeared to have been damaged or stolen. With a stable lad in tow to guide me through the complex of buildings, I made a second very detailed examination. It took some time, but I found no one.

Afterwards, I detailed my actions to J.J. Stern and advised him that if other uninvited guests trespassed on his premises, he should take care to record a detailed description of the visitors, and to obtain the registration number of any suspect cars that were around. So many people fail to do this when they see a suspect car — a car number in these circumstances is vital to an investigation and can very swiftly help to trace the culprits.

He thanked me and said he would issue instructions to his staff to follow my advice. Then he asked if I'd like a coffee. It was at this point that I remembered Mary's wish for some manure — and at this very moment I was surrounded by a huge amount of surplus horse muck.

I hesitated to ask, but he had guessed I was about to make a request of some kind. He must be plagued with people asking for winning tips, but I was not seeking this kind of information . . .

He smiled as if not to discourage me.

'Er,' I began. 'While I'm here, I was told you had some horse manure to get rid of.'

'Manure? Tons of it! Want some, Mr Rhea?'

'I wouldn't mind some, not a lot . . . I'll pay,' I offered. 'I can help myself . . .'

'Nonsense. It's free to any good home! We just want shot of it. Look, you've earned a coffee for your advice, so come into the office and I'll get young Christine to pop some in your van. Are the rear doors open?'

'I'll unlock them,' I said, and I did, leaving them standing open.

In the office, he picked up the intercom telephone, dialled an extension and a girl answered.

'Christine,' he said. 'There's a police van in the yard. Pop some manure in the back, will you? The doors are open.'

She agreed and he replaced the phone. 'She's new here,' he said. 'Only sixteen, but she's mad on horses. It's only her first week, so it'll do her good to see what goes on.'

He organised a cup of coffee, asking if I would like a touch of Scotch with it, but as I was on duty and driving, I declined the latter offer. The coffee would be fine.

We chatted for about quarter of an hour, him telling me about his life in horse racing, and me trying to explain a little about the work of a rural constable. He was a charming man, I decided.

Just as I stood up to depart, his telephone rang so I excused myself and left him to deal with his caller. When I got outside, the van doors were closed and there was no sign of Christine; I had never even seen the girl and could not even thank her for her trouble.

But when I opened the driver's door, I was horrified. The stench that met me was appalling, and as I stared into the rear compartment, I saw that it was full of hot, fresh horse manure. It was neatly spread across the width and along the length of the back of the van.

She had filled every space, but she had not bagged it; she had simply shovelled muck into the back of the van, as a farmer would have shovelled muck into a cart. I could have died on the spot. What on earth could I do?

I thought fast, closing the door to shut off some of the stink; if I returned to complain to J.J. Stern, he'd probably fire the girl . . . and it would look as if I was rejecting his generosity . . . I decided to drive away.

Gingerly, therefore, I climbed into the malodorous interior, already feeling itchy as flies were buzzing around, and began the trip home. The weight in the rear was enormous and it affected the steering, making it dangerously light as I took to the winding lanes to avoid being seen.

I opened all the windows and found that the flow of fresh air did keep some of the powerful pong at bay, but it was a terrible journey. My uniform and hair would reek of the stuff when I emerged.

After radioing Control to say I had searched Keldhead Stables but had found no intruder, I decided to sneak home and remove the muck. But on the way, I got a call to a road traffic accident about two miles from Aidensfield. Groaning, I could not avoid this duty; happily, it was not serious and no one was hurt. A farm lorry and an old Ford Cortina had collided on a junction near Briggsby, but the lorry had been carrying farm manure too, several tons of it. Due to the accident, it had been catapulted from the lorry and had almost smothered the car and peppered both drivers.

The Cortina, a battered old vehicle, had been carrying a drum of waste oil on the back seat. The oil drum had overturned inside the car, resulting in a terrible mess to both the car and its driver. The fulsome smell surrounding this scenario was dreadful, so much so that the contribution made by my uniform and van was of no consequence. After dealing with the accident and arranging for the load, the vehicles and the mess to be removed, I chugged home.

There is no need to explain the effects of this combination of events upon my person and upon the little van, save to say that Mary and I spent the next three hours frantically trying to remove the muck and then attempting to rid the van of the lingering effluvium.

But the manure had filtered into every possible crevice; try as we might, we never did remove it all.

I bathed and changed my uniform for the second half of my patrol, but the miasma remained; I cleaned the rear several times afterwards, using all kinds of disinfectants and smelly things, but it seemed that for ever afterwards, the mini-van smelled of horse muck. Some of the other drivers, including Sergeant Blaketon, did from time to time refer to the redolence; I said it had come from dealing with the accident to the muck-carrying lorry, some of which had penetrated our official vehicle. I'm sure he did not believe me, but he never questioned me further. After all, it was I who had to live with the unwholesome results of my manure venture.

In spite of everything, we should not criticise that young girl — after all, she had obeyed her boss's instructions to the very letter. However, the incident did teach me that orders must be precisely and clearly given if they are to be properly obeyed. And so Mary got her muck and the garden did benefit from it.

* * *

On another occasion, another car landed me in trouble, but it was not a police car this time. It was my own.

Even though we had been issued with our little van, the faceless powers-that-be felt it was prudent that, from time to time, we patrolled on foot.

I think this idea came to them because there were, inevitably, occasions when two rural beat constables were on duty at the same time, when both simultaneously required the official van.

Clearly, we could not patrol together, consequently when our duties overlapped in this way, one of us was scheduled to work a foot patrol, perhaps for four hours or even for eight. Now, in a city or town, this is a splendid idea and there is no finer way for a constable to meet the public and for them to meet him. But it does not quite operate the same way in rural North Yorkshire.

For one thing, villages or centres of population are several miles apart. Another thing is that such centres may contain only six or eight houses and a telephone kiosk, added to which many of the farms which created our work were located some distance away from these little villages. Furthermore, our patrols were governed by the location of telephone kiosks because we had to stand beside a nominated kiosk every hour on the hour in case our superiors wished to contact us, or in case there was an emergency.

How we would have travelled to any emergency was never discussed, but this system meant that we spent about an hour walking along deserted country lanes between villages, following which we stood beside a telephone kiosk for five minutes. After that, it was time to walk to the next village which meant we never had time to meet people or time to perform any duty of more than a minute or two's duration.

To my simple mind, it seemed very silly to spend periods of almost one whole hour beyond communication with the public. Virtually the only companions I had upon those long country walks were the beasts, birds and insects of the fields and hedgerows. Cars carrying people did flash past and occasionally one would halt to ask whether I required a lift anywhere, but such occurrences were rare. More often than not, I simply left one village telephone kiosk and walked to the next without meeting a solitary person.

From a purely selfish point of view, it was marvellous. It meant I was getting paid for regularly taking a most enjoyable walk through some of England's most beautiful countryside, a pleasure for which many were prepared to pay considerable sums or to travel long distances. But from a police efficiency point of view, it was ridiculous. The amount of official time wasted was considerable and besides, what aspects of police work could I engage upon in such circumstances? The answer was nil, other than a spot of musing upon aspects of the profession.

I had a word with the Inspector about this ludicrous situation, but his response was simply. 'If it says foot patrol on the duty sheets, then that's what you must do.'

I attempted to defend my logic by saying that an hour spent in every village *en route* would be far more beneficial than an hour spent plodding along an empty road; if I spent time in a village, I could meet the people and undertake the traditional role of a village constable.

There were always enquiries to complete about local crimes or happenings, investigations to be made and contacts to be established. But my reasoning fell on deaf ears. Foot patrols were foot patrols and there must be no arguments against the system. Try as I might, I could not persuade anyone to change the useless ritual. Then, one foul and rainy day, I hit upon a solution.

Rather than endure many hours walking to nowhere in the pouring rain, I decided to use my own private car to transport myself between the villages. I would not claim anything by way of expenses from the police authority; I would quietly drive between points for my own convenience and peace of mind. This would enable me to spend the best part of an hour in each of the villages upon my route, so giving me a greater opportunity for solving crimes, meeting people, getting acquainted with the locality, absorbing knowledge about the area and its personalities and, in fact, doing all those varied jobs a police officer should do.

None of my superiors knew about this little scheme, and so when I was next detailed to undertake a foot patrol of this kind, I decided I would once again use my own car to transport me between points. Upon arrival in each of the villages, I would conceal it well away from the telephone kiosk, just in case the Sergeant, the Inspector or the Superintendent called on me and objected to my enterprise. So far as they were concerned, I was still spending all my time on foot.

I almost fell foul of the Superintendent on one occasion because I arrived in Elsinby by car, only to find him standing at the telephone kiosk, awaiting me. And he was a witness to my arrival in this very unofficial transport.

With some apprehension, I parked and walked towards him, throwing up a smart salute upon my approach. He chatted amiably for a while and then threw in the barbed question,

'Why are you using your private car, PC Rhea?'

'I've a firearms certificate to renew, sir, at Toft Hill Farm. It expires this week. It's a mile and a half out of the village, and I wouldn't have had the time to do that, and then walk to my next point on time.'

It was true, as it happened, and he accepted my excuse.

'Well, so long as you don't do this regularly, PC Rhea. Remember this system is designed as a foot patrol.'

'Yes, sir.' I had become too wise to argue and quietly determined that I would studiously ignore this instruction, albeit with the knowledge that he would inform the Inspector of my transgression. But I could easily conceal the car in countless hiding places at every village I visited. And so that is how I conducted my foot patrols.

Then, on a damp, cold and foggy evening one November, I was performing yet another of these marathon patrols. This one, whether by accident or design I am not sure, took me to the more remote corners of my patch. I had started at 5pm, and was due to patrol, on foot, through those remote lanes until 1am with a refreshment break around mid-way.

In my view, to patrol on foot along unlit roads in the foggy darkness was rank stupidity. It was both dangerous and futile, and so I decided to use my own car. Things went well until I arrived at my 8pm point in Ploatby; in that time, I had managed to call at local inns, to chat to residents and to conduct a miscellany of minor enquiries. And then, as I stood beside the lonely kiosk in the thickening fog, the Inspector arrived in his official car.

'Ah, Rhea,' he smiled, 'Nasty night. Anything to report?'

I detailed some of the duties I had performed since starting work at five and he expressed his satisfaction. Then, after signing my pocket-book to record this conference, he appeared to have an attack of benevolence.

'Shocking night, Rhea.' He regarded the deepening fog. 'Where's your next point?'

'Nine o'clock, sir, at Waindale, then I'm off duty at ten o'clock at home for my refreshment break.'

'With a long, wet walk in between, eh? In that case jump in. I'll give you a lift to Aidensfield, you can make your nine o'clock point there instead of Waindale. Then you can patrol your own village until refreshment time. I'll inform Control of the change. It's silly tramping these lanes in this fog.'

For a moment, I wondered if some of my earlier protestations had had an impact, then I realised with horror that it would mean leaving my own car abandoned out here.

And if I left my car here, it would mean a long walk back for it! Or, I might cadge a lift . . . As I dithered in my momentary indecision, he unlocked the passenger door and waved me in.

'Come on, Rhea, I haven't got all night.'

As he issued his order in those curt words, all thoughts of refusing his offer evaporated and so, with my heart sinking at the thought of a long trek back here, I settled in the warm and comfortable front seat of his fine vehicle. He drove confidently and smoothly away and within quarter of an hour was dropping me in the splash of light outside the Brewers' Arms in Aidensfield.

'Goodnight, Rhea,' he said, and vanished into the misty darkness.

He left me standing in the pool of warmth outside the pub, so I went in, half deciding to regard this as an official visit when I might chase out of the premises any stray underage drinkers, and half to see whether any of the Ploatby farmers were in. Maybe I could persuade one of them to give me a lift back to my car? But I was out of luck. The pub contained no one from that part of the dale and I had no wish to intrude upon the drinking-time of anyone else.

By the time I'd chatted to some of the locals about crimes reported in the national papers, to others about the state of the weather, refused several offers of a drink and checked two youngsters for their ages, it was nine-thirty.

A quick peramble around the village took the time around to ten o'clock and then I knocked off for supper. I had a grumble to Mary about the Inspector's actions, but she didn't offer much sympathy.

'If they say foot patrol they mean foot patrol,' she said with feminine simplicity. 'You haven't forgotten I need the car early tomorrow, have you?' she added. 'I'm going to see my mother and I must get some shoes for Elizabeth. She's got a hole in hers.'

I decided not to pursue the matter; I would endeavour to retrieve my car sometime during the remainder of this tour of duty. After all, when I resumed my work at 10.45pm, there would be a couple of hours left before 1am, and I might still beg a lift from some of the pub regulars. But when I looked at my points and predetermined route, I saw it took me well away from the local pubs. The short second half of my patrol took me through some lonely poachers' territory, not villages.

At the end of this marathon shift, therefore, I still had not recovered my car. Tired and footsore at 1am, I trudged into my little office beside the house and rang Eltering Police Station to book off duty. The duty PC wished me goodnight. Mary was in bed and had left a mug and biscuit on a tray; I would make myself a cocoa. But she needed the car first thing tomorrow . . .

And there was no local officer performing night shift who might come to my aid . . . I daren't ring Kit Clough at Falconbridge who was in possession of the official van. He'd completed a 2pm–10pm shift and was due out at 6am so he'd be fast asleep; I couldn't rouse him for this and did consider rising early myself, to beg a lift from him as he began his tour. But I couldn't guarantee he'd be free to do the trip — the Inspector might go out early to meet him or there might be some other commitment.

It was my very own problem, so I crept out of the house and started the long, weary, wet and dark walk back to Ploatby to collect my car. I've never known such a long, foot-weary trail. In the pitch darkness and in thickening fog, I slowly made my way to Ploatby, the time ticking away and my energy being sapped at every step.

But I made it. Somehow, I managed to reach it and with a sigh of relief, opened the door and sank into the driving seat. For an awful moment, I thought it might not start due to the damp atmosphere, but it burst into life and carried me safely home.

As I sank into bed just after two o'clock, trying desperately not to rouse Mary, she muttered, 'Busy night? Working late?'

'Yes,' I said, drifting into a blissful slumber against the warmth of her resting body.

That night, I dreamt I was trekking to the North Pole in my sore, bare feet.

CHAPTER 3

Aye, marry, is't; crowner's-quest law.
Hamlet, WILLIAM SHAKESPEARE, 1564—1616

The romance and excitement of finding buried treasure was something fairly common in the countryside around Aidensfield. It happened to residents and visitors alike, and I become involved in many of these occurrences because of the fascinating and ancient law surrounding treasure trove.

The reason for so many discoveries is that the district around Aidensfield is rich in historic ruins. They include castles, abbeys, churches and even battlefields and, over many centuries, these have attracted pilgrims and travellers both from our country and from foreign lands. Because those ancient visitors were careless like the rest of us, lots of them mislaid things like coins, swords, jewellery and other personal valuables, then through the passage of time these became buried in the earth. Many years later, due to the use of modern technology in the form of metal detectors, deep ploughs or sheer good fortune, these were found amid scenes of great excitement.

One source of discovery was the humble footpath. Linking these establishments, and indeed linking the tiny villages between them, were footpaths and bridleways through woodland and along the banks of our streams and rivers. Those villages also boast origins which can be traced across the centuries, and in more than one case, evidence can be found in the village churches, some of which date as far back as the seventh century.

For example, modern visitors can examine two tiny minsters; one can be seen at Kirkdale (*circa* AD 654) over whose doorway is a Saxon sundial, the most complete in the world, which bears the longest-known inscription from Anglo-Saxon times. The other is at Stonegrave (*circa* AD 757) and each gives some indication of the immense span of English heritage which is present in this beautiful area of Ryedale in North Yorkshire.

This sense of history continues with abbeys founded some five hundred years later, such as those at Rievaulx and Byland, whose grandeur was reduced to ruin by the Reformation, while some four hundred years after their destruction more abbey-building took place at Ampleforth.

Castles like those at Ashfordly, Eltering, Elsinby, Helmsley, Pickering and Gilling East add to the majesty of the locality, and it was to these places via remote villages and hamlets that travellers came. They have travelled these byways for many centuries, rich and poor, royal, noble and common, British and foreign. And in many cases, they lost their personal belongings, perhaps the odd coin or jewel, or even a goblet or defensive weapon.

In the case of places liable to be raided either by villains or tax-gatherers, however, the people concealed their hard-earned wealth. They hid coins in the walls of castles and abbeys, up the chimneys of cottages and mansions, or buried them in earthenware jars in the gardens or fields. And, of course, many local folks lost the occasional coin.

The result of all this is that the fields, woods, paths and gardens of Ryedale, and indeed the whole of England, are rich with buried treasure. Every year, thousands of pounds worth is discovered, some by accident, some by the use of metal detectors, some during road works or building construction and some by sheer good luck. There are many recorded instances when ordinary people have suddenly found themselves in possession of a fortune — one example occurred when workmen were excavating the site of a new building at York University. They uncovered 2,880 Roman coins, while in 1966, a hoard of twelfth-century coins then worth £30,000 was found near Newstead Abbey in Nottinghamshire. Twenty years later, treasure-hunters at Middleham in North Yorkshire found a unique fifteenth-century jewel of gold with a sapphire inset. It was sold for £1,430,000. In cases of this kind, the rule is not 'finders keepers', because when certain treasure is found the law of England, with its curious provisions for dealing with treasure trove, steps in. And this is how the police and the coroner become involved.

The coroner generally concerns himself with sudden or violent deaths, so why does he supervise the laws on found treasure? The answer lies far back in our history and a little explanation is now called for: in dealing with several cases of this nature and to satisfy my own curiosity, I delved into the reason for this odd aspect of our legal system and discovered a fascinating trail of legal history.

The first thing to remember is that treasure trove is defined as gold or silver, whether in the form of plate, coin or bullion, which has been deliberately hidden in the earth or in a house or in any other private place. This immediately rules out other valuables such as precious gems, bronze, pottery and glassware etc, unless these are set in either gold or silver. It also rules out gold or silver coins, plate or bullion which have been *lost*. The law on treasure trove does not concern itself with lost articles, but merely those which were hidden, however long ago.

If the owner is not known, treasure trove belongs to the Crown, i.e. the State, but before being handed over, a decision must be made as to whether a particular item is or is not 'treasure trove', i.e. *hidden* treasure which has been found.

This is the duty of the coroner who must hold an inquest (that is an enquiry) to determine whether or not the gold or silver object in question was lost or hidden. This can often be determined by the circumstances of its discovery. In very simple terms, a gold coin found under two inches of earth beside a well-used footpath was probably lost. There is no clear evidence that it had been concealed, therefore it would not be declared treasure trove, and would probably belong to the finder or perhaps to the landowner.

On the other hand, if a cache of gold coins was found in a leather bag or a container of some kind, perhaps buried beneath a tree or lodged up the chimney of an old house, then this suggests a past and deliberate concealment.

These are the kinds of decision which must be made by the coroner, usually based on evidence obtained for him by the police. The reason for his involvement goes back to the twelfth century at least, and possibly further. Once known as the crowner, the origins of the coroner are lost in time, but the office was mentioned in 1194 in Richard I's Articles of Eyre. They provided for the election of three knights and one clerk as custodians of the pleas of the Crown. From this, the early coroners were known as Keepers of the King's Pleas (*Custos Placitorum Coronae*) and their duties were to keep 'the pleas, suits and causes which affected the King's Crown and Dignity.'

The task of an early coroner was really to record matters rather than determine them, but one of his jobs was to ensure that any 'chance revenues' were paid to the King. These included money from 'the forfeited chattels of felons, deodands, wrecks, royal fish and treasure trove.' In other words, the early coroner was little more than a tax-gatherer, although he did enquire into sudden deaths and did supervise the disposal of a deceased's lands and goods. Indeed, his official interest in sudden deaths was then to ensure that the Crown received all its dues.

The forfeited chattels of felons were the belongings of a man who had committed some felony (i.e. serious crime like theft or murder). If he was convicted, all his belongings were forfeited to the Crown and it was the coroner's job to see that it was done.

It is now easy to understand why the coroner had to enquire into every sudden death — it was to determine whether or not it was the result of a murder so that, when a culprit was convicted, the Crown would receive its dues. Deodands are now obsolete: these were the objects which had caused the death by misadventure of a person. For example, if a cart accidentally ran over and killed a man, the cart or even just the offending wheel might be declared deodand and forfeited to the Crown. In days of old when this happened, the King would donate the object to the church or to the family of the victim, so that money could be raised for the sufferers. This scheme was abolished in 1846 when it was feared that entire railway trains or ships might be forfeited!

Wrecks at sea are now subject to their own procedures which were recently updated by the Protection of Wrecks Act 1973 and the coroner is no longer involved. So far as royal fish are concerned, it was Edward II who ruled that all sturgeon caught in British waters belonged to the sovereign and it was the coroner's duty to make sure this was done. I know of no modern law which enforces these provisions, but the practice continues as a matter of courtesy and custom. These, plus treasure trove, were the chance revenues which had to be handed to the King; of them, only treasure trove legally remains, and even now, if objects are declared treasure trove, they must still be handed to the Crown. But now, of course, this means the British Museum.

Upon the coroner declaring a discovery to be treasure trove, the goods will be handed to the British Museum who will then determine the current market value of the find. The finder will then be paid that sum, which shows that, in this case especially, honesty is by far the best policy. In recent years, many rewards totalling hundreds of thousands of pounds have been paid to lucky finders.

The old common-law misdemeanour of 'concealment of treasure trove' has been abolished, but if anyone now finds treasure trove and does not declare it, they can be charged with theft under the Theft Act of 1968 and their find will be confiscated. No reward will be paid either. It is so much wiser to report any of these discoveries, both from a criminal liability aspect and from the nation's need to conserve treasures which might otherwise be lost for ever.

It is not the job of a coroner to determine *ownership* of any treasure found on private land or in private premises; if it is *not* declared treasure trove, it might belong to the finder or the owner of the land or occupier of the house, or indeed to anyone else. That kind of decision is a matter for the civil courts if there is a dispute and so, with this background in mind, I found it both interesting and simple to deal with people who found things in their homes, or in the fields and surrounding countryside. And the number and variety of things discovered was truly amazing.

* * *

It is not easy to select the most interesting of the finds which occurred in and around Aidensfield — every one was fascinating in its own way. Mundane objects like old bikes, oil drums and even motor-car spare parts were constantly being located in the lakes, ponds and streams while our woodlands produced cast-off refrigerators, ovens, settees and a bewildering selection of household offal, most of which resulted from the actions of those ghastly people who dump their unwanted rubbish in the countryside. In our streams and waterways, old guns have been found too, and so have Victorian lemonade and beer bottles which are so desired by collectors. There were modern ones too, along with kettles and bedsteads, and in one miraculous case, a diamond wedding ring was discovered in a tiny beck. This was returned to the owner who had lost it several years earlier; she had reported the loss to the police, and our records turned up her name. Needless to say, she was delighted.

But none of these objects was remotely within the scope of treasure-trove rules, neither was an antique flintlock pistol found in the thatch of a cottage, or a beautiful unmarked glass goblet which had been tucked into a hole in a wall, and then boarded over for a couple of centuries. Because our area had been colonised by the Romans, we were often told of discoveries from that era; items of pottery galore like bowls, plates and urns turned up, usually broken into fragments, although very occasionally a complete and flawless example would be found.

These caused immense excitement, and although such finds were always of tremendous archaeological interest, they were generally not of police interest, nor was the coroner officially involved. Sometimes, however, we had to bear in mind the likelihood that any found object might be the subject of a crime — people did steal valuables and then dump them, but in most of our cases they were genuine discoveries from the distant past. Our procedures referred the finder to a local museum or archaeologist; sometimes, Roman coins would be unearthed and we had all coins examined by experts to determine whether or not they were struck in gold or silver; I don't think we ever dealt with a gold or silver coin from Roman times, although I understand that the Anglo-Saxons made gold copies of some Roman coins — these are now very rare. Most of the Roman coins we dealt with looked a dull bronze colour with the head of an emperor crudely portrayed on one side with various inscriptions on the other. None was particularly valuable and there seemed to be so many different types.

In one case, a very enthusiastic and slightly dishonest hunter discovered a hoard of Roman coins on private land and kept them; he was charged with stealing them from the landowner, as he had not obtained permission either to go on to the land nor to seek the coins. Some bore the head of the Emperor Septimius Severus who died at York around AD 211; this gave them a very local interest, but because they were neither gold nor silver, they were not treasure trove.

There was a burst of tremendous excitement at Elsinby when a local farmer turned up an ancient sword. He was ploughing close to the stream which flows through this pretty place when he struck the long, stout metal blade. His fields occupy a patch of land beneath the castle walls where there are strong links between Elsinby Castle and the Civil Wars; it was a regular occurrence for Fred Pullen to find relics of this kind. He regularly turned up cannon balls, musket balls, buckles from belts and spearheads.

But this sword was different. Although the long, heavy blade and hilt had suffered years of rust, he was alert enough to notice two narrow bands of what appeared to be gold which had been incorporated in the hilt. He brought this discovery for me to examine but I could not determine whether or not the bands were fashioned from real gold. That could only be decided by an expert, so we arranged for the sword to be examined.

And those bands were of gold; furthermore, the expert who hailed from the Yorkshire Museum said that the sword was not from the Civil War period. It was very probably an Anglo-Saxon warrior's sword dating from the seventh century, and he believed the gold bands had once bound a leather handle to the sword. But those tiny bands of gold made all the difference to Fred's discovery — because of the gold content, I now had to consider the law on treasure trove and this meant that Fred could not keep the sword — unless the inquest decided it was *not* treasure trove.

I made a formal report on the matter and included a detailed statement from the museum's expert together with the circumstances of its discovery in that field beside the stream. The coroner said he would hold an inquest at some future date — he always kept such matters on file until a number of cases had accumulated, and he would then hold several treasure trove inquests on the same day. Each lasted but a few minutes.

In this case, he decided the sword was not treasure trove — clearly, it had not been deliberately hidden and had, more than likely, been abandoned or even thrown away. And so Fred Pullen was allowed to keep it, but he donated it to the museum for display.

'It'll be safer yonder, Mr Rhea,' he said with simple logic. If I keep it and then pass on to that big hayfield in the sky when my time's up, it could get chucked away again. Folks round here don't recognise history, tha knaws, 'specially them relations o' mine. They see sike stuff as nowt but old bits o' junk. In my mind, them bits an' bobs are all a part of history and should be kept where folks'll appreciate 'em and where they'll never get lost again.'

I told him I couldn't agree more, and from that time, he donated many more pieces to local museums.

If Fred's discovery was rather unusual, so was that of Mrs Dolly-Ann Powell, a delightful lady of mature years who earned a living by lecturing upon and arranging beautiful displays of flowers in hotels, shops and other places.

Dolly-Ann was a tiny, slender and very pretty widow of about forty-five who lived in a picturesque thatched cottage at Briggsby. When dressed in her best clothes, she reminded me of one of her own flower arrangements, so delightfully neat and attractive was she. Our paths seldom crossed for she went about her business in a brisk and efficient manner and her work was something that rarely, if ever, warranted attention from a policeman. Every so often, however, I would spend time patrolling around her village and very occasionally I would find her in the garden, tending her beautiful collection of exquisite flowers. Many of these were used in her work and I do know that she sold lots to florists for wreaths and bouquets, or even to customers who came to the door. To say that her house and garden were a picture was a great understatement — they were a sheer delight. On such occasions, we would chat amiably over the hedge, passing the time of day and issuing the customary British small talk about the weather and gardening.

One of Dolly-Ann's strengths was that she did most of her own renovations to the cottage; rather than employ builders or craftsmen, she would tackle most jobs and, surprisingly, achieved a great deal. It was while undertaking one of her improvements that she made a discovery which puzzled and then intrigued her.

It occurred when she decided to re-lay the sturdy path of sandstone paving-slabs which led to her honeysuckle-covered porch and front door.

Over the years, they had become rather uneven and maybe dangerous, and so she decided to level them all. To make a good job, she lifted every one, including that which formed the threshold. It was here that she made her discovery. Underneath the threshold she found an old glass bottle dirty with age. Some six inches tall with a wide neck, its top contained a large cork which was thoroughly sealed and had remained intact in spite of many years in the ground. She had wiped off much of the grime to find the bottle contained some very strange objects and ingredients, so strange in fact that she was baffled by them.

By chance I arrived just after she had cleaned the bottle, when she was endeavouring to determine the contents, so she invited me in for a look at it. She put the kettle on and sat me in her pretty kitchen among countless vases and arrangements of flowers.

'So here it is.' She plonked it on the table before me. It was a clear bottle, although the glass had a faint greenish tinge to it, and I could see a dried-up, dark and almost glutinous substance covering the bottom. This had congealed many years ago, judging by its appearance, but there were other small metal objects stuck into it, rather like pins or nails, some rusted and others still clean; I could see what appeared to be human hairs and nail clippings too.

And then I knew what it was.

At that point, she arrived with a mug of hot tea and settled down at my side.

'Well, Mr Rhea, have I discovered hidden treasure?'

'Not really,' I smiled, thanking her for the drink.

'Oh.' Her face showed just a hint of disappointment.

'You've no idea what it is?' I asked.

'Not a clue,' she was honest.

'Well, suppose I asked you if your house is troubled by witches?' I smiled at her. 'What would you say?'

'Witches? No, of course not!' she laughed. 'Why, was this a witch's cottage?'

'On the contrary, witches were not welcome here!' I told her. 'This little device was to stop them, to ward off witches and to prevent them from bewitching the house or its occupants. It's obviously done a good job!'

'Really?' She opened her eyes wide with surprise and smiled at my attempt at joking. 'I had no idea!'

I explained my own interest in the folklore of the North York Moors and how, even until little more than a century or so ago, the country folk believed in witches and the power of the evil eye. Even today, some cottages contain witch posts whose original purpose was to protect the occupants from the attentions of witches, and there are other devices which served this purpose: for example, iron nails in beams or bedsteads, circular stones with holes in the centre, horseshoes on the walls of houses and outbuildings and even rowan trees planted close to the dwelling. All were used to deter witches.

She listened as I explained, and when I had finished, asked, 'So what is this bottle?'

'It's a witch bottle,' I told her. 'It was customary to bury them beneath the threshold, or sometimes under the hearth.'

'Really?' She picked it up and tried to identify the contents. 'What's inside?'

'Do you really want to know?' The ingredients were rather revolting and I wondered if she was squeamish.

'Something odd, is there?' she asked, suspicious of what was coming next.

'Ordinary things, really,' I smiled. 'But gruesome at the same time.'

She plonked the bottle on the table and stared at it, her pretty face screwed up in concentration.

'Go on, Mr Rhea,' she said at length. 'Make me squirm!'

'I'm not sure precisely what's in this particular bottle,' I said. 'But the sort of ingredients they put in would include samples of human hair, nail cuttings and metal objects like pins or nails. They'd put urine in too, and human blood . . .'

'Urggh . . .' she shuddered.

'And!' I was in full flow now. 'Some of them contained the liver of a live frog stuck full of pins, or the heart of a toad which had been pierced with the spikes from the Holy Thorn of Glastonbury.'

She stared at the bottle on her table.

'How revolting!' she shuddered again. 'Why did they make such horrible things?'

'They really worried about the effect of witches on their children and cattle,' I explained. 'If things went wrong, things that couldn't be easily explained, they would blame the local witch. She was usually some poor old woman who dabbled in herbs or reckoned to foretell the future. And to stop any evil that she might perpetrate, they made these bottles as safeguards.'

'So the contents acted as a charm?'

'Yes, they were put under the door to prevent entry by evil spirits or witches. The presence of iron has long been a means of keeping witches at bay, hence the horseshoes, nails, pins and so on. The hair and human nail-parings come from the most indestructible part of the human body, and they believed that if included in a bottle, their presence would stop the witch injuring the family. I'm not sure what the blood was for. The addition of the urine was a terrible thing — they believed this caused the witch's death because she would be unable to pass water!'

I went on to say these charms were used beyond our shores too, examples having been found in Sicily and Germany, and that in some cases three earthenware jars were used with similar contents, in this case each being buried beside a churchyard footpath seven inches below the surface and seven inches from a church porch.

When I had concluded my lecture on local witch lore, she smiled. 'So what am I going to do with this bottle? Is it something you should know about, officially, I mean?'

'No, but thanks for showing it me. You could replace it!' I suggested. 'Or keep it as an ornament . . .'

'No thanks! I wouldn't want that collection of stuff on my shelves!'

I mentioned the local Ryedale Folk Museum and felt it would be a suitable place to keep this bottle and its odd contents. She agreed.

'Mind you,' she smiled with a twinkle in her eye. 'I suppose that if I remove it from the house, I'll then be open to the machinations of the local witches? They might ruin my flowers, cause them to wilt or die, or even create havoc in the house itself.'

'That's the risk you take,' I confirmed with a chuckle. 'It seems this cottage has been free from strife over the years!'

'It's always been a happy house,' she said. 'Always.'

Draining my mug of tea, I left her to make her decision and never asked what she had decided. I felt I should not mention the bottle again, and although I did see her from time to time, she refrained from bringing up the subject. But I have never seen that bottle in the folk museum, and so far as I know Dolly-Ann's cottage and business have remained free from trouble. And her front path is now neat and level, with the threshold firmly in place.

Among the other discoveries was a magnificently ornate silver spoon which a householder discovered buried in the thatch of his cottage; this was identified as a seventeenth-century dessert spoon worth around £2,500, and the coroner decided that it *was* treasure trove. He said due to the peculiar place in which it was found, it must have been deliberately hidden for reasons which we shall never know. So much treasure seemed to be discovered in the thatched cottages around my beat that I was almost tempted to buy one!

But perhaps the most satisfying discovery was the one that occurred at West Gill Farm, Aidensfield, the centuries-old home of Reg Lumley and his family. Only months earlier, I had seen Reg devastated by a terrible outbreak of Foot and Mouth Disease. It had resulted in the slaughter of his entire herd of pedigree Friesians, a herd which had taken him twenty years to establish but which had been wiped out in hours by that most dreaded of cattle diseases. The story is told in *Constable Along the Lane*.

I knew that Reg, his wife and son Ted, were struggling to re-build their lives but no new cattle had yet appeared on the farm. I did not like to pry into their affairs nor discuss matters like insurance or compensation, nor did I wish to cause anguish by reminding them of the outbreak, so it was a pleasant surprise when I received a call from Reg. On the phone, he sounded in unusually high spirits.

'Can thoo come, Mr Rhea? Ah've summat to show you.'

'Sure Reg, when's a suitable time?'

'Any time, we're about t'spot all day.'

'How about just after two o'clock?'

'Champion,' he said and rang off.

When I arrived just after lunch, I found the family in the kitchen. They were sitting around their massive scrubbed pine table with huge mugs of tea, and in the centre was a tray full of muddy coins and bits of broken pottery.

Reg, beaming with happiness, shoved a mug into my hand and pulled out a chair. I settled on it, staring at the treasure before me.

'That's it, Mr Rhea. How about that?'

'Reg!' I said. 'Is this yours?'

'That's for you to say, Mr Rhea. Our Ted dug it up wiv 'is plough this morning, down in oor fifteen-acre.'

'Did he now!' I couldn't resist running my fingers through the pile of ancient money. The coins, most of which appeared to be of silver and from the sixteenth and seventeenth centuries, tinkled and rattled back on to the tray, and there seemed to be thousands of them. Upon some of them, I recognised names like Carolus I, Jacobus, Elizabeth, Edward VI and Carolus II. So they were from the reigns of Charles I and II, James I, Elizabeth I and Edward VI. I believe at least one was from the reign of Henry VIII.

'Wonderful!' I beamed. 'Absolutely wonderful.'

'Are they worth owt, Mr Rhea?'

'They must be,' I said, 'but I'm no expert.'

'Can I sell 'em? We could do wiv a bit o' cash.'

'I'm afraid not, Reg. But you could still get money from the find, although it'll take time,' and I told them about the procedure relating to treasure trove. Ted showed me where he had ploughed them up and I noted the place, then took a formal statement from him.

Next, we counted the coins. It took a long time because there were almost 2,000, and I had the unpleasant task of taking them away from the Lumleys in a large sack. I gave a receipt for 1,985 coins. I explained they would have to be examined by experts to determine whether or not they were silver or even gold. The Lumleys probably thought it was the last they'd see of them, knowing they were now subjected to red tape and officialdom.

As expected, the coroner declared them treasure trove which meant they were handed to the British Museum, and they would make their customary valuation based upon the prevailing market prices. It was some months later when I got a telephone call from Reg.

'Can thoo come, Mr Rhea. I've summat to show you.'

'Not another batch of coins, Reg?'

'Nay, summat else,' his voice contained an air of mystery. 'Thoo'll like this.'

'I'll be there in ten minutes,' I said, curious to learn about his latest discovery.

This time, there was a whopping glass of whisky on the kitchen table when I arrived and the family sat around with huge grins on their faces. Even Mrs Lumley was smiling.

Reg made sure I was settled and insisted I drink the whisky, even though I was in uniform. I didn't like to offend by refusing! After this performance, I was handed a letter. It was still in the official buff envelope which had been opened, but it bore the logo of the British Museum.

'Tak a leeak at yon, Mr Rhea,' invited Reg.

I did. I read the formal letter and was astounded. It itemised every single coin and identified them by year, reign and designation, and an individual valuation had also been added. The letter said that the total official value of the hoard of coins found at West Gill Farm, Aidensfield was £47,884 and a cheque for that amount was enclosed.

I held the cheque . . . I'd never seen, let alone held, such a huge amount of money.

'Whew!' was all I could say.

'That caps owt, Mr Rhea,' said Reg. 'That really caps owt.'

'It does, Reg. It really does cap owt. And I'm delighted for you all.'

Mrs Lumley, a woman of few words and a severe hair-do, just smiled again.

'Nay, it's thanks to thoo,' said Reg. 'I read summat in t'*Gazette* aboot thoo and another inquest on summat found at Elsinby, so thowt I'd better tell thoo. If thoo hadn't said what we had ti deea wiv 'em, Ah might have stuck 'em in t'loft and said nowt. I mean, thoo can't spend 'em, so in my mind they were worth nowt.'

That was a typical Yorkshire attitude, and he continued, 'Ah mean to say, who'd have thowt they were worth all this? So we'll have a party, Mr Rhea. Your missus'll come, eh?'

'We'll be delighted,' I said, and I meant it.

'It'll be soon,' he said. 'I'll ring wi' t'date.'

'Don't spend it all on a party!' I cautioned him with a laugh. 'Make the money work for you!'

'Ah shall, Mr Rhea. Starting next week, me and Ted'll be off to a few cattle marts. There's a few young pedigree Friesians we'd like to get oor hands on.'

I was so happy for the Lumleys, and their party was marvellous. With a farmhouse full of friends and relations, it was a wonderful event, especially as Reg seemed to have overcome the depression which had plagued him for so long. And he did get his new herd started. Now, when I drive past his farm, I see his fields once again full of beautiful Friesians and Reg has still not retired. He continues to build that 'new' herd with just a little help from some past occupants of his lush farmland.

But of all the discoveries made on my patch, it was the one involving Mrs Ada Jowett which was the most intriguing. Ada, a stout and oft perspiring lady in her late sixties, was the church cleaner at St Andrew's Parish Church, Elsinby, a job which she did voluntarily. She had been St Andrew's cleaner for more years than anyone cared to recall, and the lovely building sparkled through her efforts.

The brasses always gleamed, the altar cloths were ironed to perfection, the surrounds were tidy and neat, and she managed to ensure that the flowers were always fresh and readers' lists and other notices were tidily displayed.

In short, Mrs Jowett was a treasure.

The church, always short of money and in need of constant maintenance and repairs, was soon to learn just how much of a treasure she really was. Conscientious as ever, she decided one year to spring-clean the hidden corners of the church. In addition to her normal brushing and polishing, this meant clearing out cupboards and corners, getting rid of years of accumulated rubbish and paper and generally ridding the church of unwanted junk. The job was long overdue, but no one had dared suggest it to Mrs Jowett. For all her skills, she cleaned only what could be seen . . .

No one knew what had prompted her to tackle the cupboards and corners, but she attacked the job with much gusto, lots of mops and dusters and gallons of perspiration. The stuff that was thrown out was bewildering — old curtains and cloths, ancient notices and posters, stacks of battered hymn books and a load of assorted jumble which would have graced the best junk-sale for miles around. It is just feasible that some important documents got lost in her enthusiasm, but she operated like a whirlwind. There was no stopping her once she had started and for days the church was almost lost in a cloud of dust or bonfire smoke.

And then, right at the back of a massive oak cupboard in the vestry, she found a chalice. It had obviously been there for years for it was dirty, very battered and full of dust. Like most other discoveries, she decided to throw it in the bin, so removed it from the shelf and took it outside. Then she had a second look in the strong daylight and for some reason changed her mind about casting it in the bin. It was at that precise moment that I arrived. I was undertaking a patrol around Elsinby and had noticed the frantic activity within the church. Attracted by the piles of rubbish outside, I thought I'd pop in to see what was going on and to pass the time of day with Ada.

As I strolled up the path towards the porch, I saw Ada clutching the chalice; she was peering intently at it.

'Morning, Ada,' I greeted her. 'Still busy, eh?'

'Never been so busy,' she grumbled. 'Wish I'd never started this. The more I chuck out the more I find inside, it's never ending. Makes you wonder where it comes from.'

'You're doing a good job.' I decided to praise her efforts. 'It must be benefiting the church. So, what's that you've found?'

'An old cup,' she said, holding it up for me to see. 'Been stuck in the back of a cupboard for years, it has. Junk I'd say, by the look of it. It's made of tin, I think, been battered about a bit. They'd never use this sort o' thing now for communion.'

She passed the chalice over to me and I held it, weighing it in my hand.

'It's pewter, I think,' I told her. 'And very old by the look of it.'

'It'll not be worth owt, then? It's not gold or silver, is it?'

'No, so what are you going to do with it?'

'I was thinking about chucking it out,' she said. 'Then when I got out, I had second thoughts, I'd like to show it to t'vicar, but he's away at a conference.'

The Rev Simon Hamilton, Vicar of Elsinby, was away at a Diocesan Conference; I knew that because he'd told me that the vicarage would be empty for a whole week and had asked me to keep an eye on it during his absence.

Still holding the chalice and turning it in my hands, I said, 'I think he'd like to see this,' and then, in the strong light of that morning, I noticed the faint engraving on the face. It was very difficult to determine but it looked rather like a crowned sovereign in a sailing ship; he was carrying an upright sword and a shield.

'You take it and get somebody to look at it,' she said quite unexpectedly. 'Then I can tell t'vicar what we've done. You deal with found treasures, don't you?'

'Yes, if they're treasure trove.'

'Well, mebbe it's a good thing you turned up like you did. Do you happen to know anybody that'll look at it, say what it's worth or summat?'

'I'm going into York tomorrow,' I said. 'Off duty, but I've a pal who's in the antique business. I'll show it to him if you like.'

'Aye.' She looked relieved, for the decision had now been taken out of her hands.

And so I took the chalice from her. I found a piece of brown paper among the rubbish and wrapped it up, then placed it in the cubby-hole of the mini-van. Next day, I popped it into a carrier bag and took it to York. Mary and I did a little shopping, had a meal and then I remembered the old chalice. I went back to my car and removed it, then walked along Stonegate to my friend's antique shop.

'Hello, Paul, how's things in the antique world?'

'Hi, Nick,' he said. 'Things are bloody fine. So what brings you here?'

'This,' I said, and I placed the battered old chalice on his counter. 'I think it's pewter but wondered if it's worth anything!'

He took it and held it very carefully, turning it in the strong light of an angle lamp as he first studied the cup itself, and then examined the engraving on the front.

'Bloody hell!' was all he said. 'Where's this come from?'

'One of the churches on my patch,' I said. 'The cleaning lady found it in a cupboard. Been there years by the look of it.'

'Centuries more like,' he said, and I saw his face was flushed. 'You've no idea what this is?'

I shook my head and said lamely, 'A chalice?'

'A chalice, yes. But what a bloody chalice! Worth a bloody fortune,' he whistled. 'A bloody fortune, or I'm stupid. You say she found it in a bloody cupboard?'

I explained the circumstances of its discovery, and then asked why he was so enthusiastic about it.

'Here,' he said. 'Take a look at this engraving. What is it?' he shone the light upon it and pointed to it.

'I think it's a king in a ship.'

'Right, with a sword and a shield, eh? The sort of arms you'd get on a bloody coin, not on a bloody pewter chalice!'

'Oh,' I said.

'This might have belonged to a king, see? Or to the priest who was the king's confessor or something. Henry IV it would be,' he continued. 'Reigned 1399 to 1413, he did. And see this?' He pointed to the shield, but I could not determine precisely what he was showing me. 'His shield, it's only got three fleurs-de-lis, not four. He changed his royal arms, you see; coins with only three fleurs-de-lis are so bloody rare it's unbelievable. And see this rudder on the ship? There's a star on it. Now most rudders on Henry IV coins are blank, but some have crowns on and some have bloody stars. Nick, if I'm not mistaken, this is a bloody rare find — a really rare bloody find.'

'No kidding?' I was awestruck by the thought.

'No kidding,' he said. 'You need expert valuation of this, my lad. Try Sotheby's.'

'I don't know anybody there.'

'I do, and he's a whizz-kid on medieval pewter. I'll fix up a bloody appointment, right now if you like.'

'The vicar hasn't even seen this yet; if it's what you think it is, no doubt he'll want to be involved, and maybe even bring his bishop or the Archbishop into this find.'

'Too bloody right he will when he finds out what it is. Right, show it to him, tell him what I said, then ring me and I'll fix up an appointment at Sotheby's for it to be expertly assessed. Somebody'll have to take it down to London.'

'Right, Paul, thanks. I appreciate your advice.'

'And if your church wants to sell this bloody thing, let me know! I'd mortgage my shop to get my bloody hands on that.'

When the vicar returned, I informed him of this conversation (although I omitted Paul's colourful flow of expletives) and he promptly rang the Archbishop of York who suggested we let the Sotheby expert have sight of it. And, he said, the diocese would pay the train fare of the person who took it. We nominated Ada, with the proviso that she be told to take great care of the chalice at all times. Simon Hamilton felt she could be trusted to look after it — after all, who'd think this countrywoman was carrying treasure?

'I'm off to London,' she said next time I saw her. 'With that cup, Mr Rhea. To show a chap down there. I've never been to London, you know, never even been on a train.'

And so, dressed in her heavy brown shoes, lisle stockings, headscarf and her only overcoat, which was of heavy tweed, Ada Jowett set about the journey of a lifetime. Excited both at the prospect of travelling to London and of riding on a train, she was driven to York Station by the vicar and would be met at King's Cross by the man from Sotheby's. He'd promised to care for her during her visit, bearing in mind the circumstances. I've no idea what he made of Ada when they met, but she had a most enjoyable day. Upon her return that same evening, she was collected from York by taxi and the vicar invited me to go along and hear how she'd progressed at Sotheby's.

The vicar's wife had arranged a late supper for her and I was invited. And when Ada came in from the taxi, she was carrying the chalice in a brown carrier bag; in fact, she'd put one bag inside another to give greater protection to the chalice! That was her notion of taking care of it.

'Well, Ada,' began Simon Hamilton. 'How did it go?'

'By, yon train goes fast,' she said. 'And then in London, they rushed me down some stairs under t'ground and there was more trains, coming every few minutes . . . I've never seen owt like it . . . and folks! Thousands of 'em all pushing and shoving . . . there's no wonder folks get bad-tempered with all that rushing about.'

'Yes, but the chalice . . .'

Ada ignored the vicar and continued to enthuse about London, giving her highly colourful interpretation of life in the capital. She rambled on about guards in funny hats at Buckingham Palace, messy pigeons, Eros, Big Ben, the Houses of Parliament, the department stores, the different nationalities she noticed, buses that came every few minutes instead of twice a week and trains whose doors shut without being pushed by the travellers.

Eventually, she ran out of talk of the city and Simon took the opportunity to mention Sotheby's and the chalice.

'They would have nowt to do with it, Mr Hamilton.' She shook her heavy grey head. 'Didn't want to know. This young chap met me off t'train and took me in a taxi where I saw the chap you mentioned, him what reckons to know summat about cups like that.'

'And he examined it?'

'He did, in a manner o' speaking. It took nobbut a minute or two, and that was that.'

'And what did he say?'

'Not a lot.'

'You offered to leave the chalice for a more thorough examination, as I suggested?'

'Oh, aye, I made that clear. I said I'd leave it for him to have a better look and he could mebbe post it back, but he said he'd have nowt to do with it, Mr Hamilton.'

'Nothing to do with it?'

When I heard this, I wondered about Paul's assessment — Paul would never have allowed Ada to go all the way to London with a dud. I was sure Paul knew his antiques . . .

'Nay, nowt. Summat to do with insurance, he said. He wouldn't take it off me, so I had to fetch it back.'

And she dug into the paper carrier bag and lifted it out.

'Is that all?'

'Well, he said he'd be having words with you about it, I told him your telephone number. Tomorrow, he said, all being well. He'll ring.'

There was clear disappointment on Simon's face and I knew mine also showed similar feelings. It seemed that the so-called experts in London had merely fobbed off poor old Ada. The vicar should have gone, he should have taken it and presented it in a more sophisticated manner.

'Leave it with me, Ada,' said Simon. 'We'll see what they say tomorrow, eh?'

'Aye, and it's my bedtime now. See you tomorrow,' and off she went.

I remained with Simon for a while, each of us expressing our sorrow at her apparently callous treatment in London, and then I went home. Then at lunchtime the following day, I got a call from Simon Hamilton.

'Can you spare ten minutes, Nicholas?' he asked.

'Of course,' I said. 'I'll come now.'

When I arrived at the vicarage, he showed me into his kitchen where Ada was seated at the table. Mrs Hamilton was also present and I noticed a glass of wine at each place setting. And in the centre was the dirty old chalice.

When we were all gathered together, Simon said, 'Ada, PC Rhea, I'd like to thank you both for your work in rescuing this chalice. I've had a call from Sotheby's this morning, Ada, and they thank you for taking it to them.'

'The cheek of 'em!' she pouted. 'Nearly threw me out they did . . . didn't want to know about me . . .'

'I think you have misunderstood them, Ada.' He spoke softly. 'They did a proper and expert examination; it's a Henry IV pewter chalice, a very rare object and more so because of the arms which it bears. It seems pewter chalices were used in medieval times, but most of them were buried with the priests when they died. Very few from this period have survived, especially of this quality. Now, did he say what it was worth?'

'Well, he muttered on about it being worth summat in the region of half a million pounds. Now I ask you, Mr Hamilton! Half a million pounds for that bit of awd tin?'

'And you didn't believe him?'

'I did not! I reckoned he was having me on 'cos I'm a country woman who doesn't know about such things.'

'Ada, he does genuinely believe it would bring that amount in a sale at his auction rooms. It is unique, Ada, a real treasure.'

'You're all having me on!' She flushed deeply now and looked very embarrassed. 'That's why I said nowt to you about what they'd said it was worth. A bit of awd tin can't be worth that much, it just can't.'

'No, we're not teasing you, Ada, none of us. His problem was that he could not keep it overnight because he was not insured for that particular cup. So you took it sightseeing . . .'

'Aye, and I nearly lost it over London Bridge, an' all,' she said grimly. 'Can't say I'd have missed it.'

'So you've a problem now.' I put to him. 'Your church will never afford the premiums to insure this!'

'I must speak to the Archbishop,' he said. 'This is a real shock, Ada, a massive shock. I'm reeling from the thought that this has been standing in my vestry for years and, but for you, would have been thrown out . . .'

'Half a million pounds!' she said. 'For that bit of awd tin? I'd not give it house-room!'

She was steadfastly refusing to accept the truth of that statement, and left the vicarage shaking her head. After being assured Simon would place it in a bank vault for safe keeping, I followed her out, stunned that I'd carried it around in my car and had left it unattended in a York car park!

It would be about a month later when Rev. Simon Hamilton called me again. 'I thought you'd like to know the outcome of the chalice saga,' he said.

'Love to,' I said, and drove to his vicarage for a coffee with him.

When I was settled, he said, 'As you've been involved with this from the start,' he strode up and down his spacious kitchen, 'I thought you'd like to hear the Archbishop's decision about the chalice.'

'Yes, thanks, Simon. I appreciate that.'

'It is a problem, Nicholas,' he said. 'We cannot keep it because of the risks and the necessarily high insurance premiums. We could not afford them. And, as you know, we do need a regular supply of money for upkeep of our church.'

I let him take his time on this explanation.

'If we allowed Sotheby's to auction it on our behalf, it might raise that huge sum; half a million pounds does seem excessive, but I am assured it could bring as much as that on the open market, maybe from international buyers.'

'So you're selling it?' I asked.

'Not by public auction. As the Archbishop says, if we did sell it through Sotheby's, it might go out of the country. There is no telling where it might get to. We don't want that — we want such a unique chalice, our chalice, kept in England, Nicholas. It must never leave these shores.'

'But you're in a cleft stick, Simon,' I said. 'You can't afford to keep it, and you can't dictate where it goes if it is sold. You cannot issue conditions for sales of that kind.'

'A solution has been reached, Nicholas,' he said. 'A museum has offered us £45,000 for it; it will be put on display and kept in this country for all time.'

'But that's a fraction of its true value,' I protested.

'Perhaps, but it's all that museum can afford. If we invest that cash, it will give the church a very nice income for years ahead and that will safeguard it and permit us to maintain it in the manner it deserves. After all, we want nothing more than that. You see, this method pleases everyone because the chalice can be viewed by the public, we get some income from it and it will never again be lost or taken out of England. It's an admirable solution.'

'But you're throwing money away!' I said.

'Not really, because we're getting more than we've had before, and we don't really need half a million, Nicholas.'

'It's a real Christian decision,' I heard myself say.

'It was made by the Archbishop, I might add,' said Simon as if that explained everything.

Today, Ada's name is upon the notice which provides a history of the chalice as it stands in a famous museum, and soon after the sale, Ada got a new apron, some new brushes and dusters. So the chalice was of benefit to her as well.

And she still refuses to believe that such a 'piece of awd tin' was worth so much money.

CHAPTER 4

'They inwardly resolved that . . . their piracies should
not again be sullied with the crime of stealing.'
Tom Sawyer Abroad, Mark Twain, 1835–1910

The crime of theft, known legally in England as larceny until 1968, is among the earliest of criminal offences; not only is it a crime, however, it is also a sin, and as such features in the Ten Commandments. 'Thou shalt not steal' could hardly be a more direct prohibition.

A universal loathing of theft has, over the centuries, provided it with many penalties, some of them dreadfully severe. Some five hundred years before Christ, for example, the Romans hanged those who stole crops at night. They were executed at the scene of their crime as a sacrifice to Ceres, goddess of the harvest. Here in England during Danish times, a thief could be killed without fear of having to pay compensation to his family because his act of stealing had rendered him valueless. During medieval times, theft continued to be a capital offence along with others such as murder, treason, arson, burglary and robbery; Henry II, however, said that crimes which involved the theft of five shillings (25p) or less could be punished by amputation of a foot instead of death.

By the middle ages, reforms were gradually reducing the barbarity of our penal system, although as late as the seventeenth century a woman was drowned in Loch Spynie in Scotland for committing theft, and across the Channel in France the infamous guillotine was utilised against thieves.

After many tests, France's wonderful new death-dealing machine was perfected by Tobias Schmidt and fitted with a slanting blade on the advice of Louis XVI. In fact, he was later to die by that very blade. However, after being installed on 15th April 1792 as the official method of execution, the guillotine's very first victim was a thief. He was Nicholas-Jacques Pelletier who was guillotined at 3.30pm on 25th April 1792 by the Executioner of Criminal Sentences, Charles-Henri Sanson. The machine was thoughtfully painted red and white, and Pelletier's execution had been delayed so that he could have the honour of being the first to be executed by the guillotine.

Even by the early years of last century, some forms of theft in this country carried the death penalty. In 1810, the reformer Samuel Romilly was horrified by the number of offences which did carry the death penalty, and he tried to introduce bills in Parliament to change these laws. At first, he failed; he tried, for example to remove the death penalty which had been reinstated for stealing objects up to the value of five shillings (25p), and also for stealing objects to the value of £2 from houses and for stealing from ships in navigable waters.

He achieved partial success when Parliament abolished the death penalty for stealing from bleaching-grounds. In spite of his efforts, in 1819 there were still over two hundred capital offences on the statute book, one of which was impersonation of a Chelsea Pensioner!

Examples of the contempt in which theft was held occurred in 1827, when a man called Moses Snook was awarded ten years transportation for stealing a plank of wood, and another man was sentenced to death for stealing 2s 6d (12½p). But the spirit of change was moving, and

Robert Peel, founder of the modern police service, made a tremendous impact upon legal reform. His influence reduced three hundred Acts of Parliament to only four, and drastically reduced the number of capital offences. The death penalty continued to exist however, even for some crimes of theft such as stealing goods to the value of £2 or more from a dwelling-house.

But the juries hated the death penalty for such crimes and they would deliberately undervalue the stolen goods to save a criminal from death. One jury valued a £10 note at £1 19s 0d (£1.95) to save a criminal from death; other examples involved sheep-stealing and horse-stealing, both of which carried the death penalty. A jury found a thief guilty of stealing only the fleece of a sheep instead of the whole beast, and guilty of stealing only the hair of a horse instead of the entire animal.

By 1956, when I joined the Force, theft, in its many and varied forms, carried penalties which ranged from a maximum of five years' imprisonment up to and including life imprisonment, although fines were often imposed in the less serious cases. It was then called larceny, a term which still creeps into some publications.

Stealing from one's employer, for example, carried a maximum penalty of fourteen years' imprisonment; an officer of the Bank of England who stole securities or money from the bank could get life imprisonment. The stealing of horses, cattle or sheep carried up to fourteen years, while stealing postal packets carried life imprisonment. In 1957, a murder committed during the course of or in the furtherance of theft carried the death penalty, and on 13th August 1964, Gwynne Owen Evans and Peter Anthony Allen, two Lancastrians in their early twenties, were hanged for murdering a van-driver during the course of theft. These were England's last judicial hangings.

In 1968, the law of theft was completely overhauled. The definition of the crime was both altered and simplified, and from that time it has carried a maximum penalty of ten years' imprisonment, with associated offences such as burglary and robbery carrying a maximum of life imprisonment in some cases. Those penalties still apply, for theft is still regarded by some as a sin, by others as a major crime and by yet more as a normal part of life.

People help themselves to 'souvenirs' from hotels, restaurants and cafes; they take stuff home from work and fiddle expense accounts. They 'borrow' with no intention of returning, lift plants from garden centres, purloin precious objects from stately homes and have expeditions to our cities for shop-lifting. And it is all theft with a ten-year maximum jail sentence.

In our modern society, the scope for theft is infinite; hundreds of thousands of such crimes are committed daily but massive numbers go unreported because they are accepted as 'normal', and so the true incidence of theft in this country can never be known nor even estimated. But taken as a whole, and supported by most police officers, this will suggest that we live in a very dishonest society.

A statement of this kind, taken from knowledge but unsupported by statistics, will anger politicians who are to the left of centre, but such a claim will be agreed by most business and professional people. They know that thefts occur from their premises and many are dealt with internally, so why report those for which there is no chance of detection? A cafe-owning friend of mine cheerfully told me that he had about a hundred and twenty teaspoons and thirty-six ashtrays stolen *every week,* but he never reported any of these crimes to the police. The incidence of unreported theft would make a marvellous study for a university student . . .

But while the Church continues to denounce theft as a sin, and socialists continue to regard it as a symptom of a society deprived of its basic needs, police officers continue to regard it as a crime committed not by those in need, but by those who like to get their hands on something for nothing and don't mind who suffers in the process. I must confess that I know few, if any, thieves who genuinely had to steal in order to survive; they stole out of pure greed. And that is why thieves are so despicable.

Although so many thefts are not notified to the police, considerable numbers *are* formally reported and investigated before being fed into the nation's crime statistics. For the operational police officer, however, such academic matters are of little importance; his work involves knowing what constitutes a theft, and how to catch the villain responsible. Statistics are of little interest to him.

The 1916 definition of larceny was as follows, and this was the wording which we had to learn parrot-fashion. It was the equivalent of learning the Lord's Prayer or the alphabet, and although I learned this more than thirty years ago, I still remember it. Since then, of course, I had to learn the new definition of theft, which is contained in the Theft Act 1968, but the old words stick in the memory. The 1916 wording may seem ponderous, but it does have a certain rhythm and indeed one poet wrote it down in verse form.

The definition is as follows, according to section 1 of the Larceny Act 1916, now repealed. 'A person steals who, without the consent of the owner, fraudulently and without a claim of right made in good faith, takes and carries away anything capable of being stolen, with intent at the time of such taking permanently to deprive the owner thereof.

'Provided that a person may be guilty of stealing any such thing notwithstanding that he has lawful possession thereof, if, being a bailee or part-owner thereof, he fraudulently converts the same to his own use or to the use of any person other than the owner.'

I frequently imagine a Shakespearian actor quoting this definition, with due pauses at all the commas and full-stops, but our task was to learn it and understand it, along with all the other variations of larceny such as stealing by finding or by intimidation, stealing by mistake or by trick, larceny from the person, larceny of trees and shrubs, and a whole range of other associated crimes like embezzlement, burglary, housebreaking, robbery, false pretences, frauds by agents and trustees, blackmail, receiving stolen property, taking of motor vehicles, etc.

It was fascinating stuff and the precise interpretation of that definition has kept lawyers occupied and earning fat fees for years. We had to know it in our heads so that we could instantly implement its provisions in the street, even if our actions did result in appeals to the High Court or House of Lords in the months to come. But in a volume of this nature, there is no space to enlarge upon the wonderful range of legal fiction which resulted from this and similar statutes. But imagine a thief maliciously cutting someone's grass and leaving the clippings behind on the lawn . . . would it be larceny? Were the clippings 'taken and carried away' or indeed, is grass capable of being stolen? And, how many crimes would be committed? One only? Or one for each blade of grass? Was there intention permanently to deprive the owner of his grass? Or was the whole affair a crime of malicious damage? Such points could keep a class of students occupied for hours and reap rich fees for lawyers.

But police officers tend to deal more with the ordinary crime than the exotic, and few interesting cases of larceny came my way at Aidensfield. Most of them were very routine, often committed at night by pilferers who sneaked around the village picking up things left lying around. For example, one farmer had a brand-new wire rat-trap stolen from his barn, a householder had a selection of pot plants stolen from his greenhouse, a child's tricycle was stolen having been left outside all night, and someone managed to steal a full-size horse trough. Coal was occasionally nicked from the coal yard, wood was taken from the timber yard and, as happens in most villages, there was a phantom knicker-pincher who stole ladies' underwear from clothes-lines. It seems that almost every village, and in towns every housing estate, has a resident phantom knicker-pincher, most of whom are peculiar men who operate under cover of darkness, many of whom are usually caught in the act of satisfying their weird addiction. When their houses are searched, a hoard of illicitly obtained exotic and colourful underwear is usually found. Publicity rarely brings forth claimants because many ladies are too shy to report the initial theft or to admit ownership of some of the magnificent and strikingly sensual underwear thus recovered. The courts are then left with the task of ordering suitable disposal.

Apart from the mundane thefts, several interesting cases did cross my path and one of them involved a picture hanging in a village pub.

It was one of those background pictures, some of which are delightful, which adorn the walls of village inns but which are seldom appreciated until someone steals them or mutilates them in some way during a fit of pique or drunkenness. In this instance, however, the picture remained safely in its position above the black cast-iron Yorkist range, enhanced in the colder seasons by the flickering flames of the log fire below and in the warmer seasons by a vase of flowers positioned on the mantelpiece.

The picture was an oil painting of Winston Churchill as the British Prime Minister and it depicted him with his famous cigar between his lips. It showed him at the height of his powers, a confident and forceful personality who had guided our nation to victory during World War II. In the picture, he was contemplating something across to his left (maybe the Labour party!) and was shown seated in his study with books around him and papers scattered across his desk. It was a fine picture of a widely respected statesman and it had been in the Moon and Compass Inn for several years.

It was one of those pictures which brighten the bars of our village inns, and many a glass had been raised to Winston, later Sir Winston, in his silent pose above the cosy, welcoming fire of the Moon and Compass. During my official visits to the inn, Sir Winston was still alive and I had admired the picture and complimented David Grayson, the landlord, upon its merits. This pleased him, although he had acquired the painting with the fittings of the pub.

The possibility that there could be a problem associated with that picture never entered my head until I received a visit from a tourist. He arrived on the stroke of two o'clock one Wednesday afternoon just as I was about to embark upon a tour of duty in the mini-van. I noticed the sleek grey Jaguar 340 glide to a halt outside my house and a smart man in his sixties emerged. He was dressed in light summer clothes of the casual kind, and his wife remained in the car. I met him in the drive to the police house.

'Good afternoon,' I greeted him.

'Ah, I've obviously just caught you, Constable. Are you in a hurry? You can spare a minute or two?'

'Yes, of course,' and I offered to take him into my office, but he said he could tell me his business where we stood in the front garden.

'You know the Moon and Compass Inn, at Craydale?' he put to me.

'Yes, it's on my beat,' I said.

'Ah, well, there is a problem. A delicate one, I might add,' he began. 'I hate to make accusations which I cannot substantiate, but I feel you ought to be aware of this . . .'

I wondered what was coming next but waited as he gathered his words together.

'It's the picture of Winston Churchill,' he said eventually. 'You know it?'

'It hangs over the fireplace in the bar,' I informed him. 'A nice picture, very realistic. I know it well.'

'And so you should!' His voice increased in pitch. 'It was commissioned from a special sitting — Churchill actually posed for that picture, Constable. It's not a copy, not a print but the original by Christopher Tawney. It's the only one in the world, Constable.'

'It must be valuable, then?' I said inanely.

'I have no idea of its value,' he said shortly. 'No idea at all; it's not an old master so we're not talking in huge sums, but I'd guess it can be measured in thousands, if not tens of thousands. And this is why I've called, Constable. That painting has been stolen. It should not be there; that pub has no right to that picture, no right at all.'

'Stolen? But it's been in that pub for years,' I told him. 'Long before I came here. Eight or ten years even. Are you sure it's the one you think it is?'

'I've never been so sure in my life, Constable. You see, I had it done, I was the person who commissioned the artist and persuaded Winston to undertake that sitting. I know that picture like I know my own belongings. If you care to examine it, you'll see Tawney's signature in the bottom left-hand corner too.'

'You'd better come into the office,' I said.

I asked Mary to make a cup of tea, and to include the gentleman's wife who waited in the car. She was persuaded to come into the lounge where Mary and the children entertained her as I discussed this matter with her husband.

His name was Simon Cornell and he was a retired director of one of Britain's largest and most famous manufacturers of cigars.

'I retired about six years ago,' he said. 'And now Jennie and I spend a lot of time touring England, seeing places we've never been able to visit until now. Always too busy, you know, leading the hectic life of a businessman.'

'So what about the painting?' I was taking notes. 'What's your involvement with that?'

'It was done for an advertisement series,' he said. 'Winston was happy enough for us to use that picture in our adverts — restrictions weren't so rigid then, although he did ask for us to give the equivalent of his fee to a charity of his choice. So we had the oil painting executed by Christopher Tawney; several prints were run off it and you might have seen copies of them on cigar-box lids, adverts in the papers and magazines and so on.'

'Yes,' I admitted. 'I thought I'd seen that picture before. To be honest, Mr Cornell, I didn't pay a great deal of close attention to it . . .'

'Exactly, because there are so many copies still around, a lot of them hanging in pubs, by the way, like this one. They're the same size too. But the one in the Moon and Compass is the original. I can vouch for that.'

I took a long, handwritten statement from him which confirmed what he had told me, and then noted his address and telephone number for future use.

I did extract from him that he was not acting in any official capacity on behalf of the company for whom he had worked; he was merely drawing police attention to a theft which had occurred many years ago. He did inform me that, so far as he could recall, the picture had been hanging in the boardroom and it had been painted soon after Churchill had won the Nobel Prize for Literature in 1953. Some time around 1956, it had disappeared.

'Company records will give the exact date of its disappearance,' Mr Cornell informed me. 'But that's roughly the sequence of events.'

'So it might have been here at least ten years?' I said. 'And I do know the present landlord has been here only four years. He bought the picture with the inn, by the way; he told me that when I was admiring it some time ago. He did not bring it with him — it was part of the fittings.'

'So who does it belong to now, eh?' smiled Cornell.

'I think that's a matter between the company and the landlord of the Moon and Compass,' I said. 'But clearly, you'd be interested in tracing the thief?'

'I think that would be impossible now,' he said. 'But perhaps you will contact the company and inform them of my discovery, and perhaps warn Mr Grayson, your landlord, of this conversation?'

'Yes, of course. And I'll let you know what progress I make.'

And so Mr Cornell left me with this problem.

As he drove away, his wife chirping with delight at her warm reception by our little brood of four children and I was left with the thought that David Grayson had no idea he was in possession of stolen property. I was equally aware that the matter could not be ignored but knew that if I mentioned the affair to Sergeant Blaketon, he would charge into action like the proverbial bull in a china shop. His heavy-handed, rule-bound methods would wreak havoc every inch of the way as he had me arresting everyone in sight for theft or for receiving stolen property. It was my belief that this allegation, for it was nothing more than an allegation at this stage, required some rather delicate handling.

And so I waited for Sergeant Charlie Bairstow to come on duty. I felt he would adopt a more reasoned approach. It meant a delay of just one day, but I felt it was justified. I caught him during a quiet moment over an early-morning cup of coffee in the office at Ashfordly and presented him with the story. He listened carefully and I showed him the statement made by Simon Cornell.

'A tale of villainy if ever there was one,' he smiled. 'What do you reckon?'

'About the truth of it, you mean?' I asked.

'Yes, is Cornell having us on, or is that picture the genuine thing as he says.'

'I believe him.' I spoke as I felt and, of course, I had witnessed Cornell's reaction as he had relayed his tale.

Sergeant Bairstow thought for a while and I knew he was weighing up all the problems that might accrue, both emotional and legal, and then he said, 'We'd better go and have a look at it. And we'd better warn Grayson of this.'

'He bought it legally,' I pointed out.

'Yes, and that gives him a claim to the painting,' he said. 'A claim of right made in good faith, as the Larceny Act so aptly puts it.'

And so we drove out to Craydale and popped into the Moon and Compass. David was working in his cellar when we arrived, stacking crates and cleaning out his beer pumps. He was happy enough to break for a coffee.

'Well, gentlemen.' He took us into the bar which was closed to the public as it was not opening hours. 'This looks business-like, two of you descending on me.'

'It is a problem,' Sergeant Bairstow said. 'Nick, you'd better explain.'

I told him of Cornell's visit and allegations, and he listened carefully, a worried frown crossing his pleasant face as I outlined the theft of the picture from the cigar company. We closely examined the painting and it was clearly executed in oils and signed, and on the back was a certificate of authenticity. It was the genuine thing; of that, there was no doubt. David kept looking at the image of Sir Winston and was clearly upset at our unpleasant news.

'So what do I do now?' he asked us both, looking most anxious and apprehensive.

'Nothing,' said Charlie Bairstow. 'Just sit tight; there's no suggestion that you stole it, we want you to know that. Our next job is to contact the cigar firm and tell them the picture has been found. But you do have a claim to it, David, because you bought it in good faith, as part of the fittings of the pub.'

'When did you say it was stolen?' he asked.

'1956, as near as we can tell,' I said.

'That was two landlords ago,' he added. 'I took it over from Jim Bentley, and he came here in 1959. I'm not sure who was here in 1956.'

'Our liquor licensing records will tell us,' said Bairstow. 'We'll chase up that angle.'

'But I don't want that bloody picture hanging here if it's worth a fortune!' he cried. 'Somebody might pinch it!'

'It's been there years without that happening,' Bairstow said. 'Anyway, I'd say it's yours now, David, but you might need a solicitor to do battle for you, from the ownership point of view, especially if the cigar people decide they want it back and make a claim upon it.'

'I think I'll hide it upstairs,' he smiled grimly. 'So what happens now?'

'Leave it with us,' said Charlie Bairstow. 'We will contact the cigar company and see what they say.'

'Thanks for telling me all this first,' David was clearly grateful for our action. 'So I might be sitting on a fortune after all this?'

'Cornell thought it was worth a lot of money,' I said. 'But he wouldn't commit himself to an amount. Don't forget that this is the original, David.'

'How can I? It's funny this has arisen,' he added. 'I've often said to Madge — my wife that is — that this looked like an oil painting and not a copy. I know some copies look so realistic now, even down to a rough surface, but well, this did have a genuine feel to it. I never thought of looking at the back for that certificate!'

'Well,' said Sergeant Bairstow. 'You hang on to it, and we'll see what happens next.'

'Thank you, Sergeant,' and we left him to his thoughts.

Back in the office, I compiled a report on the matter for despatch to the Chief Constable of Surrey Constabulary in whose area the cigar factory was based. In the terminology of the time, I asked him if he would allow an officer to search his records in an attempt to locate the report of the original theft, and then allow an officer to visit a senior official of the cigar company to inform him of the painting's present whereabouts. Sergeant Bairstow also asked me to include a paragraph to ask whether, in view of the passage of time, Surrey Constabulary required any further action by us in this matter.

The reply came ten days later. A detective sergeant in Guildford had established that the crime had been reported on 28th April 1956, the picture then being worth £850.

The original's disappearance had not been noticed for some time because one of the copies, in an identical frame, had been substituted. It had never been recovered, nor had the thief been arrested. Enquiries at the time had revealed that one of the suspects had been a salesman who had subsequently resigned from the company, but nothing had ever been proved against him. That man's name was not supplied, but Surrey Police did say the file had never been closed; they went on to add that it would be appreciated if steps could be taken to ascertain the name of the person who had sold the painting to the landlord of the Moon and Compass.

We did trace the long-retired landlord, an old character called Ralph Whalton who now lived with his married daughter in a bungalow at Eltering. He did not remember anything of the painting, but his daughter did. A plain girl approaching her thirties, she remembered its arrival.

'Oh, yes,' she said. 'You must remember, Dad!'

The old man shook his head. 'I'm too old now, Jill. They gave me all sorts of publicity stuff, I stuffed most of it in the cellar. I couldn't put it all up in the bar.'

'Well, I remember it well. I was about eighteen or nineteen at the time and helping behind the bar. A salesman came in, not the regular one, with a box of those cigars you always bought. And he had that picture of Churchill. He said every pub was being given one and he hoped we would display it in a public area.'

'Was I there?' he asked, clearly puzzled.

'You might not have been,' she now realised. 'Maybe not, maybe that's why I was helping out. Mebbe you'd gone away somewhere. Anyway, we took a picture down, it was one of those pen-and-ink drawings of a Scottish mountain scene, and hung Sir Winston instead. He's been there ever since.'

She was unable to provide a description of the salesman and did not know his name. We passed this information to Guildford Police and it was about three weeks later when I received a telephone call to say that Guildford Police were closing this file because (a) the picture had been located and (b) their suspect salesman was now known to have died in 1962. Apparently, their records showed he was working in the North Riding for a short period during the spring of 1956. He was a very positive suspect.

So who did the picture now belong to? I knew that if someone was convicted of stealing it, the court could make an order for its restitution to the cigar company, but this was impossible in this case because several innocent buyers had since been involved and, apart from that, no one had been convicted of its theft. This latter fact alone ruled out this form of restitution through the criminal courts; now, of course, no one would ever be convicted for stealing it.

David Grayson, landlord of the Moon and Compass, now had a strong legal right to that picture, and I do know that he changed his mind about hiding it upstairs.

He was very proud of it, particularly as it had spawned so many copies throughout the country, and he told me that the cigar company had eventually offered him one of the many surplus copies in an identical frame, but he had refused. They desperately wanted the original to be returned for display in the company head office, but they did not offer him any money or compensation for it. After all, he had paid good money to acquire it quite legally and perhaps the company should have made some form of financial gesture.

Instead, following David's refusal, the company had made a half-hearted threat of attempting to recover the painting through the civil courts, but that was never proceeded with. I don't think it would have succeeded. So even now, if you go into the bar of the Moon and Compass at Craydale, you will see Sir Winston Churchill's image beaming over the customers. And no one knows how or why it came to be in this remote North Yorkshire pub.

One theory is that the salesman managed to steal it from his head office and that he mistakenly gave it away while delivering the advertisement copies. Or, of course, he might have become terrified at the thought of being captured with it in his possession and decided to get rid of it in this way, hoping that no one in remote North Yorkshire would realise it was something special. But David Grayson did tell me that, when he decided to leave the pub, he would return the picture to the company for display in their boardroom above a little notice saying, "Donated by Mr David Grayson."

I thought it was a nice gesture, a moral compromise and a means of ensuring the picture never again went astray.

* * *

While that episode caused more than a flicker of professional interest, there were countless mundane crimes and one of them, or to be more accurate, a series of them, involved the village store at Crampton. It was a typical village store, the kind of emporium found in every self-respecting small community. It dispensed almost everything from lawnmowers to tins of beans by way of socks, bread loaves, paperback novels, eggs and some of the finest cooked ham in the area. The high walls were filled with shelves of wines, exotic foods and sweets, tins of fruit, boxes of screws, nails and washers, dishcloths and kitchen utensils.

The owner was a small sprightly bachelor of indeterminate age. He was called Mr Wilson and had run his well-stocked shop for as long as anyone could remember. No one seemed to know his Christian name because everyone called him Mr Wilson and no one knew much about his private life. A secretive but marvellously tidy little fellow, he seemed to be involved in no social or community activities, for his entire life was spent running his shop. It was his pride and joy, and if he could not supply any requested item from stock, he would always obtain it from somewhere. On one occasion, I asked if he knew where I could find a belt for our twin-tub spin-dryer, for the existing one had become worn and stretched until it would not properly turn the pulleys. Mr Wilson had one in stock.

His range of cheeses was remarkable, as were his liqueurs, chocolates, fresh fruit and beautiful vegetables, and I know one man who even bought a wheelbarrow wheel from Mr Wilson's stock — and it was the right size.

During the course of my duties, I learned that people respected Mr Wilson highly and relied upon him to cater for all their daily requirements. 'You'll get it at Mr Wilson's,' was the slogan, and so I was a frequent visitor, both on duty and off. He never complained, never seemed flustered or worried and was always in complete control of his stock and in touch with his customers' changing needs.

And then, one breezy day in May, he rang me and asked if I would pay him a visit, preferably between 1pm and 1.45pm when he would be closed for lunch. I was asked to go around the back, to his cottage door, because he wished to discuss a matter without interruption by his customers.

Intrigued by this, I drove across to Crampton and knocked on his cottage door. When he met me, he had a deep frown on his small, pink face and for the first time, to my knowledge, his immaculate head of pure white hair looked untidy. I detected worry in his eyes and there was no doubt he was more than a little agitated.

'Come in, Mr Rhea,' he invited. 'You'll have a coffee with me? Have you eaten?'

'Yes, thanks, I had lunch before I came out, but a coffee would be very welcome.'

He led me into his neat living-room; it was very plain and lacked the touch of a woman. There were no flowers, for example, and everything was in its place, untouched by children, visitors and family. There was not a speck of dust anywhere and his collection of brasses sparkled in the light of the bright spring weather. He indicated a plain leather easy chair and I settled in it as he busied himself with the coffee.

'You'll be wondering why I've called you in,' he said, sitting opposite me and crossing his legs. I was surprised at the tiny size of his shoes, so highly polished and well kept. I'd never seen his feet before because he was always behind his counters. Now, without those protective barriers, he was like a little elf as his bright blue eyes scrutinised me.

'It must be important,' was my response to that remark.

'Yes, and confidential,' he said. 'Er, am I permitted to discuss something with you unofficially, off the record in a manner of speaking?'

'Of course, we are allowed discretion, you know. We do not enforce every rule by the letter — that would make it a police state!' I wondered what was coming next.

'I have a shop-lifter among my customers'. He drew in a deep breath and then spat out those words. 'A clever and persistent shop-lifter, Mr Rhea. I do not know what to do about her.'

This problem was the scourge of many city shops, and it was also affecting some rural ones which encouraged self-service by their customers. Mr Wilson's was such a shop, for the three counters which formed an open square as the customers entered each bore a selection of goods upon their tops. Sweets, cakes, delicacies, preserves, novels in paperback, spoons, fruit and so forth occupied space upon them.

'You know who it is?' I put to him.

He nodded. 'Yes, it's been going on for some time now, months perhaps, but I've been keeping a careful eye on things recently. I have made myself certain of the identity of the culprit, Mr Rhea.'

'You've confronted her about it?' I asked.

He shook his head this time. 'No, that is the problem, that is why I need your advice.'

'So what's she been doing?'

'General thieving, I think you'd call it,' he smiled a little ruefully. 'She is a good customer, Mr Rhea, a very good one. But I noticed that she began to linger in the shop when other customers were present, allowing me to serve them while she examined my stock. Then she would make her purchases, but I began to realise things had disappeared from my counter surfaces after each of her visits. She was picking things up while I was busy, you see, and hiding them in her shopping-bag.'

'Valuable things?' I asked.

'Not really, more like silly things. Apples, plastic teaspoons, tins of sticking-plasters, tubes of toothpaste, indigestion tablets, bars of chocolate or tubes of sweets, a bottle of wine on one occasion, biscuits, cakes . . .'

'If I am to prosecute her, I'll need to catch her in possession of the stolen goods,' I said. 'I cannot take a person to court without real evidence.'

'No, I don't want that,' he was quick to say. 'I don't want to prosecute her, that's the problem. I just want to stop her.'

'Confrontation would be advisable in the first instance,' I advised him. 'You'd have to catch her in possession of something that you could positively identify has having been stolen from your shop. Then threaten her with court action. That might stop her.'

He hesitated and then said, 'I did halt her on one occasion,' he said quietly. 'I had placed a bottle of French perfume on the front counter, where I knew she had been taking things from, and it disappeared when she was in my shop. As she was leaving, I said. "Miss Carr, the perfume, that will be £3 17s 6d please".'

Unwittingly, he had revealed the name of the shop-lifter but I did not comment on this just yet.

'And what did she do?' I asked.

'She looked at me full in the face and said, "Mr Wilson, I have no perfume, I never use that horrid French stuff".'

'And did you search her bags?'

'Oh, no, I couldn't do that,' he said. 'That would drive her away.'

'You want her driven away, surely?' I put to him.

'On the contrary, Mr Rhea, I do not. That is my dilemma. You see, she is a very good customer. She spends heavily in here, buying all sorts and she always pays cash, except for the silly things she steals. She is not like some customers, Mr Rhea, who run up bills and need pressing to pay them. She pays cash for every honest purchase, so she's a very valuable customer in that sense.'

'You couldn't afford to lose her then?'

He shook his head. 'No, but there's more, you see. She is aunt to lots of people around here. She's one of a very large family, the Carrs, most of whom live around Crampton. Farmers, villagers, professional people — you'll know them as well as me. They're related to the Bennisons, the Tindales, the Haddons, the Newalls, the Lofthouses and others too. Many have accounts with me, Mr Rhea, they're all good spenders. She buys for them, as well; she's very generous you see, always buying things for her army of nephews and nieces, always giving them presents from here. Bottles of wine, expensive cheeses, perfume, tins of exotic fruit and so on. They're things she pays for, by the way.'

'Are you saying that if you banned her, they'd all stop coming as well?'

'It's a fear at the back of my mind,' he admitted. 'They are a very close family, Mr Rhea, and I know they'd never believe that their generous Aunt Mabel was a cunning thief.'

In some ways, it was the classic case of a nasty thief taking advantage of a kindly village storekeeper, and in real terms this was a case which well justified prosecution. I explained to Mr Wilson that we could secrete a camera inside the premises to catch her actually stealing an item, and then take her to court by using that film as evidence. Or we could mark certain objects with a fluorescent powder which would adhere to her hands and clothes, and which would glow under certain lights. By using technology, we could catch her in the act — all this presented no problems.

'No, I couldn't bear that,' he said. 'Not for such a good customer, Mr Rhea, and I must think of her reputation and that of all her relations. The publicity would be terrible in a community of this size.'

'So how can I help if you do not want official action?' I asked.

'I thought you might have knowledge of other methods of prevention, Mr. Rhea. I know shop-lifting is a problem, and I thought you might know of some way I could prevent her, for her own sake really, without resorting to court action.'

'I could have a word with her,' I offered. 'I could try to warn her off. Maybe a lecture from a policeman would help. I could frighten her off, maybe.'

'She might take umbrage, Mr Rhea, and boycott my store if she thought I'd been making accusations behind her back.'

'So we've reached an impasse,' I said. 'You will not confront her with your suspicions, and you will not allow me to confront her either. Really, Mr Wilson, if you do not want official police action, the remedy must come from you. You've got to decide either to let her continue, or to ban her from the shop, with all the possible consequences.'

'Oh, dear,' he said. 'I know that if I do ban her, the others will boycott me, and I could not afford that. There are some very good customers among her relations, Mr Rhea. It seems I must grin and bear it, then.'

'Sorry,' I said. 'I only wish I could be more helpful.'

'Well, I had to talk it over with someone impartial,' he said. 'I shall keep a closer eye on her, that's all.'

And so I left him to his worries. But later that afternoon, as I drove around my picturesque beat, I felt I'd let him down. Even though he did not wish me to take official action, I felt there could have been some advice or help I might have produced. But what?

How could I involve myself in this problem in an unofficial capacity? In some ways, Mr Wilson had placed me in a dilemma too and as I drove around, I passed Miss Carr's fine house. A magnificent detached stone-built house, it occupied a prime site about a mile out of Crampton and as I drove past, she drove out of her gate in her new Volvo.

Money for Miss Carr was no problem; a confident, fine-looking woman in her early fifties, she paid her way and was openly generous to her nephews and nieces and indeed to others who needed help. The village could tell of many acts of kindness by Mabel Carr. For these reasons, it seemed very odd that she was systematically stealing from this hard-working little shopkeeper. My own instinct was to prosecute her for this unkindness towards him, for I felt it was the only answer. I drove on, and it would be about a week later at lunchtime when I was next in Crampton. Mr Wilson's shop was closed so I decided to walk around the village, then pop in to see him. And as I walked among the pretty cottages and flowering meadows, I had an idea.

'Ah, Mr Rhea,' he beamed. 'Good of you to call.'

'Good afternoon, Mr Wilson,' I smiled. 'How's things?'

'Very well, thank you,' he said. The shop was empty, so we chatted about the weather for a while, and engaged in our usual small talk, and then I asked about Miss Carr.

'Is she still stealing?' I asked.

'I'm afraid so,' he said. 'As bold as brass, really. She got away with a small liqueur on Monday, slipped it into her shopping-bag as quick as lightning. I think she's getting bolder, Mr Rhea. I do wish I could find a way of halting her.'

'I think I have an answer,' I said. 'Highly irregular, I'm afraid, and very unofficial, but it might work.'

He smiled. 'I'll listen to anything.'

'First, I must ask this, you're not making it easy for her to take things, are you? Putting temptation in her way? Placing things where she can't resist them?'

He shook his head. 'No, the stuff she takes is my normal stock which is regularly on the counters for sale. I've always displayed it there, Mr Rhea; in fact, I've been trying to make things a little more difficult for her by putting out larger items, like the bottles of liqueur. But after she'd been in, one was missing. She was too quick for me, Mr Rhea; it had gone in a twinkling and she was out of the shop before I realised what she'd done. That's how she operates; I have kept an eye on her and she knows it, but she's too quick and clever, a real expert. I can't clear my counters because of her; besides, that kind of open sales technique is a valuable source of income.'

I knew that his neat and tidy mind would instinctively realise when something had been taken; he'd know if a solitary tomato or roll of mints was stolen from his stock, so organised was his mind and his business.

'I had to ask,' I said, 'because it's the sort of question that you might get asked by her relations if you implement my little scheme.'

'Short of banning her, Mr Rhea, I've done everything to make it harder for her to steal. So what is your plan?'

'Her relations, nephews, nieces, cousins and so on, how many of them are your customers?'

'Most of them who live hereabouts,' he said, opening a drawer behind the counter. 'I'll check for you.'

He lifted out several small red notebooks, each with a customer's name on the front, and sorted through them. He put several to one side, and then counted them.

'Seven,' he said. 'Seven have monthly accounts with me, these are their books.'

'And are there others without accounts?' I asked.

'Just one,' he said. 'Mrs Ruth Newall, Mabel's elder sister. She pays cash for everything. Why do you ask?'

I side-stepped that question for the moment by asking, 'And are they fond of their Aunt or Cousin Mabel? They'd not want her to get into trouble with us, the police?'

'Oh, they love her, Mr Rhea, they're a lovely family, so close.'

'Good, so this is what I suggest. I suggest that every time Miss Carr steals something, you add its cost to one of those relations' accounts. In other words, you make the family pay for her sins through a form of communal responsibility.'

'They'd know they hadn't bought the goods in question, Mr Rhea, and query it. It's almost dishonest . . .'

'But that's the idea, Mr Wilson, to encourage them to query their account. Then you tell them why, you tell them it's for a bottle of liqueur that Miss Mabel, er, took, without paying. You tell them quite clearly what she's doing, Mr Wilson.'

'I think they'd be very upset.'

'Yes, but that's where you score because you say that she's been stealing for many months, that you've done all in your power to stop her, and short of taking her to the magistrates' court, this is your only redress. I'm sure they'll appreciate your actions in not prosecuting her — after all, she is giving them presents and money . . . besides, that bottle of liqueur, for example, might well be sitting on one of their own shelves right now . . .'

'Yes, I suspect it is, Mr Rhea.'

'The idea is that the responsibility is placed upon her family; it lifts the burden from you and it means you are not losing money or sleep because of her actions.'

'I'll think about it,' was all he said.

It was several weeks later when he called me into his cottage behind the shop.

'Mr Rhea,' he said over a coffee. 'That system you suggested for Mabel Carr. I thought I'd let you know that it is working very well.'

'Is it? Then I'm delighted!'

'I must admit I was uncertain at first, and indeed I ignored it, but then she got away with a full bottle of brandy. I put it on Mrs George Haddon's bill — George is a nephew, and I explained why. It seems Mabel had given him the bottle anyway! But he called a family conference and they invited me up to the Haddons' house to explain things to the whole family, without Mabel's knowledge, of course.'

'That's an excellent move, so they took it well?'

'Yes, very well, they were sorry that she had placed me in such a position, but they fully understood. And they agreed to my actions. They were pleased I had told them.'

'And they will be trying to persuade her to stop shop-lifting?' I smiled.

'Er, no,' he said. 'They do not want to upset her, so we will all allow her to continue, and they will pay for everything she steals. They feel it is a symptom of her time of life, you see, and that she will overcome it eventually. So they're keeping my actions secret from her.'

'And does this please you, Mr Wilson?' I asked.

'Yes, it does, Mr Rhea, and thank you.'

In the days that followed, I wondered whether the actions of Mabel Carr now amounted to the crime of theft and felt this could produce a marvellous challenge for a defence lawyer if such a conspiracy ever reached court. But it never did. Mabel's huge complement of relations continued to pay for her indiscretions and I heard no more about it.

Years later, though, I did learn by sheer chance from one of her sisters that, throughout her youthful and indeed middle-aged years, Mabel Carr had conducted a very one-sided love affair with Mr Wilson. And not once had he shown the slightest romantic interest in her — I don't think he ever knew of, or suspected, her yearnings and devotion.

Maybe her shop-lifting was a last desperate attempt to attract his attention?

CHAPTER 5

> Where is the man who has the power and skill
> To stem the torrent of a woman's will?
> ANONYMOUS

It was Shakespeare who said that a railing wife was worse than a smoky house, and Thomas Moore who wrote in his 'Sovereign Woman' that 'Disguise our bondage as we will, Tis woman, woman, who rules us still'. Those poets, and the anonymous gentleman who wrote the opening lines at the head of this chapter, must have had some personal knowledge of the awful effect that a nagging wife can have upon the happiness and peace of mind of a husband.

Down the ages, and in spite of modern scientific progress, it has been impossible to stop some women from nagging. One terrible attempt was made by the introduction of the brank; this was an iron framework which was placed upon a woman's head and padlocked in position. At the front, it had a plate from which protruded a spiked or sharp edge, and this fitted into the mouth of the woman. If she moved her tongue, therefore, she injured herself; if she kept quiet, she was not hurt.

With this upon her head, the scold, as she was called, was paraded through the streets by one of the community officials. This object, known variously as the brank or scold's bridle, was thought to have been first used in 1623 in Macclesfield, although there are hints that is was used in Scotland as early as 1574. In 1600, it is thought, the brank was used in Stirling to punish 'the shrew.'

Around the country, some branks are preserved in our museums, and a famous one is linked to the church at Walton-on-Thames. It was presented to the parish in 1632 by a man called Chester because he had lost one of his estates through the actions of a lying and gossiping woman. Mr Chester presented the brank with this accompanying verse:

Chester presents Walton with a bridle
To curb women's tongues that talk too idle.

It is difficult to ascertain when the brank was last used, although there is an account of one in the early part of last century. At Altrincham, a woman who caused great distress to her neighbours by her ceaseless and malicious gossip was punished by being paraded around the town wearing a brank. But she refused to walk with it on and would not agree to this punishment. As a result she was then placed in a wheelbarrow and wheeled around the principal streets and market place. History assures us that this had the desired effect of curbing her tongue.

Another device for dealing with scolds was the ducking-stool; this varied in detailed construction but was based on something akin to a long plank, rather like a see-saw, which had a chair or seat at one end. It was positioned with the chair over a pond or river, and so the scolding woman, after being tied into the chair, was lowered repeatedly into the water to cool her tongue. This punishment usually attracted a crowd of local folks who came along for the so-called fun.

One account dated 1700, written by a Frenchman upon a visit to England, says, 'The way of punishing scolding women is pleasant enough,' and he then describes the ducking-stool, after which he adds, 'They plunge her into the water as often as the sentence directs, in order to cool her immoderate heat.'

Like the brank, the ducking-stool's last known use occurred in the early years of last century, probably in 1809 at Leominster. The lady was called Jenny Pipes and the first thing she did upon release from the stool was to utter a string of foul oaths as she cursed the magistrates.

Of these two methods, contemporary reports said that the brank was better than the ducking-stool because 'the stool not only endangered the health of the party, it also gave her tongue liberty 'twixt every dip.'

The nagging woman has been a topic of writers, poets and comedians for years, and remains so. I like the story of a man who called his wife Peg, when her real name was Josephine. Someone asked him why he called her Peg and he said, 'Well, Peg is short for Pegasus; Pegasus was an immortal horse and an immortal horse is an everlasting nag.'

There is also a view that nature has given man the apparatus for snoring to compensate for the woman's capacity for nagging. She nags him during the day, so he retaliates by snoring at night, for which she nags him during the day . . . and so a type of noisy if uneasy balance is achieved.

But not all naggers are married to snorers and not all snorers are married to naggers, which means that many innocent people suffer from vitriolic and poisonous tongues while others must tolerate nights of oscillating and very tuneless olfactory muscles.

One would hardly expect the village constable to become involved in marital battles of this kind, but in fact all police officers, whether rural or urban, do find themselves involved in what the police call 'domestics'. These are breaches of the peace which generally occur among families; if the battles remain behind closed doors, we are not too concerned, but when warring women spill into the street armed with frying-pans, rolling-pins and sharp tongues, then we are sometimes called in to quell what could otherwise develop into a breach of the peace in a public place. As a rule, we try to avoid these because the moment the peace-making constable arrives, the sparring partners both turn upon the unfortunate constable. But at least that stops the quarrelling and perhaps personifies the constable's unsung role in maintaining public tranquillity. He keeps the peace while being attacked from all sides.

It would not be possible in this book to list all the 'domestics' in which I became officially involved, but they did conform to this pattern and few terminated in court. They were usually settled by a stern talking-to or threats of having 'binding-over' orders levelled against the parties, for most were of a sudden and temporary nature.

But there were cases when nagging wives caused domestic upsets of a more permanent kind. One involved a man called Joseph Pringle who had a wife called Roberta. They lived in a neat little bungalow in Aidensfield, just off the Elsinby Road, where it nestled cheerfully among trees with a fine view to the south. With no children, the Pringles were a quiet couple who rarely involved themselves in village matters. Mrs Pringle's socialising was done in York.

I first became aware of Joseph when I noticed his car halting outside the Brewers Arms at Aidensfield around seven each weekday evening. He always popped in for a swift half of bitter on his way home from work, and sometimes I came across him when I was on official business in the pub. If I had any confidential enquiries to make of any landlord, I would pop in before the customers filled the bars. And so I became acquainted with Joseph Pringle.

Aged about forty with a balding head of greying hair, he was one of those insignificant men who are hardly noticed among a crowd of three. Of average height and average build, he wore average clothes and drove an average car at an average sort of speed. He lived in an average house on an average income, but, as I was to learn later, he suffered from a higher-than-average amount of nagging. He had married a true virago, a real warrior of a woman who constantly and cruelly nattered him during his every moment at home. She never gave him a moment's peace; she nagged and nagged and nagged.

Roberta Pringle was a loud-mouthed, energetic and very forceful woman who played hell with everyone; good-looking in some ways, she was approaching forty and had a fine figure topped with an equally fine head of dark hair which framed a handsome, rather than pretty, face. Slightly taller than her husband, she was always very well dressed, but went about her daily routine playing hell with the postman, the dustman, the milkman, the paper-boys, the butcher, the grocer, the vicar, the policeman, her neighbours and anyone else with whom she had any dealings. And of course, when they were not available, she played hell with Joseph.

Because most of them learned, by experience, to keep out of her way, Joseph bore the heaviest burden. He was continuously told off because of the government, the rates, the parish council, the state of the nation, the cost of living, the sloppy work of builders, plumbers, electricians, motor mechanics, doctors, dentists and nurses; she played hell about the roads, snowploughs, weather forecasters, British Rail, bus timetables, canteen ladies, rubbish bins, cafe proprietors, village shops, the post office, tinned beans, the telephone system, television, women's fashions, men's trousers, hotel beds, the water supply, long grass, bruised apples, cold Yorkshire puddings and fatty ham.

And she never stopped complaining and nagging, which meant that her range of subject-matter was never exhausted. Indeed, it expanded, with the meek Joseph having his ears lambasted during all his precious moments at home.

As a result, of course, he started to come home later, a ploy which enabled him to avoid some of her vitriol and which was part of the reason he paid his nightly visit to the Brewers Arms. It gave him peace from both work and wife.

Joseph owned and ran his own gentlemen's outfitters in Eltering. It was a modest shop which sold fairly cheap clothes whose quality was not of the highest. He now faced competition from the major department stores in York and elsewhere for they stocked good clothes within the cheaper range, while those men with money patronised their own bespoke tailors. Joseph had no drive and ambition; he did not wish to become the owner of a chain of shops nor did he strive to change his own dwindling circumstances. He seemed content to let things drift downwards, and I began to learn of his shrinking fortune in the course of my patrolling.

Some hint of his problems arose when I popped into his shop to buy some black socks. He was on the telephone, and was saying words like, 'Yes, dear. No dear. Yes, I will. No, I will not be late tonight. There isn't much in the till today. Yes, I know the car needs attention, the brakes, yes. I'll see what the garage says.'

When he saw me at the counter, he said, 'I have a customer, dear. See you tonight,' and he replaced the handset.

'Women!' he said, recognising me. 'All they think about is money and status! Well, Mr Rhea, what can I get you?'

'Two pairs of black socks please, Joseph,' I said.

He obtained them and I paid, then he said, 'There are times I wish I had your job, Mr Rhea. A regular salary, interesting life, varied work and the means of travelling around the district. I'm stuck in here, day in and day out, it does get a bit monotonous.'

'It's funny, you know,' I said. 'Lots of policemen say they'd like their own business.'

'It has some advantages, Mr Rhea, but times are not good for my trade. Multiple stores, cheaper mass-produced clothes, foreign imports — small shops are finding it hard, very hard to compete. I'd pack it in tomorrow if I could.'

'You surprise me,' I was honest when I said that.

He seemed anxious to talk so I did not rush away.

'Roberta likes to live well, to dress well, to socialise and have a nice home. I can't give her all she wants, Mr Rhea, it does worry me.'

'Could you sell up and try another business?'

'I would have trouble selling this shop, I feel. But you don't need burdening with my worries! Thanks for listening,

I needed someone to say that to. Not that you can help, but at least you did listen.'

'I'll listen whenever you want, Joseph.' I tried to show a little understanding. 'Maybe I will come across someone who wants a shop just like yours. As you say, I am out and about a lot.'

'Thanks, I'll buy you a half next time you're in the Brewers Arms,' he offered with a sad smile.

Further hints of Joseph Pringle's problems came to me over the next few months. A businessman friend from York, for example, asked if I knew the Pringles of Aidensfield; my friend's wife was a member of a York Ladies Luncheon Club where Roberta Pringle was also a member. It seemed she had told her fellow members that Joseph ran a men's clothing manufacturing business with outlets all over the country. In fact, there was an internationally known manufacturer of men's high-quality clothing at Eltering, but it was not Joseph's business. Roberta's skilful story-telling had led her friends to believe he was a very successful businessman and that those premises were his. I began to see that Roberta was living a life of fiction, a life of fantasy, a life of dangerous expense for poor old Joseph.

It explained why she socialised away from home, why she kept away from those who knew her well, why she dressed so expensively, why she was always nagging at the tired Joseph to improve his status and income. And, as eventually I learned, she was spending all his cash.

I met him on a walk one Sunday morning and he wanted to talk again. 'You've not found anyone who might want my shop, Mr Rhea?' was his opening gambit.

'Sorry, Joseph.' I had asked around and had in fact come across a retiring police sergeant who was thinking of starting a shop in Eltering. Not a clothes shop, however, although he did express interest in the premises. But he never went ahead.

I promised Joseph I'd keep my ears and eyes open on his behalf.

'I'm getting to the point where I can't pay my bills,' he said. 'I can't get credit to buy my stock . . .'

'How about a sale?' I suggested. 'Why not sell off some older stock?'

'I have,' he said. 'It's Roberta, you see, she is a partner and she never stops buying clothes for herself. She does need them, you see, for her luncheon clubs and theatre outings and so on, and it's not fair if I stop the only enjoyment she has in life. She has to be smart. She's mixing with the right people, you see . . .'

It's all right telling a man to be firm with a wife who is ruining him, but it's a different thing persuading that same man to take positive action. I never knew why Joseph did not take a firmer stance for I'd heard that she demanded a new outfit every month so that she could keep up her social appearances . . . poor old Joseph. Much of his dilemma was due to his own fault and his weakness with his awful wife, but I could only commiserate with him. Tentatively, I asked whether Roberta might help in the shop, perhaps by selling other lines, baby clothes, for example, or ladies' wear.

'Oh, no, she wouldn't do that, Mr Rhea, not Roberta. She doesn't believe in women having to work.'

'But if it's to save your business, your livelihood . . . ?'

He shook his head. 'She won't, I've tried that idea. In fact, I think a general clothes shop would go well, but I'd need finance to establish it, and I'd need staff to run it, but can't afford either.'

Surely Roberta would have worked with him, for no wages, to establish a thriving business and to enable her to continue her desired way of life? But she would not. He was adamant about that. After this chat, there was no doubt in my mind where his problem lay. Over the weeks that followed, I saw him spending longer and longer in the Brewers Arms, not getting drunk because he wasn't that kind of man. He just wanted relief from her nagging, but then she started ringing the pub. She began nagging at George, the landlord, demanding that he send Joseph home, and when Joseph got home, he was faced with more nagging.

Roberta continued to nag George day in and day out until, whenever poor Joseph went in for a quick half, George would say, 'Come on, Joseph, don't spend all night here, I don't want that wife of yours hogging my telephone and nagging me. Folks come here to get away from nagging.'

Poor old Joseph. There was no escape.

As for Roberta, she continued to strut around the village in her finery, holding her head high and nagging at everyone she met until the end came. Joseph went bankrupt. It was all done quietly with very little noise from Roberta, but his ailing shop closed, and they sold their bungalow. But this did not stop Roberta.

I was to learn that they had moved into York where, according to Roberta, Joseph had become a director of one of the city's department stores but where, in fact, he was an assistant on the men's shirt counter.

And she continued to attend her important social functions in the finest of clothes. Looking back, she would have been a fine candidate for the brank or the ducking-stool, and I'm sure plenty of volunteers could have been found to administer that punishment.

Since then, I've always felt sorry for the Josephs of this world, but really, who was to blame?

* * *

Another case of a nagging wife had a very different outcome. Benjamin Owens was a hill farmer in a fairly small way and his untidy clutch of ramshackle buildings occupied a remote hillside in Rannackdale. Always in need of painting, glazing, tidying-up and general maintenance, his mediocre spread barely earned him a living. He managed to scrape together a few pounds every week by selling milk from his small herd of cows, and by selling eggs, poultry, sheep for mutton and some wool when he sheared his little flock of moorland sheep. A tiny patch of land was cultivated and he would sometimes sell turnips, potatoes or cabbages to the local shops. He earned just enough for subsistence; he never bought clothes nor went out socially, except once a month to Eltering Market to sell his stock and to buy more.

Even then, he went in his scruffy old clothes which he'd worn every day for about fifteen years.

Benjamin, who was about sixty-two years old, had farmed at Helm End, Rannackdale, all his life; his parents had run the tiny farm before him and his grandfather before that, so there was no mortgage to worry about. The farm had been handed down from father to son for generations, but Benjamin had no heirs. His massive wife, Kate, who was perhaps a couple of years younger, had never produced a litter, as he once said.

The income from such a small hillside small-holding did not allow luxuries or extras; Benjamin ran a battered old pick-up, an even more battered old tractor and his untidy wife never worried about dusting the house, washing their clothes regularly or doing any form of extra housework. She did the essentials like baking, cooking their meals and some shopping, but little more.

As I got to know them better, I realised they never went anywhere together. Benjamin's only outing was to Eltering Cattle Mart once a month. The rest of his time was spent at home. Kate, however, did go out once a week. Dressed in her long, scruffy overcoat and black Wellington boots, she caught the bus to Eltering every Friday to do her shopping and seemed to enjoy these trips. She also went to the WI meetings once a month and on special occasions, such as the Anniversary, would visit the chapel high in the dale.

In those early days, I wondered whether they shared a bed, for they seemed to live separate lives, seldom speaking to one another but never fighting. Each got on with his or her own work as they had done for years, and they ate together, their main meal, a hot dinner, being at twelve noon prompt.

It was a mutual understanding, a convenient arrangement and neither seemed to mind this form of life.

I saw them once a month when I went to inspect their stock registers, and Kate always produced a mug of hot tea for me, along with a plate of fine home-made scones or rock buns. Benjamin would join us at the kitchen table, we'd discuss business and local matters, and then I'd leave.

I must be honest and say that I never noticed any discord between them but, on reflection, never noticed any warmth in their relationship. They seemed to exist side by side, to live beneath the same roof without any overt problems, but without the love or understanding that one finds in most families.

But, as I grew to know them better, and as I gained the confidence of other local farmers, especially those in Rannackdale, I learned more of the Owens' way of life.

'Never slept in t'same bed ever,' one stalwart informed me. 'She's never let him near 'er; poor awd Benjamin's nivver covered that missus of 'is, nivver. He was a bit of a stallion as a lad, but she's kept him short. It's a bit late now, mind, cos t'farm'll etti be sold up when they're called up ti yon small-holding in the sky.'

As I was realising, I'd never heard of a child of their union, he continued.

'Ah doubt she'll produce a lad noo. She's ovver awd for that sort o' caper; if she was a coo, they'd have her put doon. She's neither use nor ornament, if you ask me.'

He was right, because Kate was far from pretty. In fact, she was downright ugly, a large, loose and untidy woman with hairs on her upper lip and a floppy body which seemed to spill at random out of her ill-fitting clothes. Her iron-grey hair was pulled tightly back into a bun behind her head and she had awful teeth, many of which were rotten or missing. I could fully understand why Benjamin had never 'covered her' as his colleague so aptly put it.

But Benjamin wasn't much of a catch either. A wiry fellow with freckles all over his balding head of thin gingery-grey hair, he looked more like a retired jockey than a farmer. Bandy-legged, thin as a lath and often unshaven, he was not the kind of man who would appeal to a woman.

I was to learn also that Kate nagged him. She nagged him about getting more work done about the farm. The poor little fellow seemed to work every hour except those trips to mart, but Kate demanded more. On one occasion when I called, I could hear her lashing him with her tongue.

'If thoo didn't spend si much time messing aboot wi' these coos, you'd have more time ti spend on yon field, growing crops, selling tonnups, cabbages and t'like.'

'Coos need care,' he countered. 'We need coos for t'milk cheque . . .'

'That's a woman's job, our Benjamin. Coos is for milkmaids, not fellers.'

'Then you do it.'

'Nay, Ah've enough on what wi' t'hens and t'house.'

From what I gathered in my rounds, she did nag at him, her chief antic being that whatever he was doing at any particular time, she thought he should be doing something else. If he worked on his sheep, she thought he should be working on the cows; if he was with the cows, he should be in the fields, and if he was in the fields, he ought to be tending his sheep. If he settled down for a rest at night, he ought to be fixing the tractor, and if he was fixing the tractor, he should be tidying the garage.

I understand that poor old Benjamin had tolerated this for years. Her constant irritation had led him never to argue or talk with her, except when it was essential during moments like 'Pass t'tea pot, will yer?' or 'Get us a roll o' binder twine if you're in Atkinson's.'

Then I had a spell doing pig-licence duty at Eltering Cattle Mart and noticed Benjamin with his cronies. He was in a group of farmers of his own age and was clearly enjoying himself. He noticed me and came across for a word.

'They've let you away from t'missus an' all, have they?' he said, grinning from ear to ear.

'Now, Benjamin,' I greeted him. 'Good to see you out and about, getting away from that busy spot of yours. And, yes, they have let me loose for today!'

'That's what cattle marts are for, Mr Rhea, to get us fellers away from them wimmin folk. Ah mean to say, we could sell cattle in other ways, but, by gum, it's a grand way of having a day out.'

'You've left your missis at home then?' I knew he always came without Kate but used the phrase to make conversation with him.

'Aye, she's better off there. Couldn't fetch her here, tha knaws. If she saw me standing here, she'd say Ah should be standing ower there, and if Ah was looking at them Red Polls, she'd say Ah should be thinking of Jerseys and if Ah took her into t'Black Swan for a beef sandwich, she'd want to go to t'Golden Lion for a ham sandwich. As things are, Ah can do as Ah like; Ah allus does, mind, cos I don't let that nagging get to me. It just maks her go on a bit more, but doon here, wiv me mates, I can have a day off nagging.'

'Enjoy it,' I smiled.

'Don't you worry, Mr Rhea, Ah shall.'

I could appreciate his genuine need to get away from the farm, and then, as I performed more of those market duties, I noticed that Benjamin's group of market friends included a tall and very attractive blonde girl. She would be about twenty-five years old at the most, and I noticed he spent a good deal of time talking to her.

So fascinating was her style and beauty that most of them were taking a keen interest in her, and I noticed that she attended every mart. My own curiosity was such that I wanted to find out more about her, and the opportunity came through Benjamin himself. He came to my little wooden shed at the mart for a pig-movement licence, saying he thought he'd try a few store pigs for fattening in the hope that the bacon factory would eventually buy them from him.

'Who's your friend, Benjamin?' I asked him, nodding towards the direction of the tall blonde.

He blushed just a fraction when he realised I was speaking particularly of her, then said, 'Oh, yon's awd Harry Clemmitt's lass. Rachel. Fine lass, that. She does all his buying and selling at mart; knows her beasts, she does. Ah gets all my stock from her, Mr Rhea. Knows his breeding stock does Harry Clemmitt, and she does, an' all. You can rely on Harry Clemmitt for good breeding stock.'

'She's taken a shine to you!' I laughed, for she seemed to be very happy in Benjamin's company, even if their ages and appearances were poles apart.

'Ah used to be a good 'un at chatting up the wimmin, Mr Rhea,' he chuckled. 'Ah reckon Ah've lost nowt o' me touch!'

'I can see that!' I said, and he walked off, beaming with pride at his achievement with the girl. But I was not to realise, until some time later, that Benjamin and the girl were considerably more than just good friends. For one thing, they met here regularly and he took her to lunch.

The full realisation came to me about six weeks later when I called at Helm End Farm to make my routine check of the Owens' stock registers. I went into the untidy kitchen for my customary mug of tea and buttered scone, and was welcomed by Kate. As she fussed over me, the door opened and in walked Benjamin, followed by the tall blonde girl.

'Morning, Mr Rhea,' he beamed. 'Good to see you.'

'Hello, Benjamin.' I couldn't take my eyes off the girl; even when dressed in her rough working-jeans and old smock, she was gorgeous. Her erect bearing, long blonde hair, smooth skin and lovely features were so out of place here. I could even visualise her on the catwalk of a fashion show, such was her elegance and stylishly slender build.

'This is Rachel,' he introduced her. 'My new milkmaid.'

'Milkmaid?' I said, puzzled.

'Aye, Kate said coos were wimmin's work, and cos she wouldn't take 'em on, Ah thought Ah'd better get a milkmaid.

Rachel here knows about coos and got a bit sick o' working on her dad's farm, so I've takken her on. She sleeps in, Mr Rhea, so she's part of t'family now.'

'Hello, Rachel,' I said to the milkmaid.

'Hello, Mr Rhea,' she said, moving sensually across to the cupboard for a jug of milk for our tea.

It was impossible to guess what was going through Kate's mind at this time, but I think she felt this stunning girl would never be interested in her thin, scruffy and ageing husband. But Kate was wrong.

One night, she came back early from a WI meeting because the speaker had failed to turn up for his engagement, and poor Kate caught Benjamin and the girl together in bed. The outcome was not one of the famous 'domestics' we were so accustomed to on council estates, but merely a rapid and discreet exit by Kate. She simply packed her bags and left that same night, without a fight and without an argument. She stayed that night with a friend, and told her, 'I would never let him touch me, the filthy old brute, so she can't be very choosy! I'll not live in the same house as a hussy like that and he's welcome to her!'

Even now, I do not know what happened to Kate, for no one saw her again. So far as I know, she never returned to the district and I never heard of any divorce. But Rachel Clemmitt continued to live with Benjamin at the remote farm, and during my monthly calls, I noticed the transformation to the premises, and to Benjamin himself. The entire place was smartened up, the house was cleaned from top to bottom, new licks of paint were added, the farmyard was tidied up and the whole enterprise appeared to be buzzing with new life. Rachel had transformed the farm.

She had transformed Benjamin too. Uncharacteristically, he appeared in the pub one night with Rachel, and he sported a smart new jacket and trousers; his face was bright and alert and he behaved like a prosperous farmer, and a happy one. I was later to learn that he was prosperous; in spite of outward appearances, Benjamin had made lots of money.

Another benefit of his life with Rachel was that he looked and behaved as if he were ten years younger, and in time, Rachel started to call herself Mrs Owens. She looked very happy too and it wasn't long before she was pregnant. At this news, Benjamin strutted around like a proud bantam cock, as pleased as any man could be, and in due course, a son was born.

I called about a month afterwards and saw the baby in his smart new pram. Rachel was fussing over her son, whom she called Patrick, and Benjamin insisted on lifting him out for me to examine.

'Marvellous,' I congratulated them both. 'How marvellous for you both. You must be very proud!'

'Ah allus said t'Clemmitts had good breeding stock, Mr Rhea, and Ah was right. There'll be a new line of Owens to continue this farm now. Ah did it just in time.'

I smiled and said, 'So you did, Benjamin.'

'Ah was a bit oot o' practice, mind, but wiv a bit o' training, Ah soon got caught up again. Like a lad Ah was, in full strength. And see that, a fine lad, as bonny as you could wish to see anywhere. And he's mine, all mine.'

'And mine,' said Rachel gently.

I was pleased for Benjamin, but even now I cannot understand why such a lovely young woman had given herself entirely to this curious old character. She'd seen him as a poverty-stricken, unkempt old hill farmer during his visits to the mart and she knew his background and his age.

In spite of all that, she had fallen in love with him and had then transformed his life. Albeit at the unfortunate Kate's expense, it was something of a miracle and it only served to make me more curious about the way a woman's mind operates. That is something I have not yet discovered! But Benjamin became a local legend because of this romance; his prowess as a lover was the talking-point of the market and of the surrounding villages, and none of the eligible young men of the area could understand why they had lost to this ageing Lothario from Rannackdale. Nor could anyone else.

As one envious old farmer said to me. 'He got shot o' that nagging awd bitch of a wife and won hisself yon fit-looking lass who looks good enough for a duke and fit enough for a young buck of a lad. And he did it all without missing one hot dinner.'

* * *

Another character with a chattering wife was Horace Pitman who ran a small garage and taxi-service in Waindale. His was an old-fashioned garage which had been operating since the first cars came to these dales. Stocked with spare parts in neatly marked and carefully arranged boxes, and with a pair of tall green petrol pumps outside, Horace's garage was always busy. He worked from seven each morning until ten each night, except when he was on rural or county council business. On those occasions, he would take a day off and hire a driver/pump attendant should anyone require a taxi or some petrol.

I seldom saw Horace dressed in anything but a pair of navy-blue overalls heavy with grease and equally greasy black boots. He did all the mechanical work himself and somehow coped with everything that came his way.

Horace was a big man. In his late forties, he must have weighed at least sixteen stone and had a jolly, calm face which never seemed troubled by anything or anyone. Balding on top, and with a monk's hair-style of sandy hair, he wore rimless glasses and, oddly enough, always sported a crisp white shirt and coloured tie beneath his overalls. I think that was in case he got a sudden taxi job — he could throw off his overalls and put on a blazer type of jacket he kept hanging in his garage.

Everyone liked Horace, which is probably why he found himself elected to the rural district council, and then to the county council. With so little spare time, he did manage to accommodate his council duties, and often went to meetings at Northallerton in his white shirt and working clothes.

These comprised a pair of dark crumpled trousers, that blazer-like jacket which he kept in the garage, and his greasy black boots. One snag with his trade was that his hands were never clean; black oil had engrained itself into the skin of his hands and his fingernails were always black. Scrub as he might, he could never get his hands clean. Those who knew him paid no attention to his mode of dress or dirty hands, but I often wonder what the other councillors thought.

But Horace was a good man, a fine councillor and a very able person in every respect; perhaps in other circumstances, he would have become a top-flight businessman or even a politician. But he was utterly content with his busy village life — he loved cars and he liked being a councillor, and his way of life gave him the best of both his chosen worlds.

His wife, Dora, was an ideal companion for him. A tiny, virile woman in her early forties, she was a bundle of energy who had a family of three fine teenage children and who busied herself with the Red Cross, Women's Institute, night classes and various other charities. She was secretary to countless village organisations, including the parish council and parochial church council, and she also did the office work and accounts for Horace's garage.

And she was a non-stop chatterer, unlike Horace who was a man of very few words. What he did say usually made sense, but she could not stop talking, and the village knew that if she cornered anyone for a two-minute chat, it would continue for half an hour if her time was short, and for well over an hour if things were progressing in a more leisurely manner. Horace, however, allowed her flow of constant chatter to drift away to oblivion over his head and he had that happy knack of saying 'Yes, dear,' at frequent intervals while never listening to a word she said. For Horace, Dora's voice was nothing more than background noise, there to be ignored where possible.

He did respond when she called 'Coffee's ready,' or 'Dinner' or 'Tea's up,' usually by simply arriving at the table or desk where she placed his morning cuppa. Even in council meetings, he said very little, consequently when he did say something, everyone listened. With his wife, however, no one listened, least of all Horace.

For all her chattering, she was a lovely woman and he was a fine man; they were a popular and hard-working pair of people who deserved the best. If anything, Dora was perhaps a little more ambitious than Horace although not in the same league as Mrs Pringle. Dora loved and respected her husband and felt that his work for the council, both at local rural level and at county level, deserved some recognition.

But Horace was not interested; he went along to the meetings, said his brief piece and came home to his garage. And that, in his mind, was that. He rarely told Dora what had transpired and if she asked what had happened, he would usually say, 'Nowt much.'

I caught a hint of Dora's ambitions one day when I was in his garage. I was asking about stolen cars, and had provided him with a list of their registration numbers in case any were brought in for petrol; he would ring me or our Divisional Headquarters if he spotted one. As we chatted, Dora came in with his coffee and invited me to have one. I agreed, and she joined us, chattering non-stop.

'I mean,' she said, 'they never say thank you, not one of them out of the whole village and they expect Horace to trek over to Northallerton month in and month out to say his piece for them and to fight their fights about rates, drainage, the water works and sewage and I mean, he does do well for the village, don't you think, Mr Rhea? More than some I know, more than some who make much more of a fuss about it and you'd think they would make a bit of a fuss about a man who works so hard for other folks and who's got a business, two businesses in fact, taxi and garage, to run as well. It's not as if he's retired or on a private income, you see . . .'

I wanted to say that councillors did not work for thanks, but she would not let me get a word in.

'Dora . . .' I began.

'Well, you would think they'd do something for people like my Horace, Mr Rhea . . .'

And so she went on, so I drank my coffee while Horace rubbed at a piece of car engine with some emery paper.

She rabbited on for a long time and I found myself becoming like Horace. Everything she said drifted over my head and once I caught sight of Horace, smiling to himself. This was a regular event for him.

I could see that his wife had some social ambitions for Horace even if he did not have any for himself, and it would be about a month later when I next came across the voluble Dora. I was on duty in Waindale when she was shopping and she spotted me; before I could leap into the mini-van to avoid a marathon session of her brand of verbal diarrhoea, she had presented herself before me.

'Ah,' she began a little breathlessly. 'Just the man who might help me. Mr Rhea, I know you are familiar with the county council and how they operate because our Horace never tells me a thing because he just goes along to those meetings and says nothing, then comes home and says nothing has happened until I read in the paper that they're building new schools here, police stations there, libraries and fire stations, new roads and putting the rates up and he would know all that and yet he never says a thing to me about it. You'd think he would, wouldn't you, I mean I am his wife but the reason I've stopped you, and I won't keep you because you must be a very busy man with lots of enquiries to make and jobs to do apart from talking to women like me, is that I thought you might know something about the Buckingham Palace thing. I met this lady at WI whose cousin is a councillor from Malton just like my Horace and he's been on years, she says, sitting on the Finance Committee and the Highways Committee and really getting involved . . .'

'The Buckingham Palace thing?' I was baffled and managed to register my curiosity as she turned to smile at a friend.

'Yes, you know,' she said. 'You must know, being a policeman, but that lady didn't know much about it because her husband had never gone on it and I wondered if you know what it was, Mr Rhea, and whether I, well, Horace really, could go along as well, I mean, it would be nice, wouldn't it? It would be a sort of thank you for Horace for all he's done, and I could wear a new hat and lovely coat and meet the Queen and all those important people. I've always wanted to go to a posh place like that, Mr Rhea, in one of those large hats with a wide brim, you know, the sort society ladies wear at races and operas and things like that . . .'

As she chattered on, I began to gain a glimmer of understanding.

'You mean the selection procedure for the Garden Parties?' I said during another momentary lull in her chatter.

'Yes, so you do know! How marvellous. What do I have to do, well Horace really, what does he have to do? I mean, does he write to the Queen or how does he get there? I mean, I'm sure Her Majesty has never heard of my Horace even though he does do an awful lot of good work for the council and the village but he's so quiet about it and never makes a fuss while other folks who don't do so much seem to get down to the Palace for tea with the Queen.'

Now I realised what she was talking about because my own grandfather, himself a County Councillor, had once been invited to Buckingham Palace for a garden party.

Dora stopped chattering to say a long "Hello" to a passing friend, and this gave me the chance to say, 'Horace will have been told about the system, you know.'

'He never tells me anything, Mr Rhea, you know my Horace, tight as the proverbial duck's, well, you know what and he always says nothing's happened at the meetings, then I hear of Mr and Mrs So-and-So, then Mr and Mrs This-and-That going off to London to meet the Queen and I ask myself why isn't our Horace getting himself there, and why isn't he taking me? I would love to go and wear my new hat, Mr Rhea, I really would, it's not as if I get far, you know, what with the business and my other interests, so this would be a once-in-a-lifetime outing, a really lovely one . . .'

'There's a draw for tickets,' I managed to tell her. 'I'm not sure when it's done or how often, but according to my grandfather, all councillors who want to be considered must put their names forward, and then a draw is made. Those drawn out of the hat, in a manner of speaking, are then invited to the Palace Garden Party. But Horace would have to find out exactly how the system operates. Get him to put his name forward, Dora. But you realise it's something of a lottery — not everyone can go, so there's no guarantee Horace would win an invitation.'

She beamed with happiness.

'Oh, Mr Rhea, I know he'll get there if only he'll do something about it . . . I will have a word with him straight away; now I mustn't keep you, I know you're very busy.'

She kept me standing there another ten minutes, saying how busy I was and how busy she was, and then she sailed away home in a very cheerful mood. Horace, I knew, was in for a session of chatter from her, with strict instructions to put his name forward next time Buckingham Palace asked the County Council for Garden Party nominees.

It would be four or five weeks later when Horace mentioned this; I had popped into his garage on a routine enquiry and he said, 'Mr Rhea, our Dora said summat about you suggesting I put my name down for t'Buckingham Palace jobs?'

'Yes,' I said. 'She was asking how councillors like yourself managed to get invited to Buckingham Palace, so I told her about the draw they have.'

'Aye, well, I can't say sike affairs are much in my line, but my name's gone down. They asked us at t'last meeting, and a few councillors sent their names in. I thought I would, then if our Dora goes on at me, I can allus say I put my name forward. That'll keep her quiet, cos I shan't win. I never win owt, Mr Rhea.'

I was surprised that he had bothered to actually do this, for it would have been easy to tell a white lie, to tell Dora he had submitted his name even if he hadn't. But the surprising thing was that Horace won. His name was drawn from the list and he was notified by a telephone call, following which detailed instructions about the event would be sent to him.

Dora spent hours rushing around the village telling her friends, and then she went off to York to buy an entire new outfit, including one of those huge wide-brimmed hats that were her heart's desire.

Then the formal instructions arrived by post.

And Dora's world fell apart.

Horace had certainly submitted his name, but he had failed to understand that he had also to nominate his wife; he had failed to include her name, and so the invitation was for him and him alone. A maiden lady councillor from Whitby had also won an invitation — she had been issued with the one that should have gone to Councillor Horace Pitman's lady.

Dora's anger and disappointment were acute and she kept herself hidden from the public for some weeks after this bad news. Then on the day before the event, I saw Horace getting into one of his cars, and went across. He was dressed in the dark blazer he used for taxi-driving; he had on a dark tie and white shirt, and some crumpled trousers which he usually wore under his overalls. His boots were clean but very greasy and he carried a brown paper carrier bag.

'Going shopping, Horace?' I asked

'Nay, it's for t'hotel tonight, Mr Rhea. I'm off to London. A clean collar and me razor and toothbrush. I need nowt else. I'm off to Buckingham Palace.'

And so he was; thus equipped, he got into his car and started the engine. I had no idea whether he intended to drive all the way to London or catch a train from York, but he sat there, smiling at me but saying nothing as he ran the engine of his car.

And then Dora came rushing out, looking like a dream. She wore a beautiful new suit, a matching wide-brimmed hat and high-heeled shoes. She carried a small suitcase and a matching handbag.

'Off to see the Queen, Dora?' I asked.

'I am not, and I'm glad I'm not, not with our Horace looking like that. You'd think he would have got some new clothes if he's to shake Her Majesty by the hand . . . no, Mr Rhea, he's not getting away with this! I'm going to London to see the sights, a play maybe, and then the shops. I wouldn't be seen dead with our Horace dressed like that . . .'

And Horace engaged first gear and drove off with a big smile on his face. I wondered what Her Majesty would make of him. Upon their return, Dora never stopped talking about her trip. She'd had a marvellous time and had crammed a host of exciting events into her short visit to the city. As for Horace, I asked him what he thought of the Buckingham Palace Garden Party.

'Not much,' he said. T'food was nowt but a load o' ket.'

A translation of that dialect word would, I doubt, not please those who arranged the teas.

CHAPTER 6

> If this be not love, it is madness,
> and then it is pardonable.
> WILLIAM CONGREVE, 1670—1729

One of the recurring duties of the sympathetic police officer involves dealing with people in distress; there are times when that distress is self-inflicted either by accident or design, and there are times it is inflicted upon us by other people or by a single event or even a series of unfortunate occurrences. Officialdom, bureaucracy and red tape can also inflict distress in their own inimitable manner, the latter being revealed when puzzled pensioners receive threatening letters from computerised accounts departments when their rates or other bills have been paid.

Minor examples of distress might include those who lock themselves out of their homes or whose motor cars run out of petrol, or who are locked out of their homes by others during arguments or stupidity, or whose cars run out of petrol because their teenage son has surreptitiously done a trip to Scotland and back. Other people can inflict distress upon us, by simple things like persistent telephone calls or playing football in our front garden, or by greed such as burglary or through dangerous actions like reckless driving, playing about with firearms or indeed anything else. The possibilities of trouble are endless, and it seems we are continually at risk either through our own behaviour or from the actions of others.

In the course of police work, therefore, the constable often comes across examples of this kind and seeks to comfort the victims where possible. A kind word and some assurance that the world isn't going to end is generally sufficient, albeit tempered with advice on how to cope with the unexpected and harrowing predicament.

In dealing with jobs of this kind, however, it becomes evident that of all the root causes of man's predilection for disaster, that which causes most problems is man's love for woman. Through their vast experience of people, police officers know that men get themselves into some of the most curious situations in their undying efforts to prove their love to the lady of their dreams. Constables know that love is one of the most powerful of urges, so strong that at times it removes every scrap of common sense from the skulls of those whom it infects. A poet who remains anonymous once said that 'Love is a passion which has caused the change of empires' — in short, men do the daftest things when they are in love, and I have mentioned some of their misadventures in previous 'Constable' books.

But because this symptom provides a never-ending series of dramas, sagas, mishaps, problems and (to be honest) a few chuckles in the process, every constable has witnessed and can recount stirring tales of love. They would fill a volume, so I thought I would place on record a few more tales of the lovelorn countryman.

One example occurred during the depths of winter. While I was the village bobby at Aidensfield, one of my less pleasant duties as Christmas approached was to man roadchecks at various lonely points. This meant stopping all cars to check them and their boots for stolen chickens, turkeys, drinks and other festive fare. We were also seeking those who stole holly from gardens and Christmas trees from our acres of local forests. It was a task that country constables had undertaken for years and the only time I found any game in a car was when I halted and searched a Rolls-Royce which, it transpired, had a boot full of pheasants. His Lordship was not too pleased; he was delivering them to his tenants.

The timing of those road-blocks varied, but they were usually of two hours' duration, perhaps starting at 8pm, 9pm, 10pm, 11pm or even midnight, and on each occasion, we selected a different check-point. Word generally got around the local pubs that the police were checking cars at Bank Top or The Beacon or Four Lane Ends which probably meant the poachers took alternative routes. But we did get results — we found cars with no insurance, drivers with no licences, cars not taxed, cars with dirty number plates and cars in a dangerous condition. We caught drunken drivers, car thieves and burglars and, once in a while, we caught a Christmas poacher with a boot full of illicitly acquired game or liquor, or a hard-up dad who had risked digging up a Norway spruce from the local Forestry Commission plantation.

We referred to these duties as turkey patrols, although I've never known an arrest for having a boot full of turkeys. On one occasion, however, I caught a youth riding a bike without lights. It happened like this.

It was a pitch-black night with no moon, and I was manning a road-check at Elsinby Plantation. It was about 8.30pm and I was alone for it was a very minor road which ran right through the centre of the conifer plantation which comprised Norway spruce, Scots pines and larches. We'd had reports of Christmas-tree thefts and so I was out to catch a thief.

Almost numb with cold, I suddenly heard the distinctive swish-swish of bicycle tyres and as I peered into the pitch blackness, I could not see any lights. And then the noise came closer and I could hear the sound of breathing as the rider pedalled up the slight gradient. And so I shone my torch upon him.

He cried with alarm, for my sudden action had terrified him. In the light of my torch, I saw it was young Ian Spellar from Elsinby and he stopped when he realised it was me.

'Oh, Mr Rhea, hello.' He was slightly out of breath.

'Now, Ian, what's all this then? Riding without lights, eh? You could get yourself killed on a night like this, you know. Car drivers can't see you; you realise you're putting drivers in an impossible situation?'

'Aye, sorry, Mr Rhea. I won't do it again.'

'Where are you going anyway? It's a bit off the beaten track up here!'

I shone my light on his bike and upon his back to see if he had anything which might carry a small tree or any other Yuletide trophy, but he wasn't equipped for transporting anything save himself. I knew he wasn't stealing.

'I'm not pinching things, Mr Rhea, honest. I'm off to see my girlfriend.'

'And who's she?' was my next question.

'Linda Thornhill,' he said. I knew where she lived and this was on the route to her parents' isolated farm.

'Right,' I said. 'Off you go but be careful. And next time, get some batteries in those lights, and get them switched on, OK? Or I'll book you!'

'Yes, Mr Rhea. Sorry Mr Rhea.'

'And be careful — remember you can't be seen!'

Knowing few cars used this quiet track, I allowed him to continue to see his love, although the lad might be a danger to other road users. Maybe I should not have relented, but I decided in his favour. Ian was a pleasant youth. Just turned eighteen, he worked in a local timber yard and was a hard-working lad from a decent working-class background. I'd had to tell him off once or twice about drinking underage, but he never got into serious trouble. Underage drinking and riding a bike without lights was the extent of his lawlessness.

Then, only a week later, I was manning another checkpoint in that vicinity, this time at Flatts End, when I heard the same swish-swish of bicycle tyres. I shone my torch upon the oncoming rider and again it was Ian.

'Same rider, Mr Rhea!' he said, halting at my side.

'Same constable, Ian!'

'Same excuse!' he countered.

'Same warning!' I said. 'Now what about those lights?'

'I never got round to putting them on, Mr Rhea, sorry,' and he bent over his lights, back and front, and switched them on. After telling him once again of the dangers, I let him go.

'It'll be a summons next time, Ian!' I shouted after him as his red rear light disappeared into the gloom.

It puzzled me that he should be riding in such darkness without lights when both his lamps were in good working-order. It didn't make sense. Then some ten days later, one Saturday night, I was manning yet another check-point, this time at Swathgill Head, and once more, I heard the panting sound of someone pedalling heavily, and the accompanying swish-swish of bicycle tyres. I groaned. I would now have to be harder with this youth.

I switched on my torch and waved him to a halt. I was right; it was Ian Spellar.

'Same cyclist, Mr Rhea,' he said, this time not so chirpily.

'Same constable,' I retorted, sternly.

'Same excuse,' he said, wondering what my reaction would be as he switched on both lights.

'Same threat, Ian!' I sounded angry. 'Now look, this is getting beyond a joke. This is your final warning, right? Next time, you go to court, I can't have you putting yourself and car drivers at risk . . .'

'If I hear a car coming, I stop and put 'em on,' he said. 'I'd never let 'em run me down, Mr Rhea, I'm not as daft as that.'

'Why ride without lights when your lamps are in working-order?' I asked. 'There's nothing wrong with them!'

He just shrugged his shoulders in reply, and I watched him ride off once again. Each time I'd seen him, he'd been on a different road, albeit within the same general area of the heights above Elsinby. Any of those roads would take him to Linda Thornhill's remote home, but his attitude defeated me. It wasn't defiance of the law; it was more a strange sort of lethargy. Now, however, I felt he had got the message. But I was wrong. Only a week later, I was again on the lane running through Elsinby Plantation when I became aware of an approaching cyclist without lights. My heart sank. I could distinguish the swishing of the tyres and the sound of a man breathing as he climbed the gradient, and so, once more, I shone my torch on Ian Spellar.

'Same cyclist, Mr Rhea.'

'Same constable, Ian.'

'Same excuse,' he recited what had become a kind of ritual response.

'Same results, Ian.'

'Same apologies, Mr Rhea.'

'And this time, it's the same summons, Ian. You're clearly ignoring my warnings, so it's a summons this time,' and I took down his name, age, address and occupation, then reported him for riding a cycle without obligatory lights.

'I'm really sorry, Mr Rhea,' and he switched on his front and rear lamps.

'Look, Ian, this is serious, you're risking an accident and putting too much faith in other drivers . . . they just cannot see you in darkness. Why are you doing this?'

He hung his head, embarrassed at my questioning, but his demeanour told me there was a reason for his odd behaviour. Even so, he did not reveal this to me. I must admit that I was against submitting a formal report against him; on paper, it seemed such a trivial matter and my superiors would probably think I'd become drunk with power. But Ian had to be taught a lesson, and so I did submit a report with an accompanying account of the reasons for my action.

And then, even before a decision had been made upon that report, I caught Ian once again.

'Same constable, Ian,' I shouted at him. 'And it'll be another summons for the same offence. What on earth are you playing at?'

'Same cyclist, Mr Rhea.' He sounded very subdued now. 'And same excuse.'

'You're going to see your girlfriend again?'

'Aye,' he said. 'I am, and well, Mr Rhea, I'm sorry, I really am. I know it's wrong, but, well, it's so important . . .'

'Go on, Ian, I'm listening,' I said.

'Well, you know where the Thornhills live, down at Birch Bower Farm?'

'I know it well,' I paid a visit to this farm about once a month and it was an awful trek from the road. The farm lay at least a mile and a half from the road, and although the first quarter of the track leading to it was surfaced, the remainder was an unmade lane full of ruts and pot-holes and littered with partly buried rocks. It was a diabolical road and Ted Thornhill never seemed inclined to repair it. Everyone who used it grumbled.

'Well, old Thornhill doesn't like me courting his lass, Mr Rhea, so I go in secret. Linda can't get out at night, you see, being only sixteen anyway, so I have to ride out there if I want to see her. She goes into her room to do her homework, you see, but she sneaks out at nine o'clock. Well, her dad might catch me riding down that lane if I show lights, Mr Rhea, and 'cos I need to adjust my eyes to ride down when it's pitch dark, I practise on these quiet roads, you see . . . I allus have lights on in the village, or on main roads, but not here where there's nowt but trees.'

I believed him. I knew the value of working without light when operating at night because one's eyes do become accustomed to the darkness.

'So you're practising that ride and using different roads to avoid me, eh?' I put to him.

'Yeh, well, when you first nabbed me, I reckoned you'd often be on that road, seeing Christmas is coming up and there's poachers about. So I went the other way round, then you were there an' all, Mr Rhea . . .'

'And I've no doubt you've been riding those roads other nights, Ian, when I've not been on duty?'

He laughed with a silly sort of giggle. 'Aye, well, you have to, haven't you? Just the quiet bits, mind, and that lane down to Birch Bower.'

'I'm not interested in Birch Bower Farm Lane,' I said. 'That's private property. I'm concerned with public roads.'

'So will they take me to court, Mr Rhea?'

'It depends on the Superintendent,' I said, which was the truth. 'He'll read my report and decide what to do.'

'Tell him I'm sorry, then. But mebbe he was a lad an' all, at one time? Going courting.'

'I'll see what he says,' was all I could promise.

The Superintendent met me at one of my rendezvous points a few days later and took the opportunity of asking me about my 'no bike-lights' report. I explained the situation and included Ian's odd reason.

'Christmas is coming up, PC Rhea,' said the Superintendent. 'Would you agree that a written caution is appropriate in this case?'

I smiled. 'Yes, sir. I think it would be very appropriate.'

And so that was Ian's punishment. Within a few days, he would receive a written caution from the Superintendent which would inform him that he would not be prosecuted on this occasion, but that the letter must be regarded as a warning. Any future offences of this nature could result in a court appearance.

I saw Ian in Elsinby one Sunday afternoon just before Christmas and told him what to expect.

'Thanks, Mr Rhea. I'm grateful.'

'Wish Linda a happy Christmas from me,' I said.

'Thanks, Mr Rhea. I will. And I'm sorry I've been a nuisance; I was daft really. But there was nowt else I could do, was there, if I wanted to see Linda?'

'I can't encourage you to break the law.' I smiled at him. 'Mind,' I added, 'I'm not sure how you'll sneak down to Birch Bower in the summer without her dad knowing.'

'Me neither, Mr Rhea. I'll have to find a way in somehow, although she might be able to go for walks when it's light at night.'

'Let's hope so, Ian. Oh, and by the way,' I said. 'We finish those check-points this coming Saturday night.'

'Thanks, Mr Rhea,' he said. 'Happy Christmas.'

One of the funniest incidents involved a man whom I shall call Ronald Youngman, a salesman who lived in Ashfordly. I was never very sure what he sold, although I think it was something linked to the building-industry like scaffolding. A dark-haired, attractive man in his early thirties, he was a lively character who played a lot of tennis, cricket, football and badminton. When he was not selling scaffolding or playing one of his sports, he was exercising his considerable charm upon the local ladies.

In the latter case, he made ample use of his company car which was a Ford Cortina with reclining front seats; he used this to take his many conquests for outings, frequently making trips to rural pubs after which he would take his charmed girl to a remote rustic location, there for mutual enjoyment. For this reason, his distinctive gold-coloured car was often to be seen parked in lonely places, sometimes with steamed-up windows and generally in complete darkness.

Most of the local police officers knew the car and they knew of Ronald's insatiable appetite for lovely ladies, consequently they never checked over the car or its occupants when they found it in a far-away place. Normally, our procedures were to check every car found in a remote place to see if the occupants were safe and sound, to see if it was someone trying to commit suicide or whether the car had been stolen and abandoned. It might contain the proceeds of crime, or it might be used for crime — there were many other valid reasons for checking such vehicles.

If I was patrolling late, therefore, and came across Ronald's car upon the moors or deep in a forest, I ignored it. After all, I didn't want to embarrass either Ronald or his lover of the evening and if neither was breaking the law there was no need to make myself a nuisance.

But late one night — in fact it was after midnight — I was working a patrol and around 1am, my route took me high into Waindale. Tucked away in the corner of a quarry behind Wether Cote Farm was an explosives store; it belonged to the quarry owner and because it contained explosives and detonators used for blasting, we had to check it regularly for security. It was little more than a very solidly built chamber, part of which was underground, and it seldom contained a large amount. But it had to be checked and our checks had to be recorded.

With this in mind, I parked my mini-van off the road near Wether Cote Farm and decided to walk the couple of hundred yards to the explosives store. The route was along an unmade lane, full of pot-holes and with the quarry gates closed, there was very little room for turning a vehicle around. It was much safer to walk. And so, in the gloom of that night, albeit armed with a torch which I did not use during the walk, I made my way along the track. Rather like young Ian Spellar, I found I could see without the light from a torch. And then, in a corner right next to the store, I came across Ronald's car. It was in darkness but I could recognise the outline. Ronald was at it again.

Having no wish to become a peeping Tom or to disturb him in his moments of bliss, I tried to creep past the car to carry out my essential check. But as I was going past, I could hear cries for help . . . and they were being sounded in a man's voice! I halted a while, listening; I thought it might be the car radio, a disc jockey fooling about or perhaps a character in a play or it could be Ronald playing games. After all, he had no idea that I, or indeed anyone else, was standing just outside his passion-wagon.

But the cry was genuine . . . and a woman's voice was calling too. Who on earth they were hoping to attract in such a remote part of the moors was beyond me, but I listened carefully, just to ensure that these were genuine cries for help. I did wonder if it was some odd part of their love-making, but in spite of being muffled by the closed windows, they were, I felt, very genuine cries of distress. And, they sounded rather weak.

I had to investigate.

I switched on my powerful torch and pulled open the driver's door. The interior light came on and there, in the most bizarre situation upon the passenger's reclining seat was Ronald. He was face down and beneath him was a woman. Both were completely naked. And neither could move.

'Who's that?' he asked, with a mixture of relief and embarrassment, unable to turn his head towards the door.

'PC Rhea, Ronald.'

'Oh, thank God . . . get me out . . .'

In the weak glow of the interior light, I could distinguish a tangle of bare legs; I could not identify the woman, and she was saying nothing. In fact, she was hiding her face by turning her head towards the wall of the car. But Ronald was saying 'My foot, Mr Rhea, my leg . . .'

'What's the problem?' I asked, baffled by this discovery.

'My legs . . . my feet . . . they're trapped . . . can you loosen them . . .'

I could now see that his right foot had disappeared through the cubby-hole of his car; it seemed he had been exerting pressure with that foot as a result of which it had dislodged the plastic back panel of the cubby-hole. His foot and much of his lower leg had then slipped through the hole to become trapped among the wires and bodywork, and he could not pull it out. That sudden action had then caused his left leg to make an involuntary movement, and his foot had gone through a gap between the spokes of the steering-wheel. That leg was also trapped due to the weight upon it.

'Interesting position, Ronald,' I said as I examined his predicament.

'I can't move, Mr Rhea. I just can't move . . .'

His entire body weight was resting upon the woman beneath; she could not roll free because the driver's seat was not in a reclining position, nor could she slide towards the rear due to the slope of the seat upon which she was trapped, and Ronald's position prevented a forward escape.

Besides, one of her legs was somehow curled between his which well and truly anchored her. Unfortunately for Ronald his own trapped position and the weight of his body meant he could neither rise nor free his own legs.

'I wish I had a camera, Ronald, this is one for the record books!'

'Give over, Mr Rhea, just get me out . . . I've been here ages . . . I thought nobody was going to come . . .'

'They wouldn't, at least not until the quarry opens in the morning — it would give the lads summat to talk about. I just happened to be coming to the explosives store. Now, let's see if I can shift one of these legs.'

I went around to the passenger side and opened that door, upon which the woman turned her face the other way. It was almost the only part of her that I had not seen, but I set about removing Ronald's foot. By pushing my hand through the cubby-hole, I could dislodge the panel which had secured his foot, and then, by heaving on that leg and getting him to bend his knee, I could release that foot. But he could still not help himself. Gradually, I eased the other foot out of the spokes of the steering-wheel, got into the rear of the car and dragged him towards the back seat by his shoulders, and then he was free. Aching, stiff with cold and very, very embarrassed, he rolled into the driver's seat.

And then the woman could move and I recognised her.

'Good evening, Mrs Stamford,' I greeted her.

She was the wife of an hotel owner in Ashfordly but she made no response, not even a thank you. As I clambered out of their car, she began to get dressed in total silence as Ronald grabbed his clothes and began to pull them on in the lane as he talked to me.

'Look, Mr Rhea, we're men of the world. I mean, I've committed no crime, no offence . . . You don't have to take action, do you? Report this, or anything? She is a respected lady from the town, you see, she's never done this before, not with me anyway. Her husband's away, He's at an hoteliers' conference in Harrogate . . .'

'There's no need to say anything, Ronald. Rescuing damsels and knights in distress is just part of our service. Well, it's made my night interesting, but, Ronald . . .'

I paused.

'Yes?' He was fastening his shirt by this time.

'I'd love to know how on earth you managed to get yourself into that position. I'll bet a contortionist would have a job to achieve that!'

'You'll not tell a soul, will you, Mr Rhea?'

'It's our secret, Ronald, ours and Mrs Stamford's.'

And I have never mentioned it to anyone. Ronald often greets me and insists on buying me a drink when I'm off duty, but the humiliated Mrs Stamford never speaks to me.

But when I returned home and booked off duty that night, I realised I had omitted to do one vital thing. I'd completely forgotten to examine the explosives store.

Possibly the most dramatic love story that came my way involved Mr and Mrs Colin Blenkiron and a notorious crossroads called Pennyflats Cross. So difficult and accident-prone was this stretch of road that my predecessor, and then I, kept a stock of blank scale-drawings of the roads for use in our accident reports. The number of traffic accidents which happened at that point kept us in regular work!

Wherever a road traffic accident occurred which resulted in a need to examine all the evidence with a view to prosecution, we had to submit detailed plan drawings of the scene. These were carefully drawn to scale and contained the positions of the vehicles involved both before, during and after impact. This was for the benefit both of our senior officers in deciding whether or not to send the case to court, and later the magistrates if it did get to court. This system helped enormously to simplify a difficult explanation of the events. A stock of neatly drawn plans depicting this road, with all the constant measurements, the position of warning signs, indications of gradients, type of road markings, etc., did save a lot of time.

At Pennyflats Cross, the main road, which had a 'B' classification, ran from Ashfordly to York and crossed Pennyflats, an area of elevated scrubland covered with small conifers, gorse bushes and heather. As it reached the crossroads, the road dipped suddenly and quite steeply, although this short gradient was well signed in advance.

Nevertheless, many drivers who were strangers to the area were, when approaching from Ashfordly, largely unaware of the undulating nature of the road. They sailed over the summit without knowing and apparently without caring what lay beyond. That in itself could be regarded as careless driving or even dangerous driving because, just over the summit, within a matter of very few yards, was a minor road. It crossed the Ashfordly–York road at an oblique angle, emerging almost unseen from a plantation of conifers at one side and a copse of young silver birch at the other.

Defence solicitors always maintained that these crossroads were badly placed and it was unfair to convict anyone of driving carelessly here. The police, however, assured the court that the crossroads was well signposted from all directions, and that, in any case, a driver should always drive at a speed and in such a manner that he or she could deal with any unexpected hazards.

But a similar problem afflicted drivers coming out of the side road on to the main road. Upon emerging on to the main road, their vision was grossly impaired by the angle of the road and the profusion of trees. The chief problem was that those on the main road often crested that hill at speed only to find a slow car emerging into their path. So short was the stopping-distance that very few could pull up in time, not even those who pottered along in a leisurely style. Fast or even moderately fast drivers had no chance at all.

Accidents were inevitable, and although we, the police, grumbled at the highway department and the district council for improvements to be made, nothing was ever done. Their argument was that the crossroads were not dangerous because no one had been killed there, and, oddly enough, that was true. There never had been a fatal accident there, although some nasty injuries had occurred. Everyone said that, one day, somebody would be killed, but happily in my time at Aidensfield that did not happen.

I was not surprised therefore, one Sunday afternoon in May, when I received a frantic phone call from a passing driver to say he had come upon two cars which had clearly just been involved in a traffic accident. He was chattering nervously as people tend to do when they are reporting urgent matters to the police, but I tried to calm him down by slowly asking the obvious questions.

I learned that the location was the infamous Pennyflats Cross, and that both drivers were injured. In his view, the injuries did not appear to be too serious although he said an ambulance was required. The road was not blocked and he had not witnessed the accident; he had come upon it moments after it had happened. I thanked him and said I would be there in less than ten minutes; I assured him I'd call the ambulance before I left home. He said he would wait and attend to the injured drivers.

The accident was one of the kind that regularly happened here. A young woman in an Austin mini-car had come out of the minor road on to the main road just as a young man in a sports car had crested the brow of the hill. He'd reacted quickly and had attempted to swerve to his right to avoid a collision, but she'd kept coming across his path from the left. He had collided with the front of her car. This had spun her off the road and she had collided with a telegraph pole while he had veered further to his offside, ending his short trip by crumpling his MGB around a sturdy ash tree.

A quick visual appraisal of both drivers showed that neither was too badly hurt; happily, neither was unconscious and I could detect no arterial bleeding; the girl, however, did say that her right arm hurt a lot and the youth complained of intense pain in his left leg. Tenderly, I examined both their injured limbs and was in no doubt that each was fractured; there were abrasions too, and some degree of shock. Hospital was a necessity for both.

At that stage, the ambulance arrived. The injured pair were well enough to tell me their names and addresses before the skilful ambulancemen lifted them out of their vehicles, wrapped them in blankets and in no time had placed them aboard stretchers. In seconds, they were being borne towards

York County Hospital for treatment. I thanked the passing driver for his assistance and confirmed that he was no longer required as he was not a witness. Then I radioed our Control Room with a request for a breakdown truck.

The rest of my action was routine. I obtained measurements of the positions of their cars, cleared the scene, swept up the broken glass and made arrangements for relatives to be informed. The breakdown truck took away both cars, lifting one on board and towing the other, and I went home. Using my stock plan of the crossroads, I entered the position of each of the cars and completed my accident report as far as I could. I rang York Police with a request that an officer be allowed to visit the hospital when the injured couple were well enough, and that the officer be allowed to obtain from each their version of events.

If they were not well enough, then other arrangements would be made; I also had their driving licences and insurance certificates to check.

When all this was done, I submitted my report to the sergeant for onward transmission to the Superintendent and I was to learn later that he recommended 'No prosecution' on the grounds that there was no independent witness. No one could say precisely what had happened, for it was a case of the man's word against the girl's. And that, I thought, was that.

But there was more to follow.

Some time during the November that followed, I received a telephone call from a Mr Colin Blenkiron.

'It's Colin Blenkiron speaking. Is that PC Rhea?' the voice asked.

'Speaking,' I confirmed.

'Ah, good, well, I wondered if you'd like to come to a party, you and your wife.'

'Me? Well

At that instant, I couldn't recall knowing anyone called Blenkiron and I was hesitant until he said, 'That accident at Pennyflats Cross last May, Mr Rhea. It was me in the MGB Hardtop.'

'Oh!' Now it all came flooding back. 'I remember now that Colin Blenkiron! Well, thanks, what sort of party and where is it?'

'It's my engagement party, Mr Rhea, and it's at the Hopbind Inn, Elsinby, a week on Thursday night. Half eight.'

'Well, that's very kind of you,' I was surprised at this. 'Very kind. I'm off duty that night,' I said. 'And I know my wife would love the outing, but . . .'

I was about to say that I was surprised at the invitation because Colin's parents' farm, which he ran in partnership with his father, was not on my beat. I did not know him or his parents, although I did know they were very wealthy and successful.

'It was because of that accident, Mr Rhea, you looked after me, and Susan. Got us to hospital, and there was no court appearance for us either. So we'd like you to come to our party.'

'She's your fiancée?' I was surprised.

'Not then, she wasn't. I didn't even know her then! She's my fiancée now, we met in hospital, you see.'

'What a way to meet!' I laughed.

'Yes, well, it was. Actually,' he chuckled, 'we met in the ambulance, but we weren't exactly on speaking-terms then! I was blaming her for the pile-up . . . I still am, by the way, and she was blaming me . . . anyway, in hospital, one thing led to another and here we are, getting engaged!'

'What a lovely tale!' I said. 'Yes, then we'd love to come and wish you a happy future!'

'Marvellous. We're inviting those ambulancemen as well, they were great. See you then.'

And he rang off.

Mary was delighted. From time to time, one of my 'customers' produced an offer of this kind, a form of genuine and heartfelt 'thank you', even if my part in their romance was very minor. We went along to the party and met their respective families, friends and relations. Susan Ascough, Colin's fiancée, was a secretary in a big department store in York and lived in Ploatby, which was on my patch. She drove into York every day. I knew her parents by name but had never met Susan until this evening.

During the party, there were ribald jokes about their method of meeting, their respective injuries, their time in bed in hospital and the prospects for their future together. It was a very happy gathering and a real tonic for me, and even more so for Mary. Diplomatically, we left the party at closing-time for I did not wish to make them feel uncomfortable if they decided to stay awhile at the pub.

'I enjoyed that,' said Mary on our way home. 'They seem a real nice couple, and their families are nice too.'

'It makes you think that that accident was fate,' I said. 'I wonder if they'd have met each other if it had never happened?'

'We'll never know,' she said. 'And thanks for leaving the pub at closing-time!' she added. 'I hate people staring at you as if you're a leper when the landlord calls time.'

'A little drink after hours always tastes better,' I said. 'It's like kids pinching apples — they're always better than the ones at home, and drinks laced with a spot of law-breaking taste all the better for it. A hint of naughtiness will put the final seal on their celebrations!'

'That's if they *do* drink after hours!' she laughed. 'You'll never know, will you?'

'I don't want to know,' I said, truthfully.

I thought that would have been the last we'd see of Colin and Susan, but it wasn't. The following March, we received an invitation to their wedding. It was fixed for the weekend before Easter in Elsinby Parish Church, with the reception at Craydale Manor. This was a fine country house which had been converted into an hotel and restaurant, and we looked forward to the whole celebration. The wedding was superb. In Elsinby's historic parish church, the atmosphere and setting were both dramatic and moving. Susan looked a picture in her long white wedding dress with its train and eight tiny bridesmaids in the most delicate of pinks.

Colin and his best man looked handsome and splendid in their top hats and tails, and the happy couple were united before a full congregation of family, friends and well-wishers. Beyond doubt, it was this district's wedding of the year. Mary and I thoroughly enjoyed the occasion; we lingered as the photographs were taken outside the church, savouring every moment and participating in the sheer happiness of the newly-weds. As the village constable, it was so nice being part of this joyful event.

Eventually, the photographer had taken all that he wished and the best man shouted for us to rejoin our cars and follow the bridal procession to the reception, after which the presents would be on display at the bride's home in Ploatby. And so we all went off to Craydale Manor in a long procession of gleaming vehicles led by a silver Jaguar car with white ribbons fluttering from its bonnet.

The reception was splendid; the excellent meal was run with flair and efficiency, Colin's speech and those of the other dutiful men were fluent and entertaining, and the toasts were drunk with style and aplomb. The wedding had started at 11.30am and by the end of this reception the time had crept around to 2.30pm.

At this time, the best man, a friend of Colin's, said, 'Ladies and gentlemen, the presents are on display at the bride's home, Sycamore Cottage, Ploatby — you are invited to view them. The bride and groom will leave the bride's home for their honeymoon at four pm. You might like to see them off.'

Mary, who always loves a wedding, said she'd like to view the presents and see Susan's going-away outfit, so we agreed to visit Sycamore Cottage, Ploatby. As we were leaving the reception, several other cars were doing likewise, and leading the first flush of departing vehicles was the silver Jaguar containing the bride and groom.

The uniformed chauffeur had been hired with the car, both coming from a York firm which specialised in this kind of service. In an orderly fashion, the procession of cars filed out of the spacious grounds of the hotel and began to speed through the lanes towards Ploatby.

I was somewhere towards the rear with perhaps ten or a dozen cars ahead of me. I simply tagged on behind and others followed me, for some of the guests were strangers and did not know the route. I made it clear I would show them the way. As we moved off, there was a good deal of merriment with people waving at each other out of car windows, flying their silk scarves, throwing confetti, shouting and laughing as we passed through the splendid Ryedale countryside.

And ahead was the fine Jaguar, its polished silver bodywork glistening in the bright sunshine of the day as the happy couple waved and blew kisses to everyone. It disappeared around the sharp corners and was frequently hidden from my view by the high hedges and the distance between us.

As we motored along Hazel Burn Lane which joined the Ashfordly–York road, I lost sight of the powerful Jaguar; its lead had become quite substantial but I did not try to keep pace with it, for I had no wish to lose those behind me who were relying on my guidance. And then we were on the main road, the B-class highway which led towards York. Driving steadily, I was approaching the dangerous portion over Pennyflats Cross, and even as I neared the place, I saw several smart-suited gentlemen waving us to a halt.

'Oh, no!' I groaned at Mary. 'What now! Don't say there's been an accident today of all days!'

With every passing yard, it was clear there had been an accident, for cars were strewn across both lanes of the highway and people were milling about, shouting at us to slow down and stop. I pulled on to the grass verge, making sure my car was clear as I went to investigate. Upon my advice, Mary remained in her seat — the fewer people about the scene, the better.

When I crested that notorious hill, my heart sank. The silver Jaguar was on its side, its roof crushed against the very same ash tree that Colin had hit only months ago. Also lying on its side in the middle of the road was a tractor and trailer, the trailer having carried a load of manure. It was spread across the carriageway and other cars were scattered randomly about the road with anxious people milling about . . .

I ran to the Jaguar.

I knew Colin and Susan were inside and the awful silence about the car made me fear the worst; I was no longer a wedding guest, but a policeman who had suddenly found himself on duty. As I ran down the road, weaving between irregularly parked cars, I saw that several had been slightly damaged. The accident was one of the shunt type when each car runs into the back of the one ahead. Seven or eight had been damaged, but I was not concerned with those. I arrived at the Jaguar to find a knot of helpers trying to reach the bride and groom who were in the rear seat. No one seemed to be worried about the chauffeur, and at this stage I was not even aware of the tractor driver's injuries.

Susan, her wedding dress stained with blood and dirt, was crying as she lay on top of Colin; he was curled up in an untidy heap as he lay among the broken glass and shattered metalwork of the car body, and he was bleeding about the head and face. I told the helpers who I was and they stood aside as I wrenched open the rear door which now lay uppermost and somehow, I don't know how, I found myself crouched inside the rear compartment, mysteriously avoiding trampling on the couple.

They were conscious but hurt; I shouted for someone to call two ambulances and to stress the urgency due to the number of casualties, then call the police, a local doctor and finally a nearby garage to arrange lifting-gear and cutting-equipment. I asked the volunteer to give a detailed account of the multiple accident; he said he would cope.

I thought Colin or the chauffeur might be trapped, such was their position in the wreckage. Each was lying on the side of the car, which was on the ground, the roof being caved in around them. I asked the gathered menfolk to care for their ladies and other guests, and to ensure that there was adequate warning for approaching vehicles. I didn't want more pile-ups and I asked them not to move their cars; their position was vital for the subsequent official report.

But I must see to Colin and Susan. Speaking to them in what I hoped were soothing terms, I managed to move Susan to a more comfortable position. Then I made a very brief and almost cursory examination of Colin. He was sighing with pain and I daren't move him in case he had broken bones or internal injuries which could cause further damage. One of his arms seemed to be trapped somewhere beneath him and careless handling could aggravate any injuries he might have.

Relieved that he was alive, I now looked to the unfortunate chauffeur; he was lying trapped too, unconscious and pale with a spot of blood on his face, but he was breathing quite smoothly. I did not touch him. This release required the skill of experts and the injured people needed medical attention. I hoped the messages for help would receive the attention they required. And I was not disappointed.

The sequence of events moved rapidly ahead. In what seemed a very short time, the emergency services arrived; a motor patrol car based at Scarborough had happened to be patrolling nearby and two capable officers, not closely known to me, came and dealt very efficiently with the multiple accident, paying immediate attention to the casualties. Two ambulances came and, with the help of us all, and the garage's lifting-gear, we soon had the casualties free and on their way to hospital.

The chauffeur was placed in a second ambulance and the tractor driver, who seemed to be forgotten by most of us, was also placed on board. The other casualties were all suffering from minor injuries and shock, and Doctor Archie McGee, summoned from Elsinby, was able to treat most of them without hospitalisation.

I sent Mary home while I remained to help the two officers with the statement-taking, clearing the scene and generally making myself useful. Under the circumstances, I'm not sure if anyone went to the house to see the presents, but we didn't. I was shattered by the awful turn of events, the enormity of which did not register until some time later.

This is a feature of police work; you deal with a harrowing incident in a cool and professional way, and it is later, when relaxing at home, that the sheer horror of the incident registers. I'm sure many police officers have wept with sorrow and anger after dealing with terrible incidents.

But this was not such a serious case for there were no fatalities. That, I felt, was another example of fate. With so many cars involved, there could have been carnage.

I rang the hospital to enquire after each of the casualties and learned that Susan had fractured an ankle and had suffered lots of bruising to her body. Colin had a broken arm, a minor fracture to his skull and lots of cuts about the face; the chauffeur, a man from York called Eric Wallis, had fractured six ribs and had facial injuries due to impact with the steering-wheel and windscreen. The tractor driver, a 56-year-old farm worker called Eddie Harper, had been knocked from his machine to suffer a broken shoulder blade, a broken arm and severe lacerations to his face and hands.

The following day, I rang the two motor patrol officers to explain about my battles to get the junction made safer either by more signs, better advance warnings and a clearer view from the minor road and they assured me this would be incorporated in their report. Their enquiries, based on witness statements, suggested that poor old Eddie Harper had pulled out of the minor road with his slow-moving tractor and trailer, and the fast-moving Jaguar had crested the blind summit of that hill driven by a man who was accustomed to city traffic, not country roads. The Jaguar had hit the tractor, and the following cars had each collided with another vehicle. Nine of them were damaged, and fifteen people had been injured.

It was the worst accident on my patch and I hoped it would result in some improvements to that road. And then, about six or seven weeks later, I received a phone call.

'It's Colin Blenkiron,' said the voice. 'We're out of hospital, Mr Rhea, Susan and me, and we wondered if you and Mrs Rhea would like to see the wedding presents? I know it's a bit late, but we're having friends in, a few at a time . . . how about Sunday afternoon, say three-ish?'

'We'd love to!' I enthused.

'Drive carefully!' he said, laughing.

It was pouring with rain as we went along to their lovely cottage and we found both of them still wearing dressings on some of their injuries and both chuckling at the absurdity of the situation.

'That crossroads has got it in for us!' Colin laughed as he poured the wine. 'It's put us in hospital twice now . . . I never go that way when Susan's with me. I'm not risking another accident, I can tell you!'

'You met me because of Pennyflats Cross!' she retorted with good humour.

'And I got put in hospital twice because of it!' he said. 'And that first accident was all your fault . . .'

'It wasn't! It was yours!' she cried. 'You were going far too fast . . .'

'Here's to the pair of you!' and as the driving rain beat upon their cottage, a flash of lightning was followed by a crack of thunder which rattled the windows.

I raised my glass to them and then, for some odd reason, I remembered the words of Samuel Beckett in, I think, *All That Fall*. I quoted them as a toast, 'What sky! What light! Ah, in spite of all, it is a blessed thing to be alive in such weather, and out of hospital!'

And Colin kissed Susan.

CHAPTER 7

A difference of taste in jokes is a great strain on the affections.
GEORGE ELIOT, 1819—80

Society will have its jokers. Throughout the ages there have been many classic pranks, some on a large scale and others of a very minor nature. In the countryside, April 1st has always been a good time for practising pranks upon one's friends, relations and workmates. I remember one joker who claimed that hens' eggs could be stretched if they were collected immediately after being laid because at that moment, their shells are still soft. He said they could be stretched to appear larger and so fetch a better price.

In our area, one newspaper printed a story that the castle at Barnard Castle was to be demolished to make way for a bridge across the River Tees, and there was a joke that almost went wrong when a man walked into a park and picked up a new park bench under the nose of a policeman. He was stopped on suspicion of theft and claimed he wanted the seat for firewood. He was promptly arrested and when he explained that it was merely a joke no one believed him. He did, however, manage to prove that the seat was his own, as he'd bought it specially for the joke only the day before.

One Yorkshire lad tricked his family and friends when he organised a spoof wedding. He and a girlfriend had apparently got married, had their photographs taken, and then driven around town in their wedding outfits for all to see.

One of my favourite jokes was the news that British time was to be decimalised. It claimed that, in order to rationalise Great Britain with the move towards metrication and decimalisation, the year would no longer have twelve months. Instead, Britain would have 10 months, each comprising 10 weeks; there would be 10 days to each week, and 10 hours to each day. Each hour would have 10 minutes and each minute would be split into 10 seconds. A year would be called a Kiloday, a month would be a hectoday, a week would be known as a decaday, while a minute would become a centiday and so forth.

Furthermore, to coincide with the change, Big Ben would become digital and there would be wage adjustments to cope with each Leap Kiloday.

Harmless, and at times very believable, jokes are great fun, such as the time our local zoo claimed they had found the Loch Ness Monster and even fooled the Scottish police into halting them at the border as they tried to smuggle out the carcase. It was in fact a huge type of seal, but the police had unearthed a byelaw which forbids the taking of certain rare species out of Scotland and so they were halted at the border in the belief they had the Loch Ness Monster in their possession!

One 'animal' which is a regular victim of April Fool jokes is the famous White Horse of Kilburn. It overlooks the North Yorkshire countryside from its vantage point just below the rim of the escarpment near Sutton Bank.

This huge white shape of a horse, over 105 yards long, was cut from the hillside in 1857 from plans drawn by John Hodgson, the headmaster of Kilburn village school. Helped by his pupils and a group of local men, Hodgson carved the horse from the hillside where it remains a landmark for miles around. It is the only hillside sculpture of its kind in the north of England and can be seen from over 70 miles away. It was filled with white lime and so the outline of this magnificent horse continues to dominate the countryside around Kilburn, not far from Aidensfield. But on April Fool's Day, the horse is liable to change! From time to time, it has been transformed into a zebra, a cowboy's horse with a rider and, in recent times, a well-endowed stallion.

I think it is fair to say that most of us enjoy a clever but harmless joke and police officers are no exception. A clever April Fool joke is always appreciated and so are jokes perpetrated at other times of the year.

I well remember one young rookie constable who was ordered to place traffic cones around York Minster one Sunday morning which happened to be April 1st. He had been told that today was the annual Archbishop's Foot Race, when every clergyman in the York Diocese was expected by the Archbishop to run a short race around the Minster, all dressed in their cassocks and surplices. The lad had therefore coned off the entire Minster moments before the regular services were due to start. If he kept his cones there, no one could enter the Minster.

The situation was rectified at the last minute when he received a radio call, supposedly from Police Headquarters, to say the race had been cancelled because the Archbishop had influenza.

Other jokes included leaving notes for the night-shift sergeant to the effect that the Chief Constable had requested an early call at 5am, and a similar one backfired when an unsuspecting constable was ordered to wake up the warden of the local dogs' home at 5am by knocking on his door. He was told that the warden had made this request and that he had insisted that the police keep knocking until he answered the door. He was a noted over-sleeper and had a very important meeting that day. The truth was that the warden didn't live on the premises; in fact, no one lived on the premises except hundreds of dogs, and the resultant continuous loud barking roused the entire town.

It was when I called at Eltering Police Station one day on duty that I found myself involved in a practical joke on a new constable who had recently arrived. His name was Justin Pendlebury, a man of about twenty-eight years of age, and he came from a very wealthy background; it seemed his family were from the stockbroker belt of Surrey, but Justin had decided to break away from both family and environment to become a constable in the North Riding of Yorkshire. We never knew why he had done this, but in fact he proved himself a very capable young officer.

But he had one annoying character trait. He was rather pompous and always boasted about the style and quality of his clothes. Certainly, he dressed well, far better than the rest of us. His suits were beautifully cut, he wore hand-made shirts and shoes, exquisite silk ties and his casual wear was of the very highest quality.

Justin certainly looked very stylish and smart, but he made everyone aware of the fact, telling us tales of how his tailor was the very best in London's West End, how the fellow made all his suits by hand and dressed film stars, politicians and city business people. Justin scorned the cheap suits and flannel trousers that we wore, saying we ought to be more clothes-conscious. But none of us copied him or ever tried to emulate his style. If our clothes kept us warm and dry, then that was good enough.

Although everyone liked Justin and admired his professionalism when on duty, we did get sick of his continual talk of fine clothes, men's fashions and popular styles. He talked of Ascot, Glyndebourne and Epsom as we talked about the back row of the Empire Cinema or the cheap end at Thornaby Races and Cargo Fleet Greyhound Track.

As I entered Eltering Police Station that day, I walked into a discussion about clothes. And, as usual, it was led by Justin. He was having an animated conversation with PC. Alf Ventress and two visiting officers, PCs George Henderson and Harry Pitts.

Alf Ventress was known to us all as Vesuvius because his uniform was always covered in ash and he was likely to erupt at any time; he was a huge, grizzly-haired constable of the old-fashioned type whose trousers always needed pressing, whose tunic was constantly smothered in dandruff and cigarette ash, whose boots always needed cleaning and whose shirts always sported crumpled collars. He was the last person to be discussing smart clothes with Justin.

'Ah, young Nick,' he said as I walked in. I had my bait-bag with me, bait being the name for my sandwiches and coffee. I was to take my meal-break here this evening.

'Hello.' I nodded at them all as they were seated around the kitchen of the police station, with the kettle boiling and a bottle of milk on the table.

'Just the chap!' said Vesuvius to me. 'Nick, a few months ago, you were telling us of a tailor you knew, one of the old-fashioned kind who makes suits by hand. He sits on his table cross-legged, you said, and you can see him at work through his window.'

'Golding,' I said. 'John Golding,' for this was his name and I remembered telling them about him.

'The best for miles around, you said,' continued Vesuvius and he winked at me in what I recognised as the beginnings of a conspiracy of some kind.

'He does a lot of work for the local folks,' I agreed. 'Yes, he turns out some good stuff, our farmers love him.'

'Justin here was saying he needed somebody local to make him a good suit,' Vesuvius continued. 'I was telling him of that chap you mentioned; couldn't think of his name or where he works.'

'Ah, well, John Golding,' I said to Justin. 'He's a bit old-fashioned, but he sits there in full view of the street making suits, jackets, trousers and so on. He'll tackle women's costumes, children's coats and, well, everything, even rugs for horses or car travellers. He's always busy.'

'Really, where's he operate?' asked Justin.

'Elsinby,' I said. 'If you're ever out there patrolling, park near the church and then go up the little alleyway just opposite. You'll see his window. It's a little stone cottage and there's a sign on the top of his window with his name, and it says "Ladies' and Gentlemen's Alterations".'

This was true; people from far around took pictures of that curious sign with its double meaning, but John reckoned it brought him customers!

'And can you recommend him?' asked Justin. 'I need a brand-new suit, you see, urgently. I've been invited to the wedding of Lord Gauvey in Westminster Abbey and I must have a new suit. Duty commitments mean I cannot get to London to be measured, and Vesuvius recommended this fellow.'

At this stage, both the other constables began to praise the old tailor and I suspected a plot of some kind.

I had no idea what they'd been saying before my arrival, so I adopted an impartial stance by saying, 'I've never had anything made by him.'

'But your local farmers use him?' Justin said.

'Oh, yes.' I knew this to be the case. 'They keep him going with their jobs.'

'Just like your farmers from the south, they are,' said Vesuvius. 'Smart, plenty of cash, and always out to impress. Gentlemen farmers, you know, stylish and up-to-date.'

Now I knew something was going on. Many of the local farmers didn't care two hoots how they dressed or what they looked like. If they had one smart suit for funerals and weddings, that was sufficient; the rest of the time was spent in any old working-togs they could muster. They would rarely buy a new outfit, the main visits to Golding being by bachelor farmers who wanted to have tears mended or patches sewn on knees and elbows of worn-out clothes which they thought had ten or twenty years of wear left in them. Those who were married received this attention from their wives.

I realised no one had told Justin that Golding's suits never fit anyone properly; they were always far too big or far too small; one sleeve or one leg would be longer than the other and the general rule was that his clothing only fitted a customer who was misshapen. Throughout the district, John Golding was known for his awful tailoring, although the material he used was of very superior quality. 'It's stuff,' said one farmer to me. 'Real stuff.'

John Golding always used the finest of materials and we never really knew his source, although it was thought he had family connections with the textile industry at Halifax, West Yorkshire. But his cloth was his strength, and those who commissioned John to tailor their clothing invariably knew the outcome. They would received an ill-fitting outfit made from the very best of materials, so they would take it to another tailor to have it altered. Because he was more than generous with his sizes, making clothes that were far too large, such alterations could usually be achieved. This system kept John in work, for his fees were modest, and at the end of the operation, the customer did have a very fine article of clothing which would last a lifetime.

The outcome of that visit to Eltering Police Station was that Justin Pendlebury did call on John Golding. He was duly measured and ordered his suit. He selected the very best Yorkshire worsted and was highly impressed by the quality of material kept in this tiny village tailor's shop.

'Amazing,' he said to me over the telephone. 'You'd never expect quality of that kind up here! It's top quality, you know, genuine too, the real stuff.'

Two or three weeks later, I received another telephone call from Justin. 'Nick,' he said. 'Can you do me a favour? I've had a call from Mr Golding to say my suit's ready. I wondered if you could pick it up for me and drop if off at Eltering Police Station? I see you're covering the whole section next Friday.'

'Yes, of course,' I offered.

That Friday morning, I called at John Golding's little shop and collected the parcel. I completed my morning's patrol and at lunchtime telephoned Justin who was on duty in Eltering until 3pm. He was working 7am–3pm that day, and I said that I had the parcel and would bring it to the police station around 3pm. I arrived just before three o'clock and Justin was already there, awaiting his treasure. The wedding was the following day, and he was to travel to London later this afternoon.

Vesuvius had obviously spread the word around because four other constables from the villages had, apparently by sheer coincidence, come into the office at that time, and Sergeant Charlie Bairstow was there too. They had brewed a cup of tea and it seemed that Justin, even though he didn't realise it yet, was about to have a fitting.

'I had one earlier, you know,' he told us when we pressed him to try on the suit. 'Mr Golding called me in last week . . . the final fitting . . . it was a really good fit . . .'

'Come on, Justin,' pleaded Vesuvius. 'Let's see how a city man should look. We know nowt about smart clothes up here on t'moors, you know. You've been telling us to dress well, so now's your chance to show us how to do it, right from scratch.'

The rest of us echoed those thoughts and pressed Justin to try on his new suit. In the face of such demands, he disappeared down the cell passage to change.

A few minutes later, he emerged in his new outfit. In a handsome dark worsted, it was a three-piece in the very latest style and it was a perfect fit. Justin was the epitome of a smart and successful city gentleman.

There was a stunned silence from his audience.

'How about that, then?' he beamed, doing a twirl. 'This is style, gentlemen,' he said. 'I never knew such clothing was obtainable in the north.'

'Bloody hell, you must be deformed!' laughed Vesuvius, going across and tugging the jacket. 'It's perfect . . .'

And so it was. We admired the suit; it was superb in every sense and the quality and fit was undeniable. Justin was so proud and, to be honest, we were all pleased for him. Looking back, it would have been a tragedy if it had been a gross misfit, and so later that afternoon he hurried away to travel down to the wedding in London.

Our joke had misfired, and perhaps it was a good job it had. But later that evening when I was relaxing at home, the telephone rang. It was John Golding.

'That suit you picked up this morning, Mr Rhea,' he began. 'Have you still got it?'

'I haven't, John, no. I delivered it to my colleague.'

'Where is it now?' he asked.

'In London, I'd say,' I told him, and explained the reason.

'Oh, crumbs,' he said. 'That's torn it!'

'Why?' I asked, wondering what John's problem could be.

'Well, it was the wrong one,' John said. 'That should have gone to a chap in Thirsk, and I reckon he's got that 'un your friend ordered. He reckons it doesn't fit him.'

'I think he's mistaken, John,' I said, trying to cover for Justin. 'Justin's was perfect, he's gone to a wedding in it and he was delighted. I saw him wearing it, he got the right suit, I'm sure. Maybe you could alter the Thirsk one and say nothing about the possible mistake?'

'Aye, mebbe I should. I'll tell yon Thirsk chap he's got the right 'un, they're t'same cloth. Thanks, Mr Rhea.'

I never told Justin he'd been given the wrong suit, nor did I tell Vesuvius and the other constables. I let Justin think we could produce the finest suits, and it was several weeks later when there was another repercussion.

'How did the wedding go?' I asked Justin one day when we were chatting.

He told me all about it and then, as an afterthought, he added, 'Oh, by the way, that suit you helped me with. You should have seen the admiring looks I got; my family and friends were most impressed, Nick, most impressed. In fact, several of them are ordering suits from Mr Golding. I can't wait to see their faces when they receive them.'

'Neither can I,' I said with some honesty.

* * *

One of the funniest jokes was the one played upon poor Douglas Gregson and his girlfriend Deirdre. Douglas was a farmer's son who lived in Crampton with his parents.

Aged about twenty-five, Douglas was not the brightest of lads; in fact he was very simple-minded and worked as a labourer on his parents' large and busy farm. He was capable of doing as he was told, and his physical strength enabled him to undertake most of the tasks about the farm. A very good worker, he was not mentally ill, but merely rather slow when it came to using his brain.

He was strongly built with powerful shoulders and a neck like a bull, although he was very gentle-natured. With his short brown hair and big brown eyes, he was a fine-looking lad, but as his father said, 'Oor Douglas was at t'back o' t'queue when God was dishing out brains.'

His parents were ordinary hard-working farmers, and his father enjoyed working with horses; indeed, he kept several on the farm, as well as a collection of fine horse-drawn vehicles including a stage coach and several traps. He would take these to local agricultural shows and galas, where he would provide rides in them for charity. Douglas was quite a capable driver too, and would often take the reins of his father's coaches, carts and traps.

Then Douglas found a girlfriend. Deirdre was the niece of a couple in Crampton and she came to visit them from time to time. She was not too bright either and was a plain but pleasant girl a couple of years younger than Douglas. She wore her dull brown hair in a bobbed cut and had pretty pink cheeks and grey eyes. Heavily built and somewhat slow in her movements, her surname was Wharton.

Deirdre lived in Middlesbrough where she had a mundane job with the Corporation and she loved to come to the countryside. Her long-standing, platonic friendship with Douglas meant she paid regular weekend visits to Crampton and there is no doubt the couple were ideal for one another. She loved to go on outings alone with Douglas and they were sometimes accompanied by his family or her aunt and uncle.

It was during one of those outings on a lovely summer day in June, that someone played a prank on the happy pair. Douglas had been allowed to take a pony and trap for a drive and this delighted Deirdre. With her sitting in the trap like a lady, Douglas had driven along the lanes until he had found a place to halt. It was a field through which a footpath led to a lovely walk along the banks of the river to an old mill, and then across the water via a footbridge and back to this field over another pack-horse bridge. The local people enjoyed this as a Sunday afternoon walk, for it took a little over an hour.

At the entrance to the field, Douglas had tied the horse's long reins to a small tree beside the five-barred gate and had then escorted Deirdre upon this delightful stroll. The horse could move around and was able to munch the grass, even though it was still between the shafts of the trap. But a prankster saw a wonderful opportunity for a joke upon Douglas. This unknown person had discovered the unattended pony and trap and had clearly known it belonged to Douglas.

He had unhitched the pony and, with considerable skill, had manhandled the light trap. This was really a governess cart of the kind used for taking children on outings; it had two seats facing inwards, mudguards over the wheels and a low rear door. Ideal for country lanes, it was very light and manoeuvrable, even by hand. The prankster was able to place the tips of its twin shafts between the bars of the gate and the gap between the bars was sufficient for the entire length of the shafts to go through. Thus the front panels of the cart were tight against the gate, with the shafts protruding at the other side, and then the joker had backed the pony between the shafts and had re-hitched it.

When Douglas and Deirdre had returned, this sight had baffled them. Neither could understand how the pony had somehow caused the gate to become inextricably intertwined with the shafts of the trap. And Douglas, not being the brightest of lads, could not see a way to undo this problem. His answer was to use his strength. The space between the bars allowed him to lift the gate off its hinges, then he put Deirdre aboard the trap and jumped up himself.

And then he set a course for home with the gate still fastened in position; its width filled the lane and provided the wonderful sight of a mobile five-barred gate being carried between a pony and trap. And that's how I found them. I was driving my mini-van towards Crampton when this sight confronted me. I could not get past on the narrow road and pulled on to the verge where I signalled Douglas to stop.

'Now then, Douglas,' I said. 'What have we got here?'

'A five-barred gate, Mr Rhea, from yon field down by t'beck.'

'Ah.' I knew the field in question. 'And how's it come to be here? Did you run into it or something?'

'Nay, I didn't, but how it's come to get tangled up with my cart is summat I shall never know, Mr Rhea,' he said with all seriousness.

'Why, what happened?' I was now very curious about it for at this stage, I did not know what had occurred. As he pondered aloud, Deirdre sat silently in the trap, frowning as she puzzled over the answer.

'Well,' he said slowly. 'I got into t'field, tied up my awd pony and set off walking. I mean, we didn't crash through t'gate or owt like that. It was in t'field by this time, safe and sound, Mr Rhea, both t'pony and t'trap. And when we got back, yon pony must have got loose or summat, because it had got itself tangled up like yon. Now how it managed to do that, I'll never know, so I thought I'd take it home and get yon gate off. I might have to saw it off, it looks fairly well fastened on, eh?'

'If we unhitch your pony,' I said. 'We could slide that gate off, eh? And then we can put it back before somebody thinks you've stolen it.'

'Stolen it? I'd never do that, Mr Rhea.' He looked very worried at this suggestion.

'I know you wouldn't, Douglas, so let's get it off.'

I felt that the best way would be to drive pony and trap back to the field, for this was the easiest way to carry the gate to its former position. To manhandle that gate off those shafts as the trap stood here on its two wheels wouldn't be easy, so I jumped aboard and Douglas drove us back to the field. There, he skilfully positioned the trap into the space between the hedges and we inched the gate into its former position. There was sufficient room for me and Douglas to manipulate it back on to its hinges while still resting upon those shafts, and when it was secure, we unhitched the pony, withdrew the trap from the gate, and re-assembled the unit.

'There,' I said to Douglas and Deirdre. 'Now you can go home without this gate.'

'By gum, Mr Rhea, that was a clever move. Who'd have thought of that, eh?'

'Who indeed?' I wondered who had done this to Douglas and guessed that, sooner or later, the culprit would approach him to find out how he'd coped with the gate. Maybe I would never know of that discussion.

But the happy couple then drove home and I heard no more about the prank with the five-barred gate. I'm still convinced, however, that neither Douglas nor Deirdre thought it was the work of a prankster. They thought the pony had done it.

* * *

Prominent among the wonderful aspects of welfare within the police service are the police convalescent homes. There are two in England and they provide facilities for serving or retired officers who are recuperating from sickness or injury. Supported by voluntary contributions from every serving officer, they are havens of rest for those who wish to recover quietly from a serious ailment or injury. Many officers make use of them, for it is here they can enjoy a relaxed and cheerful atmosphere coupled with the undivided attention of dedicated staff. These are not hospitals; their function is to consolidate the work of the doctors and hospitals by providing after-care facilities for rest and recuperation away from domestic and professional pressures. And most certainly, they do a fine job.

The following account is not mine, therefore, because it comes from a friend who spent some time in one of the convalescent homes, and I feel it is worthy of inclusion at this point as we are discussing practical jokes.

I will call my friend Dave; after a serious illness he was advised to spend some weeks in the Northern Police Convalescent Home in order to encourage a full recovery. Once inside, he was one of a group of about thirty officers, men and women of all ranks representing most of the Northern police forces. The friendly atmosphere was evident from the moment he stepped inside, and one of the things he noticed, as a constable, was that the rank structure was abolished.

In the workaday routine of the police service, especially among the provincial forces, ranks are strictly honoured, with sergeants always being called 'Sergeant' by the constables. Sometimes, very unofficially, they would be called 'Serge', but the lower rank must never address anyone of higher rank by his or her Christian name.

Sergeants and constables then address inspectors and anyone above that rank as 'sir'; inspectors call chief inspectors 'sir'; both call a superintendent 'sir', and so forth up the scale. Chief superintendents, assistant chief constables, deputy chief constables and chief constables are all 'sir' to those who are subordinate to them. In the London Metropolitan Police, the higher ranks include commanders, deputy assistant commissioners, assistant commissioners and a deputy commissioner with, of course, the Commissioner himself, all of whom are addressed as 'sir'. In the case of lady police officers, sergeants are called by that name, whereas inspectors and those of senior rank are addressed as 'ma'am'. Within the CID hierarchy, the ranks are the same, i.e. detective constables, detective sergeants, detective inspectors, detective chief inspectors, detective superintendents and detective chief superintendents.

Throughout the service, this hierarchy is strictly honoured because police officers are members of a highly disciplined body with an enormous amount of formality; inevitably, this leads to a powerful consciousness of rank through every aspect of a police officer's life.

For officers of all ranks to be thrown together into a common pool can be a traumatic experience, especially if they are supposed to be off duty and recovering from sickness in a friendly environment. No one wants his boss breathing down his neck when he is recovering from sickness. This was recognised by those in charge of the convalescent homes, and it was felt that, within those walls, all distinction between ranks should be abolished. After all, a constable could hardly feel relaxed if his table companion or snooker partner was known to be a deputy chief constable, albeit from another police area.

When officers were admitted therefore, their ranks were not known to the other residents. They were simply Miss, Mrs or Mr. Obviously, instances did occur when one officer was known to another which meant that his rank was also known, but this was a comparatively rare event because of the huge catchment area. Many officers found themselves sharing their convalescence with complete strangers, and this was the ideal situation. The decision whether or not to reveal one's rank rested with individuals.

It was Dave's misfortune, therefore, to be admitted at the same time as his own deputy chief constable. Within moments of arriving, the Home's insistence that ranks should be ignored was made known to them, and to give the Deputy his credit, his first words to Dave were, 'Ah, Dave. I'm Bill. I mean that; I'm Bill, so forget my rank. I'm Bill Short, got it?'

'Yes, sir, er . . . Bill, . . sir . . .'

'Bill,' said the Deputy.

'Yes, sir . . . er . . . Bill.'

It was very difficult to abandon that habit which had developed over many years in the service, but Bill Short did his best to make Dave relax. The others, a mixture of men and women of all age groups and from widely varying aspects of the job in distant police forces, had no trouble referring to Bill as Bill. They did not know his rank, and he did his best to ensure Dave didn't tell them. But for Dave, it was not easy; it took days for him to be able to refer to his second most senior officer as Bill.

Inevitably, he did slip up from time to time and called Bill "sir" in front of the others. They, of course, did not mind for there were other "sirs" among them, happily unaware even then of the precise ranks involved. And then there developed a strange situation which completely relaxed Dave and put his boss in a wonderful new light.

One Friday evening, the residents gathered around the notice-board to study the list of forthcoming arrivals who were due at the Home on the following Monday.

'Bloody hell!' cried Stan, a man from Lancashire Constabulary. 'See that? He'll not go along with this "no rank" idea. He's the most rank-conscious man I know — he even gets his wife to call herself Mrs Superintendent Welsh. He never speaks to lower ranks when he's off duty — he's a right pain, I can tell you!'

The rest of them crowded around the board in an attempt to read the name of this unwelcome guest, as Stan went on:

'He crawls to the bosses — he'll grovel like hell to anybody higher than himself. He'll put a right damper on this place, you'll see.'

'Who is he?' asked Bill Short.

'Superintendent Adam Welsh, the Admin Superintendent in one of our Divisions in Lancashire. Special-course man, a flier, passed all his exams and shot up the tree. He's a right toffee-nosed bastard! He doesn't know me, thank God, but we all know him!'

Bill laughed.

'Right,' he said. 'If he's coming here to flaunt his rank, we'll be ready for him. I have a plan. We can take him down a peg or two, as they say. Everyone agreed?'

They asked Stan to give a detailed account of the behaviour of the newcomer, after which they agreed they would listen to Bill's idea. In short, Welsh seemed a most objectionable man whose chief aim in life was to rise through the ranks by creeping to those who were senior to him. After hearing this, Bill took them all into the lounge and explained his system.

'Right,' he said. 'The first thing is not to react to him if he toes the Home's line; I mean, he might join in with everyone and forget his exalted rank. If he does, then we don't bring our plan into action. OK? We let him set the pace — we must give him a chance to join us.'

They all agreed to that.

'But,' he continued, 'we shall need plans if he tries to pull rank on the rest of us. To get the maximum benefit from this, you should know that, although I'm Bill to each of you, I am really a deputy chief constable. But from the moment this man enters this Home, you will let him know that I am a constable. I'm the sort of constable who has never been in line for promotion, never passed my exams, and at my age there is no hope for promotion!'

They smiled at the idea.

'Now,' said Bill addressing a man called Keith who came from Newcastle upon Tyne. 'Keith. You are a very well spoken man, if I may say so. You do not have a Geordie accent, not even a trace of one and you do have the presence of a senior officer.' Bill's ability to assess a person shone through.

'I'm originally from Surrey,' said Keith.

'You sound very like a deputy chief constable to me!' smiled Bill. 'At least a deputy, perhaps even a chief constable. You're not, I know, because I know all the chiefs, deputies and assistants in the north. So do you mind telling us your rank — for this important exercise?'

'No, I'm a constable, that's all. I never got promoted because I never passed my exams!'

'Right,' said Bill. 'From the moment this Lancashire character arrives and plays the rank game, you will be a deputy chief constable. I shall inadvertently call you "sir" from time to time and we'll see how he reacts.'

'I'll love that!' said Keith.

To avoid further confusion, the little meeting of conspirators decided that no one else would adopt a false rank, although there was nothing to prevent them pretending they were higher than superintendent if the moment justified it. They all agreed that Keith would be their deputy chief constable for this exercise, and that Bill would be a constable on a beat in Scarborough.

It was with some interest, therefore, that the company awaited the arrival of Mr A. Welsh. After being attended to by the receptionist, he settled in his room and came to join the rest of the guests in the lounge just before lunch.

His first remark, to a grey-haired man called Cyril was, 'Where are the officers' toilets, please?'

'There aren't any,' said Cyril. 'Men's and women's are separate, but we don't use ranks here, Mr Welsh.'

'This is a *police* establishment,' was his retort. 'I should not be expected to share toilets with the lower ranks. I shall speak to the management. And for lunch? There will surely be officers' tables? With linen cloths and napkins?'

'No,' said Bill Short, entering the conversation. 'We all muck in, we don't ask for ranks here, Mr Welsh.'

The cheek muscles in the taut white face of this man tightened noticeably; he was a tall, thin man with an almost gaunt expression and his fair hair was cut short and plastered back with hair oil.

He showed no inclination to smile and his eyes, darting rapidly around the room for indications of support, rested on Keith. As Bill Short had recognised, Keith, for some reason, had the demeanour of a very senior officer and Welsh addressed him:

'Is this true? Am I to believe that in this police establishment, the achievement of rank is not recognised?'

'Yes, Mr Welsh, that is so,' said Keith in his finest voice. 'We are all guests, men and women of equal status as we recuperate.'

'Then I think this is appalling. I haven't worked my way up to superintendent rank for nothing! I am Superintendent Welsh, I wish everyone to know that and to remember and respect that fact during my stay here!'

And with that statement, everyone knew what to do.

'What do you think, sir?' Bill Short asked Keith, slipping in the rogue "sir" with astonishing ease. 'Should we revert to our ranks?'

'I think it is a matter for individual choice,' said Keith. 'Speaking purely personally, I am happy to be called Keith by everyone here, including Superintendent Welsh.'

Keith played his part with such aplomb that the others almost applauded him and this set the scene. Later, they learned that Welsh had quietly sought the advice of one of the guests about Keith's rank, and was told, in the strictest confidence, that he was deputy chief constable from Newcastle upon Tyne City Police.

In the days that followed, Welsh followed Keith around like a pupil with a crush on a teacher, having been assured that everyone else here was below his own rank and therefore unworthy of his companionship. He carried Keith's golf clubs, invited him out for drinks, joined him at snooker and card games, discussed policy matters with him and generally shut the others out of his short convalescence.

For Bill Short, this was excellent and he was enjoying himself testing Welsh's reactions; he tried to win his confidence by inviting him out for a drink, by offering to play snooker with him, by inviting him for walks into the town for shopping or sightseeing, but each of Bill's overtures was politely rejected. Welsh made it abundantly clear that he did not consort with lower ranks, especially constables who drank pints and played snooker.

Stan's assessment of Welsh had been absolutely accurate for he was a snob, and a rank-conscious snob into the bargain. By the end of the week, everyone was wondering how to reveal to Superintendent Welsh the fact that he was being led gently along a path that led to nowhere in a wonderfully false world. It was learned that he would be going home on the Sunday, and in order to make the necessary impact upon him, the truth should be revealed.

The opportunity came during the dinner on Saturday night. It was made known that the Chief Constable of Newcastle upon Tyne City Police would be attending the evening dinner as a guest of the Home.

He was chairman of the management committee and was attending in that capacity. Chief constables were regular visitors, for most of them served on the management committee or supported the work of the convalescent home in various ways. As the dinner gong sounded, therefore, the residents moved into the dining-room and Superintendent Welsh made sure he shared a table with Keith. There was an even more important reason for this because Welsh realised that Keith was from the Newcastle force. Perhaps he thought the Chief Constable would come over and express interest in the health of one of his most senior officers. Everyone was seated prior to the Chief Constable's entry and, as was his custom, he toured the tables to speak to the guests before settling down to eat.

When he arrived at Keith's table, his eyes lit up.

'Ah, PC Burton, good to see you. How's it going?'

'Fine, sir,' beamed Keith. 'This break has done me a world of good. I feel much better now.'

'Summonses and Warrants is having a busy time without you, you know. I'll tell Sergeant Helm you're doing fine; I know he's anxiously awaiting your return!'

'Another week should do it, sir,' said Keith, pleased his Chief had recognised him.

'Good, well, nice to have seen you looking so fit. And you,' he now addressed Welsh. 'Are you recuperating nicely?'

'Yes, sir,' beamed Welsh.

And before Welsh could announce his name and rank, the Chief Constable moved on and stopped at Bill Short's table.

'Bill, good to see you! Are you coping with these rebels around you? It's time you were getting back, you know, your Chief hasn't had a day off since you went sick!'

Everyone in the room heard his friendly exchanges and all eyes were now on Superintendent Welsh. For a long time, he said nothing, his eyes flickering as the full import of the Chief's words began to register.

'PC Burton?' Eventually he quietly asked Keith to tell the truth. 'Did I hear your Chief correctly?'

'You did, Mr Welsh,' said Keith with an air of pride. 'I am PC Keith Burton of the Summonses and Warrants Department of Newcastle upon Tyne City Police.'

'And that other man, that Bill Short, he led me to think he's a constable at Scarborough. If my ears don't deceive me, your Chief knows him well and that smacks of a rank much higher than constable! The others haven't mentioned their ranks.' Already there was a look of impending horror on Welsh's pale face; he realised he had been deliberately tricked.

'He's a deputy chief constable, Mr Welsh. With the local force.'

For a long time, Superintendent Welsh did not speak. He ate his dinner in silence, often playing with his food and allowing the conversation to bubble around him. No one could tell what thoughts were buzzing through his head.

At the end of the meal, the Chief Constable left the room with other members of staff, and only then did the grim-faced Welsh make his move.

'I would like a word with all of you,' he said to the residents. 'In the lounge, if you don't mind, in five minutes.'

It was almost like a command, but it was clearly tempered with a note of sorrow and even regret. As the others looked to him for guidance, Bill Short nodded his agreement to Welsh's request and they all assembled, wondering what was in store. They settled on the easy chairs which lined the walls, awaiting Welsh's comments. He came in and stood before them, a tall, pale and now rather fragile figure. The arrogance had been knocked out of him.

'You've made a fool of me,' he said, without smiling. 'I fell into your trap. I am a fool,' he suddenly added with a smile. 'An utter stupid fool. It's people that matter, not ranks. So if anyone wants to go out for a drink, there's a nice hostelry down the road, and the drinks are all on me. I am sorry for my behaviour.'

There was a momentary silence, then Bill Short said, 'It takes a man to admit he's wrong, so you're on — er, sir!'

'Thanks — er, Bill,' smiled Welsh. 'You've made me realise we're human beings, not machines with pips on our shoulders!'

Everyone started chattering and then Welsh turned to Keith Burton. 'Coming — er, sir?', he asked with a smile.

'You try and stop me — er, Adam,' said PC Burton.

CHAPTER 8

I have considered the days of old, and the years that are past.
The Book of Common Prayer

In previous *Constable* books, I have provided accounts of fascinating people in the twilight of their years; some of their stories are included in *Constable Around the Village* and I thought I would elaborate upon one or two of those tales and include a few new ones.

So far as old folk are concerned, caring for them is very much a part of the village constable's life. This is not formal care of the kind expected from the multitude of welfare and charity services nor does it impinge upon their family's own responsibilities, but it means that the village constable, while on patrol, does keep an eye open for signs of need or distress among the older folk. Sometimes this continuing observation results in a telephone call to the family concerned or perhaps to one or other of the welfare services or charitable organisations. More often than not, however, the constable is able to cope with any immediate need and his work goes unpublicised, save for a word of thanks, or a cup of tea, from a grateful senior citizen.

I found that the elderly who lived in and around Aidensfield were highly independent country folk who hated the idea that they might have to depend on charity or the welfare state. In helping them, there was a need to exercise discretion and to show them that any help given was not an adverse reflection upon their own capabilities.

Having led a life of self-sufficiency founded upon hard work and enterprise, their advancing years made them less able to cope physically, although their mental state and belief in themselves remained undimmed. Many of them felt they could achieve just as much at eighty years of age as they had done at thirty, and that did cause some worries.

One shining example of this philosophy was eighty-three-year-old Jacob Broadbent. Officially, he was a retired farmer and he and his wife, Sissy (81), lived in a neat bungalow in Aidensfield. Built specially for them in their retirement, it was fitted with the latest work-saving ideas and boasted a large garden full of mature soft-fruit bushes, fully grown apple and plum trees and a patch for vegetable cultivation. The garden had once been part of a larger house and Jacob's son had succeeded in buying the plot upon which to build his parents' retirement home.

The inclusion of a large garden had been a brilliant idea by Jacob's son, Jesse, a man in his late fifties. Jesse knew that his father would require something to occupy him during his so-called retirement, and this was the garden's purpose. In spite of tending his little patch, however, Jacob made regular visits to the farm where Jesse found the old man various jobs to keep him busy. Jacob, as one would have expected, couldn't understand the new ideas and machinery that Jesse introduced, but contented himself by looking after the pigs and sheep, feeding the hens and recording their egg production as he had in years past.

The result was that in his retirement, Jacob was kept busy and that made him very happy. Sissy, his down-to-earth wife, kept out of his way. She knew better than to interfere with his daily routine. Always on the go, she fussed over her new bungalow, visited people in the village and, even at eighty-one, made sure she was involved in village activities such as the church and the Women's Institute. This kept her fully occupied, and for a couple in their eighties, they were remarkably alert, active and energetic.

There is no doubt that one of Jacob's joys was his orchard. Having grown apples at the farm, he had continued this enterprise at his new bungalow, another example of Jesse's foresight in providing something for his father to do. And so, in the autumn, Jacob supplied the local shops, hotels and village people with a variety of fresh and tasty apples. It provided him with some pocket money, out of which he enjoyed a regular pint in the Brewers Arms, a daily pipe or two of strong-smelling tobacco and weekly trips to all the local cattle markets and, where possible, sales of antiques or house-contents.

It was during a late September afternoon that I was attracted to his orchard by a cry for help. By chance, I was walking through Aidensfield, intending to call at the garage on a routine enquiry about a recent accident. The garage had recovered from the scene the vehicles which had been damaged, and because I needed precise details of the damage for my report I was on my way to inspect them.

As I walked beneath the high wall which concealed the Broadbents' home from the street, I became aware of a hoarse cry. It was very faint. At first, I could not decide what it was or where it was coming from, but as I stopped to listen more carefully, I realised it was a man and it was coming from Jacob's orchard. Sensing trouble, I rushed into the garden and hurried around the back of the bungalow to the orchard from where the calls were being repeated. And there, as I rounded the corner past the greenhouse, I found Jacob.

'Mr Rhea!' he breathed as he saw me. 'By, it's good thoo's come along now . . .'

He was lying on his back beneath a tall, sturdy apple tree and his right leg was held high in the air among the lower branches. A basket of apples was lying upturned near by with its contents spilled across the grass.

'What's up, Jacob?' I asked, hurrying to his aid.

'I tummled doon this tree, Mr Rhea, and that trouser leg's gitten hooked up somewhere . . .'

'Jacob!' I tried to sound angry as I examined his elevated leg. How did he come to tumble down the tree? But I had no time to ask that sort of question just yet. I had to release him first. The material of his trousers had "snagged" on a short, strong stump of a branch, and it had pierced the cloth. This now held Jacob's leg in the air and from his position on the ground, he could not free himself. He was a prisoner of his own apple tree!

'This is a right mess you've got yourself into, Jacob!' I said, trying to free his leg. 'Are you hurt?'

'It winded me, Mr Rhea,' he said. 'Knocked the stuffing out of me, landing flat on my back like this. But I've got me breath back now. I think I'm all right.'

'No injuries, then?' I was struggling to free the trouser leg from the tree but his weight made it difficult.

'Nay, nowt.'

'How long have you been lying here then?' was my next question.

'Ages, Mr Rhea. She's out, you see, our Sissy, I mean. Gone to see a friend, she has. I've been laid here shouting for hours . . . nobody heard me . . . I got frightened, thoo knaws.'

'Lift your backside in the air a bit, can you?' I asked him. 'Then it'll take some of the weight off this leg and I'll be able to lift you off this branch.'

His overall trousers were made of tough denim and I had to cut the cloth to effect his release. My pocket knife made short work of that problem and once his leg was free, I lifted him to his feet. He hobbled around a bit, stamping his foot and holding his aching back with his hand. I looked around for a ladder, but found none. Maybe a rung had snapped or its wood was rotten?

'How did you get up that tree, Jacob?' I asked.

'Climbed up,' he said.

'Without a ladder or steps?' I put to him.

'There's no need for owt like that, Mr Rhea,' he said with just a trace of contempt. 'Why bother with ladders when t'trees grow their own steps?'

'You shouldn't be climbing trees at your age!' I shook my finger at him in a mock rebuke. 'You could break a leg or something if you fall down — these are big trees and it's a long fall from the top! Look how a tumble bruises apples that come down! You'll be covered with bruises tonight, I shouldn't wonder.'

'Thoo'll not tell our missus, wilt thoo?' he asked with a note of pleading in his voice.

'Why not?' I put to him.

'Well, she's allus going on at me about climbing trees and picking apples, Mr Rhea, and it's only way I can pick 'em. So say nowt to her, eh? About me tummling doon.'

'So long as you're not hurt!' I submitted.

'Fit as a fiddle,' he said, straightening his back as if to emphasise his words. 'There's nowt ailing me.'

'OK, but remember, no more climbing trees!'

'You sound just like my missus!' he grumbled as he stooped to begin picking up the spilt apples, groaning with pain as he did so. I helped him and when we'd collected the lot, he went indoors.

'Thoo'll come in for a cup o' tea, Mr Rhea?' he invited me.

'No thanks, Jacob,' I said. 'I'd love to, but I've got to get on. I'm supposed to be visiting the garage!'

Happy that his fall had not resulted in any permanent damage, I left him to recover over a cup of tea. I thought little more about the incident until I saw his wife, Sissy, in the village street a couple of weeks later.

'How's your Jacob these days?' I asked after a general chat.

'Fine,' she said, 'But his rheumatics is bothering him a bit. He reckons his back hurts; I say it's with climbing apple trees but he says it's not. Mr Rhea, mebbe you'd have a word with him about climbing trees at his age. He'll fall down one of these days, mark my words, and that could be t'end of him. I shouldn't want to deal with him if he cripples hisself cos he's tummled oot of a tree at eighty-three, Mr Rhea. He's a bit awd for that sort of a caper.'

'I'll have a word with him,' I promised her.

I did speak to him and said he was too old for that sort of a caper, as Sissy had put it. But it made no difference. He continued to climb apple trees until his death at ninety-two.

* * *

Another tale involved Sidney Latimer who was eighty-six. A retired lengthman, his work had involved keeping the roads tidy and well maintained. And, so I learned from the older folks, Sidney had done a very thorough job. In winter especially, he had kept them gritted and open when others near by had been closed in the grip of the weather. Sidney had always taken a pride in "his" roads.

He lived alone in a pretty cottage just off the main street at Aidensfield and he coped very well with his daily chores, albeit with the help of a lady who popped in to care for him. Like so many of the elderly in and around Aidensfield, he would emerge on a fine day to sit on the bench near the war memorial, there to observe the passing show and to chat with three or four pals of similar age.

Then he became ill. I was not aware of this for some time, but realised that he was not enjoying his daily walk or his sojourns to the village seat and so I asked after him from his cleaning lady.

'Oh, he's in hospital, Mr Rhea, at York.'

'Oh, I had no idea! What's wrong with him?' I asked.

'Old age mainly,' she said without a hint of sympathy. 'And his waterworks are giving him pain. They're seeing to him there, he might be in for a week or two.'

I rang the hospital to enquire after his progress and was given the usual response, 'Mr Latimer is as well as can be expected.'

That did not say a great deal so, one afternoon when Mary and I, with the family, went shopping to York, I decided to pop in and see Mr Latimer. I found him in a ward full of elderly gentlemen, some in a very poor state and clearly approaching the end of their lives. Assailed by the distinctive smell from this geriatric ward, I settled at Sidney's bedside.

'Now, Mr Latimer,' I said. 'How's things?'

'Hello, Mr Rhea.' His old eyes twinkled with delight because he had a visitor. 'You are looking slim. How's Mrs Rhea?'

This was his usual greeting; whenever he met anyone, man or woman of any shape or size, he complimented them upon looking slim.

'She's fine thanks,' I told him, pulling up a chair. 'She's in town, shopping, she sends her best wishes and hopes you'll be home soon.'

'It's my waterworks, Mr Rhea, they say. I reckon I need a good plumber not a doctor. But they say I'll be home before long.'

He was very alert and we chatted for some time about village matters. He was a big man, well over six feet tall, and in his younger days must have been an impressive sight. He had married, I knew, but his wife had died several years earlier and, so far as I knew, there had been no children. Sitting propped up on that hospital bed, he did look rather vulnerable and somewhat smaller and more fragile than usual. During the course of our conversation, he said he got a bit lonely.

'It's not like being at home, is it? At home I can pop out and see folks, there's allus somebody about, or something to do, even if it's just popping into a shop or the post office for my pension. Here, I just have to lie down and do as I'm told. These old lads in here aren't much company, are they?'

He looked along the ward at his companions and sighed.

'Just lying there fading away, that's all they're doing. There's not a lot of excitement unless it's some poor sod who's cocked his toes.'

It must be awful, seeing one's companions dying one by one, but he seemed unperturbed. He was fully convinced he would be allowed home very soon.

'There must be somebody I can tell about you being in here, Mr Latimer,' I suggested. 'The village folks know you're here

'They never come!' he grumbled.

'Relations, then? Old friends? Shall I write to them and say you're here?'

'Apart from folks around Aidensfield, there's only my old schoolteacher. Taught me when I was a lad, she did. You might tell her, I allus send her a Christmas card.'

Now I thought he was going senile but wary of his reactions if I showed disbelief, I said, 'Where's she live? I'll tell her.'

He delved into his bedside cabinet and pulled out a battered old pocket diary, years out of date. Flicking through the pages until he found the place, he said, 'No 18 Ryelands Terrace, Eltering. Miss Wilkinson. Taught me my three Rs at Ashfordly Primary she did. 1886 she was there. Lovely woman. Lovely as they come. She'll be interested to know I'm here. Allus kept in touch, she has.'

To humour him, I made a note of the name and address in my private diary and promised I would tell her. This seemed to please him greatly and our next half-hour was spent in casual chatter about nothing in particular. I could see he was tiring so I said my goodbyes.

'Goodbye, Mr Rhea,' he smiled as I stood up. 'My word, you do look slim. Now, you won't forget to tell Miss Wilkinson, will you? And you will come again?'

'Yes, I'll come again,' I assured him, and left to collect my wife and family from the cafe where they'd been having tea with one of Mary's friends.

I must admit I gave no more thought to Mr Latimer's supposed schoolteacher, but a few days later, I was patrolling Eltering. I had driven there in my mini-van because I was scheduled for a two-hour foot patrol in the town; there was a shortage of local officers that afternoon. And then, quite unexpectedly, I found myself walking along Ryelands Terrace. The name had meant nothing until now and when I saw the nameplate on the wall of one of the houses, it caused a flicker of reaction in my mind. At first, I could not determine why it should interest me and then I recalled my chat with old Mr Latimer.

Pulling out my diary, I found my note about Miss Wilkinson, the primary schoolteacher who'd taught him around 1886; she had lived at No 18. Now full of curiosity, I decided to walk along to No 18.

When I got there, I found an elderly lady tidying her front garden. She was slender and small, with a neat head of tidy grey hair and she carried a paper sack. She was collecting fallen leaves which had been blown from some nearby sycamores. She smiled warmly as I approached.

'Leaves are such a nuisance, Constable, aren't they? Every autumn, they blow into my garden, and every autumn I clean them out!'

'They are!' I sympathised with her. 'My wife makes compost from them, we find them a nuisance really, but we can make use of them!'

'Yes, I give mine away,' she smiled. 'To the old gentleman who lives next door. My garden is much too small for me to worry about compost.'

I wondered if I dare ask about Miss Wilkinson, Mr Latimer's old teacher, for it was such a long time ago that she'd taught the old man. Maybe she had married and this was her daughter? Or a younger sister? Maybe this lady had no idea who lived here before her . . .

'Excuse me,' I said, 'But now that I'm here, I wonder if you know of a Miss Wilkinson who used to live here. She was a teacher in the primary school at Ashfordly in 1886.'

'That's me,' she said primly. 'I'm Miss Wilkinson.'

'You!' I did not know what to say. 'But, she must be older than you . . . she taught a friend of mine, a Mr Latimer . . .'

'Sidney Latimer,' she smiled. 'Yes, of course. He was in my class, a very good pupil and very bright. He did nothing with his life, Officer, he could have done anything he wanted, that man. Wasted his talents. Such a shame.'

I was still not sure we were discussing the same Sidney Latimer, so I said, 'Well, he's in hospital actually, in York. He's had a minor operation and asked if I would inform Miss Wilkinson, his teacher . . .'

'Yes, that's me. He must be, oh, what? Eighty-six now? He was eight when I taught him, Constable, and I would be getting on for twenty, I think.'

'So you really were his teacher?' I was astounded.

'Yes, of course! I'm well into my nineties now, you know, but still going strong!'

'But . . .'

'Sidney was a nice boy, Constable, and I've always been interested in his welfare. Always. I shall go to visit him in hospital.'

'Shall I arrange a lift for you?' I heard myself offering.

'Thank you, but no. I will use the bus. There is a very good bus service from Eltering to York and I will enjoy the outing. Thank you for telling me about Sidney, I will certainly pay him a call.'

And so she did. He was delighted and I was amazed.

I sat down and worked it out; if he was eight in 1886, he'd been born in 1878 and at the time I met him, he was about eighty-six. If she was twenty in 1886, which was feasible for a teacher in a primary school, she'd have been born in 1866 which meant she was around ninety-eight!

Even now, I find myself surprised that a man of eighty-six could keep in touch with his primary school teacher. And, following her visit, Sidney Latimer did get well and returned home to continue his life in Aidensfield.

* * *

Another sad but funny tale occurred during a summer soon after I arrived at Aidensfield. It involved a pair of twin bachelor brothers and their aged father who farmed in an isolated dale to the north of Aidensfield. The sons were Angus and Fergus MacKenzie, and their father was Alexander Cameron MacKenzie, a man in his eighties. No one was quite sure of the twins' age, but they must have been around sixty years old.

In spite of their names, they were Yorkshiremen, although I'm sure a distant ancestor must have journeyed this way from the Highlands. They occupied one of the most remote farms in the moors; it was called Dale Head and it stood high on the slopes of Lairsbeck, at the end of a long, rough track. The MacKenzies dealt chiefly in sheep, although they did breed Highland cattle, and seemed to scrape some kind of a living from their lofty farmstead. Theirs was a life of constant work with no time for relaxation.

Money was always short; they were clearly hard up and were seldom seen in the village or nearby market towns. Mrs MacKenzie had died some years ago, but the twins had never married; they'd never seen the point of having to keep one or two extra people in the house. And so, over the years, they existed in the little stone farmhouse with its stupendous views across the moors. I called infrequently to check their stock register, and that was my only contact with them. I called, drank a mug of tea, signed their book and departed. I probably called once every month or even once every two.

On one occasion when I called in late May, Angus met me and produced the necessary book which I signed. I had seen Fergus in the foldyard and on this occasion, I was not invited to stay for a cup of tea in spite of my long drive.

'We're getting set up for haytime, Mr Rhea,' Angus told me. 'It's allus a thrang time for t'likes of us.'

I knew what he was saying. Thrang is the local word for "busy", and for a moorland patch like this, every day counted. Haytime up here was fraught with risk from the weather, and so they had to work rapidly and positively to succeed, taking swift advantage of the limited sunshine and drying winds. And with only two fit men and one old man to do all the work, it was a lengthy procedure. Later, however,

I thought about that missing mug of tea. It was unusual, but at the time I did not pay any heed to this departure from the normal.

Later, I realised I had not seen the old man around the buildings either, and once more, this was unusual. Down in the dale and in the surrounding hamlets, no one thought it odd that old Mr MacKenzie had not been seen. He seldom ventured out anyway, his lads making sure they did any shopping that was necessary. I must admit that his absence did not bother me, for I knew of his habits and routine. It was more unusual to see him than not to see him! It was only after the events which occurred later that I realised the significance of all these odd facets.

It began with a call from Harold Poulter, the undertaker.

'Mr Rhea,' he said quietly over the telephone. 'I've a rum sort of a job on. I thought I'd better give you a call.'

Harold dealt with most of the local funerals and we had a good working liaison due to my own official involvement in the investigation of sudden, violent or unusual deaths. Harold knew which deaths should be investigated by the police and so a call from him had to be taken seriously.

'Yes, Harold, what is it this time?'

'It's poor awd Alex MacKenzie, you know, from Lairsbeck. He's tipped his clogs.'

'Ah', I said partly to myself, 'that's why I haven't seen him around, he must have been ill.'

'Well, I'm not so sure about that, Mr Rhea,' he said. 'But it's a funny affair if you ask me.'

'Go on, Harold,' I invited him to continue.

'Well, them twin lads of his, they've had him up there for weeks, Mr Rhea, never got around to fixing a funeral. I mean, I wonder if you fellers'll need a PM or inquest or summat. Seems he's been dead for weeks.'

'Weeks? How many weeks, Harold?' I asked.

'Dunno, and they're not sure either,' he said. 'They've had no doctor in, they say they know when a pig's dead or a cow, so they know when a feller's gotten his time overed.'

I groaned.

'Where is the body now?'

'In a pigsty,' said Harold. 'They put him there because it's a cool spot and he would keep a while. He wouldn't stink the bedroom out, so they said.'

'I'd better get up there,' I said. 'Have you told Doctor McGee?'

'No, I thought you'd best know first.'

'OK, right, I'll have a ride up to Dale Head and let you know what happens. I'll ring Doctor McGee before I go.'

When I spoke to Doctor McGee, he asked whether I thought it was a suspicious death, like a suicide, or even murder. I had to say I had no idea at this stage; a visual examination would help to determine the future police action, but in view of what Harold had told me, I felt the presence of a doctor was advisable.

'Right, I'll see you there,' he said.

I arrived in advance of Dr McGee and knocked on the tatty kitchen door. In need of a coat of paint, it was opened by Angus, a thin, large-boned fellow with gaunt cheeks and an unkempt head of sparse ginger hair which was greying around the temples. He smiled a welcome, showing a mouth full of huge yellowing teeth which looked as solid as the rocks around the farm and which had probably never seen a dentist in half a century.

'Noo then, Mr Rhea,' he said, opening the door. 'We was expecting thoo.'

Inside, Fergus, who was almost identical to his brother, albeit perhaps a little more robust in his appearance, was sitting at the end of the plain wooden kitchen table. Around him was a collection of mugs along with the teapot, a half-full milk bottle and a sugar bowl.

'Thoo'll have a cup o' tea, Mr Rhea?' Fergus asked. I was pleased to see this routine had been re-established.

'Thanks, Fergus,' and I settled at the table with Angus at my side. I waited until I had the mug in my hands and said, 'Harold Poulter would tell you why I had to come?'

'Aye, 'e did, Mr Rhea. Unusual death, 'e said. But, Mr Rhea, there's nowt unusual aboot oor father's death. 'E just passed on, like awd folks do. In 'is sleep, no fuss or bother. We've 'ad cows pass on like yon. Nice as yer like, Mr Rhea, so, well, Ah'll be honest, Ah can't understand why awd Harold wouldn't just let us git on wi' t'funeral and git t'awd man buried. It's time we did summat wiv 'im.'

'There are always formalities when a person dies.' I tried to be courteous. 'Forms to fill in, a doctor's certificate to obtain, the registrar to see, things like that. You can't bury a human being like you'd bury a sheep.'

'When they're dead, they're dead,' said Angus. He was probably harking back to the days when the procedures surrounding death were less strictured. Certainly in some remote places, people died in circumstances which today would warrant a full investigation — but all that was in the past.

'Doctor McGee is following me along,' I said. 'He must see the body . . . er . . . your father . . . and certify that he is dead. That's his first job. Then if he cannot certify the *cause* of death, I'm afraid a post-mortem must be held. That means examination by an expert who determines precisely what caused death; he'll find out if it was a heart problem, or something else. Once that's been established, the funeral can go ahead, with the permission of the coroner.'

''E's as dead as a doornail,' cried Angus. 'There's neea need for t'doctor to come and tell us that! And as for t'reason 'e died, it was age, nowt else. 'E was tonned eighty-eight, and 'e just faded away in 'is sleep.'

'I'm sure you're right, but we do have to do things the proper way.'

I could see they did not understand the need for all the fuss, and then Dr Archie McGee arrived. Fergus took him to the table and he sat down with a mug of tea, then looked at me for guidance.

'Well, Mr Rhea, what's the score on this one?'

'It seems that Mr MacKenzie, senior, died in his sleep, Doctor.'

'He'll be upstairs now, is he? I'll have a look.'

'No, he's outside, in a pigsty,' I said. 'We are waiting to take you there, after you've had your cuppa.'

'Pigsty? Did he die there?' he asked the twins.

'Nay!' said Fergus shortly. ''E died in bed, but because it was haytime, we couldn't stop work to git 'im buried. There was no time, Mr Rhea, not a minute to spare. You'll know what t'weather's been like, we daren't miss a day just for a funeral. So we laid 'im in yon pigsty till we got finished haytiming; it's not in use and we cleaned it out, them put 'im in straw and salted 'im, making sure we turned 'im twice a week. 'E's out there, as fresh as a posy, waiting to be buried. I mean, there's nowt wrang wiv 'im, except he's dead o' course. 'E didn't suffer, 'e wasn't badly, ' e never fell off a ladder or banged 'is head on owt . . .'e just faded away like Ah said.'

Doctor McGee raised his eyes as if to heaven. 'And how long has he been there?'

'Since just afore we started hay time. Four or five weeks, mebbe. Actually, Doctor, we got finished haytiming a while back, and we was that relieved we'd got all t'hay ladened in, we forgot aboot 'im for a day or two. It was only when Ah went in t'sty for summat that Ah saw 'im there, so Ah turned him over and rang Harold to git 'im buried.'

Dr McGee grinned ruefully at me, as Fergus continued,

'I thought it was time we were gitting summat done with t'awd feller. Not that 'e'd have minded waiting, thoo knaws, 'e allus was a patient chap, oor dad.'

'You are supposed to organise the funeral straight away, gentlemen,' Doctor McGee sighed. 'You must call a doctor who'll certify death and get things moving.'

'We couldn't see t'point in that,' said Fergus. 'Ah mean, once 'e was dead, there was nowt 'e could do and nowt we could do, and besides, 'e wouldn't take any 'arm waiting awhile to get buried. Ah reckon this is a fuss about nowt.'

McGee drained his tea. 'I'd better have a look at him. Take us to him, gents.'

The brothers led us to a row of pigsties and pointed to one with its door closed. 'In there,' said Fergus.

'You wait outside,' he said to them. 'I'll have a look at him, PC Rhea had better come with me.'

Inside, there was the stench of death which is always present around a corpse, but it was tempered by the stronger smell of salt and there, packed in lots of dry straw, was the body of old Mr MacKenzie. It had not decomposed as one would have expected, and no doubt the salt treatment had done something to preserve it. And the straw had kept it cool too, rather like the old system of storing blocks of ice in straw deep within the ice-houses of country mansions. Ice blocks kept in straw could survive for many months without melting . . .

Corpses were kept in mortuary fridges for months or even years, and those old ice-houses would keep game fresh for months too. This pigsty was beautifully cool and dry; it was also rat-proof and I wondered how long old Mr MacKenzie would have kept 'as fresh as a posy' in here. Maybe for months, even if it was an English summer.

Dr McGee began his examination; it was very thorough due to the curious circumstances, and he stripped the nightshirt off the stiff old man to check for wounds or marks of violence, turning the body over and meticulously inspecting it. From where I stood, I saw no marks likely to raise suspicion, but I watched the doctor's careful work.

'You never treated the old man, Doctor?' I asked as he conducted his examination.

He shook his head. 'Once, years ago, he went down with a stomach problem, but that was ten or twelve years since. Looking at him, and bearing in mind he's been out here for weeks, I'd say he died from old age, from natural causes.'

'Would you certify that?' I put the important question to him.

'It would require a post-mortem to determine that with any accuracy.' He spoke honestly. 'The pathologist would have to examine the heart, brain, internal organs, lungs, throat muscles, the lot — you know the routine as well as I do. There are ways of despatching old folks, as you well know, to make it look like a natural death.'

'So do you think this is a suspicious death?' I put him on the spot once again.

'To be honest, no. These chaps are too basic for that. Besides, if they had done the old chap in, they'd have got rid of the body, not kept it in cold storage until they could fix a proper funeral. Look, PC Rhea, if we go through all the official motions, with a PM, the coroner, publicity and so forth, these old characters are going to be made to look fools, aren't they? And nothing will be achieved.'

'Yes,' I agreed. 'They will look a bit daft.'

'I am prepared to certify first, that he is dead, and second, that he died from natural causes, from old age in fact. In spite of these odd circumstances, there is no doubt in my mind that the old boy died naturally, although, to be totally honest, we should really have a post-mortem due to the time lapse since he died. But I will stick my neck out and issue the necessary certificate, without going through all those formalities. I think it is totally unnecessary in this case.'

'Fine, that's all I need, and thanks. We can get this over now. That's all Harold needs to organise the funeral.'

And so Dr McGee wrote out the necessary certificate and gave it to the brothers.

'That's all you require,' he said. 'Give this to Harold Poulter and he'll attend to the rest of it. He'll see the registrar for you as well, leave it all in his hands.'

'Thanks, Doctor,' said Fergus. 'Ah never realised dying meant sike a carry-on.'

'I've dated the death certificate for today,' said McGee. 'That means the official date of your dad's death is today, do you understand?'

Angus nodded. 'A bit like t'Queen, eh?' he said slowly. 'She's got an official birthday and a real one, so our dad's got an official day for dying and a real one.'

'Yes,' said McGee, 'but don't mention the real one!'

'Do we 'ave to do owt else, then?' asked Angus. 'Is that it? Is t'official bit ovver with?'

'Nearly, but Harold the undertaker will see to the rest of it for you. You've done your bit.'

'Dying's fussier than Ah thought it would be,' said Angus to his brother. 'So think on, and get me buried quick if Ah goes afore thoo!'

'And we'll 'ave to get yon pigsty disinfected, we've a sow due to farrow next week, and we can't let t'young 'uns live in a sty that needs disinfecting. It's time we got oor awd dad shifted somewhere more permanent.'

And so the funeral went ahead and they made their 'more permanent' arrangements for their father's long-term rest. So if you visit the churchyard at Lairsbeck, you will see the tombstone of Alexander Cameron MacKenzie who died aged eighty-eight. The date on his tombstone is 4th July, but that is neither the date of his actual death nor of his funeral.

It is the date Dr McGee examined him in that pigsty.

CHAPTER 9

Something very childish, but very natural.
SAMUEL TAYLOR COLERIDGE, 1772—1834

Children take part in a large proportion of a police officer's work, sometimes through the fault of others such as cases of neglect or cruelty, sometimes as victims through the commission of crimes, sexual assaults, family arguments and maintenance defaulters, sometimes by accident when they are knocked down by motor vehicles or suffer death by drowning or from any other cause. Other matters within our scope were the employment of children, dangerous performances in places like circuses or theatres, harmful publications which might affect them, smoking by juveniles, their general care and protection, their education and a whole host of other matters. Abortion, child destruction, infanticide, concealment of birth and the abandonment of children all came with the realm of our duties.

Our law books and police procedural volumes devoted entire chapters to the law, practice and procedure relating to children and young persons but I cannot determine precisely what proportion of my duty time was spent on matters relating to them. It was certainly a substantial amount and indeed, the criminal law of England does rightly devote many statutes or parts of statutes to children and young persons. Indeed, it divides them into neat categories and we had to learn, parrot-fashion, a table of relevant ages at which certain crimes and offences might be committed against youngsters.

For example, a mother causing the death of her child under one year old could be convicted of infanticide; it was an offence to abandon a child under two so as to endanger life or health; there was a crime committed by suffocation of a child under three when it was in bed with a drunken person over sixteen; intoxicants must not be given to a child under five unless for medicinal reasons, and children over five must receive a proper education. It was an offence to be drunk in charge of a child under seven in a public place or on licensed premises and, at that time, a child under eight was not held criminally responsible for his or her acts. That age was subsequently raised to ten.

This table of ages included youngsters up to twenty-four, with a mass of information concerning those in their teens — there was drinking in pubs, owning and using firearms, driving motor vehicles, marriage, betting, pawning goods or dealing in rags plus a list of penalties open to them if they committed offences or crimes. Much of this legislation was designed for the care and protection of children and young persons and it was our duty to enforce those laws.

In criminal law, the word 'child' meant a person under the age of fourteen, and 'young person' meant a person who had attained the age of fourteen but was under the age of seventeen. The term 'juvenile' included both children and young persons, thus referring to all those under 17, while 'adult' was a person aged seventeen and upwards, but aspects of these definitions have now been changed.

It follows that we spent a lot of time learning the mass of laws which affected children and young persons, and we also spent considerable time enforcing the awkward laws which seemed to attract rebellious youngsters, such as drinking underage, driving underage, betting underage, smoking underage, using firearms underage, having sex underage and being employed underage. There were times when even police officers felt the law was silly — for example, a person can take the responsibility for getting married and having children at 16, but cannot buy a pint of ale in the bar of a pub until reaching 18. A person of seventeen could be in sole charge of an aircraft in motion but should not be sent betting circulars until reaching 21.

However, it was not the task of the police service to question the laws of the realm, however illogical they might be, for those laws were made by Parliament and our job was to enforce them without fear or favour. In fact, our enforcement of the law is always tempered with discretion for without that, the country would become a police state. If we rigidly enforced every law, life would be intolerable; imagine the furore if we prosecuted everyone who drank, smoked or placed bets while underage or experienced their first groping sexual encounter with someone under the permitted age. One learned judge made it clear that the latter laws were not for the prosecution of youngsters having a tumble in the hay.

But many of our dealings with youngsters were outside the scope of the law; they were simply ordinary everyday happenings which involved a policeman and a child, and I had a marvellous example of this when Mrs June Myers lost her purse. A pretty young mother with two children, she came to my police house at Aidensfield to report the loss.

When the doorbell rang that Saturday lunchtime, I answered it to find the fair-haired June standing outside with her daughter; this was Melanie and she was seven. I invited them into the office, but June turned to look behind herself, and there, hiding behind the hedge at my gate, was her son. This was Joseph and he was nine.

'I won't come in, thanks, Mr Rhea, it's Joseph, he won't come near you.'

'Why not?' I asked as the little face peered at me through the foliage.

'He's frightened of policemen,' she said. 'He thinks you'll lock him up!'

'I'm not frightened!' beamed Melanie from her mother's side.

'Of course you're not,' I smiled, 'so what on earth's given Joseph that idea?'

'Some of the kids at school, I think. He won't say much about it, but I don't like to leave him there with all the traffic passing . . . so . . .'

'Joseph is silly,' said Melanie.

'Be quiet, Melanie,' said her mum.

'I won't hurt him,' I said loudly so he might hear, 'so what's the problem, June?'

She explained how she had been to Ashfordly on the bus only this morning to do some shopping and had lost her purse. It contained a few personal belongings and about £10 in cash, too much for her to lose.

With Melanie adding her comments, I took details and promised I would see if it had been handed in. As she waited at the door, I rang Ashfordly Police Station, but at that stage, there was no record of it. However, I assured her that if it was handed in, it would be restored to her in due course. Off she went, with Joseph running ahead to keep out of my clutches and Melanie waving a brave goodbye.

That afternoon I had to visit Ashfordly Police Station on a routine matter and was in time to see a middle-aged lady departing. As I entered, PC Alwyn Foxton said,

'Ah, Nick! Just in time. That purse you rang about, it's just been brought in. Found in the market place under a seat. The finder's just left.'

I checked the contents and sure enough, it belonged to June Myers, and the money was intact. I told Alwyn I'd deliver it to Mrs Myers later in the day, and would provide her with the name of the lady who had been so honest in handing it in. And, of course, I would obtain the necessary official receipt for it and its contents.

I knocked on the door of the Myers' council house at teatime and it was opened by young Joseph.

Upon seeing me standing there in full uniform, he gave a sharp cry of alarm and bolted back indoors, shouting and crying for his mother. Alarmed at his outburst, she rushed from the kitchen and expressed relief when she saw me at the door. I gave her the good news about her purse and she invited me in while she signed my official receipt. During this short item of business, Joseph hid behind the settee, peering out at me with tearful eyes. I learned that Melanie was out playing with friends.

'Mr Rhea isn't going to hurt you!' she said to the child. 'He's brought mummy's purse back, look!'

He looked at it, apparently puzzled that a policeman should be doing something helpful, and then he retreated behind his protective settee.

'I'm not here to hurt you, Joseph,' I spoke to the unseen lad. 'I'm here to help your mum, we've brought her purse back.'

There was no reaction from him. I didn't seek him out; that would have raised his fears even more, so I left quietly with June's delight being my reward. She said she would write a letter of thanks to the finder.

It was some three weeks later when I received a phone call from Alan Myers; he was June's husband and he worked at an agricultural engineers' depot in Ashfordly. I think he was a welder and he rang me from work.

'It's Alan Myers, Mr Rhea,' he said. 'I've just had a call from our June. Somebody's pinched Joseph's bike, It's a new one an' all. We got it for his birthday . . .'

'Where did it go from?' I asked.

'Outside our house, sometime since last night. It got left out, Mr Rhea, by accident; it's our own fault, but I thought you might come across it.'

'I'll have a walk down there this morning, Alan,' I assured him. 'Is June in? I can see her for a description of it.'

'Aye, she rang me from a neighbour's, said she'd be in all day.'

'Good, I'll do my best.'

When I arrived, both Joseph and Melanie were at school and I obtained the necessary written statement from June Myers. This included an account of the bike's location, its description and a sentence to say that no one had any authority to remove it. It was a Hercules, a small blue cycle with white mudguards and a white pump. The seat was white too and it had a chainguard and lamps back and front. Almost new, it was clean and in very good condition. It was the miniature of a gents' full-size bicycle.

I promised June I would circulate its description to all local police stations and patrolling officers, and that it would appear in our monthly Stolen Cycles Supplement which was distributed to all cycle dealers. But, in my heart of hearts, I was doubtful if we could recover it.

Having undertaken these routine matters, I decided I would tour the area around Aidensfield, making a search of hedge-backs and likely dumping places. An adult could not have ridden it away; it was far too small for that, but another child might have taken it for a joy ride and abandoned it. Or, of course, a thieving adult could have picked it up and transported it away to sell for cash.

But I was lucky, or rather, Joseph was lucky. Later that afternoon, I decided to visit the village sports field at Maddleskirk, a couple of miles away. I knew it attracted youngsters from the local villages and many rode there on cycles. And there, parked behind the cricket pavilion, I found Joseph's bike. It was undamaged and there was no one on the field at the time. I was tempted to leave it and keep observations upon it, for the thief would probably return and collect it. Then he could be dealt with. But there was no hiding place for me here and if I left it unsupervised in the hope that I might later catch the thief riding it, it might be stolen again or lost forever. I decided against those risks. I had found it and it was safe, so I put it in the van and drove to the Myers' home.

When I arrived, the family was having a cooked tea and Alan answered the door.

'Hello, Alan,' I smiled. 'I've good news,' and I led him to my van. I lifted out the cycle and, of course, he was delighted. He looked at it and was pleased it had suffered no damage.

'Come in, Mr Rhea, and show it to our Joseph. He's scared of blokes like you, this might make him appreciate you fellers a bit more.'

Following Alan indoors, I wheeled the little bike into the front room and Alan called for Joseph, Melanie and June. They came from the kitchen, and when Joseph saw me holding his precious bike, his little brown eyes showed a mixture of fear and amazement.

'Here, Joseph,' I invited him to come closer. 'Come and have a look — is this your bike?'

'Go on, Joseph,' urged his mother. 'Tell Mr Rhea if it's yours.'

The little lad, brave but somewhat shy, moved towards me and I crouched down to welcome him. 'Well?' I asked. 'Is this yours, Joseph? I found it on the cricket field.'

He took hold of its handlebars and nodded.

'Yeth,' he said.

'Say thank you to PC Rhea,' said his mother. 'Thank you for finding my bike.'

'Thank you for finding my bike,' he said.

'There,' said his mother. 'That wasn't bad, was it? You see, policemen are not here to hurt you, Joseph, they're here to help you.'

'Shall I ride it for you?' He suddenly asked me.

'Can you ride a two-wheeler?' I asked.

'Yeth, of courth I can,' and he proudly wheeled it outside as I followed with June and the others.

Melanie suddenly decided she should ride a bike too, for she said, 'I can ride a bike, Mr Rhea,' and dashed back indoors for her red three-wheeler. On the footpath, I was then treated to a display of cycle-riding by Joseph who did tricks like ringing his bell while riding with one hand, riding with his feet lifted from the pedals and doing rapid turns around the lamp-posts. His shyness had evaporated; now he was a show-off. Melanie did her best to outdo him with her skills, and for me it was a pleasant few moments. Quite suddenly, Joseph decided he was unafraid of me. He halted at my side and asked, 'Do you arretht naughty boyth? There are thome very naughty boyth at our thchool.'

'We only arrest very naughty people,' I said. 'We are here to help people, really, like your mum when she lost her purse or you, when somebody took your new bike.'

'I'm ten now,' he said proudly. 'I'm big now and I'm not frightened of you any more!'

'Good, then I am very pleased. Now, you must look after your bike . . .'

I gave him a short lecture on caring for his belongings and bade the family farewell. I thought no more of the incidents until, around half past five one evening, I heard a knock at my office door. I went outside to find Joseph standing there clutching a small boy by the collar.

'Thith ith a very naughty boy,' Joseph announced as the other cringed and protested beneath my gaze. 'I've brought him for you to arretht!'

'What's he done?' I asked.

'He thtole thome thweets from a girl at thchool, I thaw him,' he said. 'That ith very naughty!'

'Really, well, you'd better come in, both of you.'

I was uncertain how to cope with this development, but the other little lad, a six-year-old whose name I learned was Simon, denied the charge.

'I never,' he said. 'She gave me them.'

I lectured Simon against ever stealing sweets and congratulated Joseph on his community spirit, albeit couched in terms he would understand, and packed them off home. I wondered if he knew what was meant by the word 'arrest' — perhaps he thought it involved nothing more than a telling off by a policeman? In that case, I had done as he had expected and honour had been satisfied. Two days later, Joseph returned with another arrested child. This time it was a girl who'd torn another girl's dress in a fight.

'Thhe'th very naughty,' Joseph told me. 'Thhe'th tore Fiona'th dreth fighting when Mith Clement said not to.'

I gave Fiona a lecture about damaging the belongings of her friends, and she cried a little. I told Joseph to take her home. Now I had a problem, because he turned up with other 'arrested' children and probably thought he was doing a good job as a very special constable. I didn't want to hurt the child by telling him off, for that might destroy all his new-found confidence and the good work that had been achieved in removing his fears of policemen.

So, in an attempt to solve this little dilemma, I decided that the easiest way was to be 'out' whenever he arrived with one of his arrests. I explained the situation to Mary and so during the following few weeks, whenever we heard his knock at the office door around teatime, she answered it. For a short time afterwards, she was confronted by Joseph and his many prisoners. One some five or six occasions that followed, she explained that PC Rhea was out on patrol and suggested that Joseph and his prisoner return later. This had the desired effect. Joseph ceased his one-man vigilante campaign, but he always spoke to me when he saw me. In fact, he matured into a fine young man and became a detective chief inspector in the London Metropolitan Police with his own lovely children. And he always pops in to see me when he's in the area — but now he doesn't bring his prisoners for me to deal with!

* * *

A farmer's eight-year-old son caused something of a flap one Christmas Eve, but it was a short-lived panic. I learned that the little boy, who was called Jonathan, had been suffering from teasing at school because he believed in Father Christmas when some of the others claimed he did not exist. Determined to settle the issue in his own mind, young Jonathan had not mentioned his doubts to anyone, not even to his parents, but after they had tucked him into bed that night, he had secretly gone out to seek Santa Claus.

I learned of his disappearance about ten o'clock on Christmas Eve when his father, Howard Sinclair, rang me. I hurried straight to the farm, which was only five minutes drive from my own home, and was ushered into the living-room. There, with the help of Jonathan's older brother, Andrew, I learned of his worries.

Andrew told us that, at school, several of the lads in Jonathan's class were boasting that they had discovered the truth about Father Christmas and Jonathan had championed those who still believed in him. Jonathan had said, before the holidays, that he would find out for sure whether Father Christmas really existed.

'Did he say how he would do this?' I asked Andrew, an alert eleven-year-old.

'No, he never said. I thought he'd forgotten all about it, Mr Rhea, 'cos it was at school, before the holidays when he was on about it.'

At my instigation, we checked Jonathan's clothes and found he had dressed in his warm clothes which comprised a pair of small jeans, warm jumper, Wellingtons, scarf, gloves, balaclava and overcoat.

'Let's search the farm buildings first,' I suggested.

'We've had a look around,' said Howard.

But if a policeman learns anything, it is how to conduct a thorough search of houses and buildings, especially for people who are deliberately concealing themselves.

I was sure the lad was out of doors, because of the clothing he had taken, and so we began our hunt. I allowed the parents to go one way while I went elsewhere, then I would retrace their steps, searching for the tiniest and most unlikely of hiding places. There was no snow yet, but it was crisp and frosty outside, so there'd be no footprints to provide any clues. After some twenty minutes of searching outbuildings, sheds and parked vehicles, I found myself in the hayloft. It was dry and cosy, with the scent of the hay filling my nostrils as my powerful torch picked out the stacked bales with hollows and passages between.

And then, as my torch beam moved across the surface of the bales, someone hissed for me to be silent.

'Sssh!' demanded the child's voice. 'You'll frighten 'em off!'

'Jonathan?' he would not know my voice.

'Who's that?' he demanded.

'The policeman, PC Rhea, we're looking for you.'

'I'm all right, leave me alone. I'm busy.'

My torch picked him out now. He was lying fully clothed on some bales of hay, peering through the loft window in the gable-end of the hayshed. The window was normally closed, having a small door to cover the gap, but now it was standing wide open. It gave him a perfect view of the farmhouse and at his side was a carpet brush and dustpan.

I knelt beside him. 'What are you doing here?'

'Waiting for Father Christmas,' he said.

'He never comes when children are awake and waiting for him,' I said gently. 'He will know you are here, so he'll keep away till you go to sleep in bed. Why do you want to see him?'

'To see if he's real,' he said simply.

'Well, as I said, Jonathan, he won't come while you are here, so you'd better come home. Your mum and dad are worried about you.'

'Are you sure he won't come?' he asked me, standing up and collecting his brush and dustpan.

'Yes,' I said, pointing the way out with my torch. 'But why have you got that brush and dustpan?'

'For reindeer droppings,' he said. 'I know Father Christmas will come to that chimney over there,' and he pointed at the house. 'And I know his reindeer like our hay, 'cos mum and dad said so; we always leave this hayloft window open so them reindeer'll come here for a feed. And I know how cows and horses make droppings, so I'll pick 'em up and show 'em to my pals. Then they'll know Father Christmas is real, won't they?'

'If you can find some reindeer droppings, I'm sure you'll convince them,' I said, accepting the brush from him and taking his hand. 'Come on, time for bed.'

'I'll never know, will I?' he said slowly.

'One day you will,' I told him, as I led him back to the house.

* * *

If young Joseph Myers misunderstood the meaning of 'arrest', it was understandable that little Martin Stokes, a small-built ten-year-old, should misunderstand one of this nation's best-known phrases. Most grown-ups know what is meant by 'London's streets are paved with gold' but Martin's vision of that big city was one of a glistening fairy-tale lane with golden footpaths and houses which contained everything a family could ever wish for, especially a dad.

Martin's mother had no husband. Martin was the result of a brief encounter with a young man who had vanished immediately after the act which had created Martin, and so the little fellow was reared by his loving and caring mother who was called Rosemary. She provided her sole offspring with lots of affection and as much comfort as possible.

She worked in a local shop which provided the barest of necessities, but at least she did work and she did attempt to give Martin the best that was within her very limited means. When the village primary school announced it was organising a trip to London for some ten-and eleven-year-olds, therefore, Martin said he would like to go. The trip was a form of celebration of the conclusion of their primary school education because next term, they would begin a new life at either a Grammar School or a Secondary Modern. In spite of the expense, Rosemary wanted Martin to go to London and she raided her meagre savings for his fare. Happily, a local businessman had said he would match fifty per cent of the total cost if the parents would raise the rest themselves.

The outcome was that a dozen children found themselves embarking on the trip of a lifetime. None had ever been to London and so the teacher, Miss Clement, told them about it. She explained about the Houses of Parliament, Big

Ben, the Queen and Buckingham Palace, the Horse Guards, the River Thames and all the traditional tourist sights. She showed them photographs too and a short film about London. And it was Miss Clement, in her lecture about the delights of our capital, who quoted from the poet George Colman (1762—1836), when she said,

> *Oh, London is a fine town,*
> *A very famous city,*
> *Where all the streets are paved with gold,*
> *And all the maidens pretty.*

At home that evening over his tea, Martin told his mum all about the golden streets of London but she tried to explain that they weren't really made of gold. She told Martin that London was the town of opportunity, where people could become rich if they worked hard because there was a lot of money in London. It was there for everyone if they worked hard and took the opportunities to find it. Martin said he understood, and the night before the trip, she'd bathed him, got his best clothes ready and packed him an old army knapsack full of sandwiches and drinks.

'Will I be rich if I go to London?' he had asked her as she'd tucked him into bed.

'Maybe when you are grown up,' she'd said. 'If you go to London and work.' Poor Rosemary; money was so short for her that her worries about it must have made an impression upon her young son. He was always anxious to earn lots of money. 'But if the streets are made of gold, there must be some for me?' he'd said.

'No, darling, I've told you. The streets aren't made of gold, not really. They're stone like our streets, but there is lots of money in London, there's lots of it about and people can find ways of getting a lot, earning a lot, if they live and work there.'

He hadn't quite understood it all, but had fallen into a fitful sleep, dreaming of the fabulous town he would visit tomorrow. Next morning at six, a small coach left Aidensfield for York Station where the train departed just before seven o'clock, thus allowing them a day in London under the guidance of the teachers and one or two volunteer helpers. They were all so eager to see the sights and to bring back lots of souvenirs. All had little bags containing their sandwiches and drinks, and I knew these would be full of trinkets and leaflets upon their return.

I was aware of the trip — a village bobby should know everything that is happening on his patch — but as none of my own children were old enough to join it, I was not really involved. The trip was an unqualified, if exhausting, success and my professional involvement came the following morning.

I received a phone call from Rosemary Stokes asking if I could call at the shop where she was working as she had a matter to discuss with me. Not knowing what this matter could be, I drove along to Maddleskirk where I found her behind the counter of the post-office-cum-grocery store. She was alone, the proprietor having gone into York to buy his weekly stock of groceries, and the morning was quiet.

'Hello, Rosemary,' I greeted her. 'What's bothering you?'

'Would you like a coffee, Mr Rhea? I've got the kettle on?' This was a good start!

I let her make the coffee without asking more questions and she settled on a stool behind the counter as I settled on another at the customers' side. If a customer entered, she would deal with him or her, and I would enjoy my drink.

'I hope you don't mind me calling you like this,' she apologised. 'But I am very worried about Martin.'

'Why, what's he done? He went to London yesterday, didn't he? He has come back, hasn't he?' I suddenly had an awful thought that he might not have returned.

'Oh, yes, he's back. He's asleep, he went straight to bed last night when he got back, Mr Rhea, he was utterly worn out. I've never seen him so tired,' and she bent to withdraw something from under the counter. It was a small khaki-coloured knapsack of the type soldiers used to carry for their rations and it was evidently very heavy. As she passed it over to me, I heard the rattle of coins.

'Look inside,' she invited.

Resisting its weight as I accepted it, I pulled open the stout press-studs and saw it was half-full of coins. Threepenny bits, sixpences, shillings, florins, half-crowns, pennies and ha'pennies. There was a small fortune.

'Somebody's been saving fast!' I laughed. 'Who's is all this?'

'I don't know,' and she looked sorrowful. 'Martin brought it back from London. He said he'd found it all. I didn't give him that money, Mr Rhea, nothing like that. I don't know where it's come from. I do hope he hasn't been stealing. I thought I'd better hand it in.'

I fingered through it; there were no £1 notes or ten-shilling notes, merely a large amount of cash. I didn't count it and learned Rosemary hadn't done so either, but there would be several pounds.

'Did you quiz him closely about it?' I asked.

She shook her head. 'No, he was too tired, he just fell into bed, exhausted and besides, I didn't like to upset him after his day out. I do know it's not his money and as he said he'd found it, I thought I'd better hand it in. I wondered if anybody had said anything to you about it.'

'No, they haven't,' I told her. 'I'm not surprised he was tired, carrying this around! I'll have to ask him about it.' I was worried in case he had taken it off the other children, although I doubted it. Martin was an honest little fellow, I was sure.

'He's in bed, at home, Mr Rhea, my mother's looking after him today, he's got the day off school. I didn't wake him to ask about it this morning. Should I come with you?'

'Your mother's there, so I'll be fine. I'll take the money to remind him!' I said, and so I returned to Aidensfield to have a chat with Martin.

Mrs Stokes, senior, Rosemary's mother, opened the door and was aware of the reason for my visit. She took me into her house, for Rosemary still lived at home, and said Martin was now out of bed and in the front room, playing with his souvenirs of yesterday in London. I went in. He was a happy boy, with a mop of curly blond hair and bright blue eyes, and showed no apprehension at my arrival.

'Hello, Martin,' I squatted on the carpet at his side. 'What have we got here?'

'Things from London,' he told me proudly. 'Pictures, books, flags; look, that's where the Queen lives and that's Big Ben . . . there's boats on the river and that's the Tower where the two princes were killed . . .'

I let him tell me all about his journey and it was clear it had made a tremendous impression upon him. At this stage, I knew nothing of his vision of golden pavements, but when I presented the knapsack full of coins, he said, 'I got them from London, Mr Rhea.'

'Did you?' I expressed surprise. 'Where from?'

'The streets,' he said. 'Everybody said the streets were paved with gold, well, they weren't, they were stone like ours, and it was mum who said there was money on the streets for everybody who could find it, so I found all that, Mr Rhea. I looked for it, and brought it home.'

'You mean you found all this, Martin?' I ran my fingers through the coins.

'Yes, Mr Rhea. On the pavements. I told mum that.'

'Was all this money lying on the pavements?' I asked, surprised at the amount. Finding the occasional coin was not unusual, but to find all these . . .

'Yes, it was,' he said. 'People were throwing money down and other people were picking it up.'

'Whereabouts was this happening, Martin?'

'Oh, all over. Everywhere we went.'

'And who was picking it up?'

'Sometimes nobody, it was just left there. But those men playing music and drawing things on the pavements, they were keeping some. And sometimes, people threw it in boxes and hats and things on the pavements. I saw a lot of money thrown away like that, Mr Rhea, so I thought I'd have some.'

'You helped yourself from the boxes and hats, then?'

'Not really, 'cos I thought it must be somebody's, but I did pick some up from the pavements when it was just lying there. There was lots lying about, Mr Rhea.'

'I'm sure there was!' I had now guessed the source of his cash flow!

And so, by asking more questions, I came to realise that Martin, through the legend that the streets of London are paved with gold, had honestly thought money was being thrown on to the pavements to be collected by poor people like himself. And so, during that trip, he had picked up pounds' worth of coins from the feet of pavement artists, buskers and newspaper vendors and no one had noticed.

Martin's grandmother overheard this and was shocked.

'Martin!' she shouted at him. 'That's stealing . . .'

'He wasn't to realise that,' I said. 'But Martin, this money did belong to those people playing the music and doing the drawings. That's how they earn their money.'

I don't think he fully understood, but his grandmother asked, 'You're not going to take him to court, surely?'

'No,' I said. 'I wouldn't, not for this! But I couldn't take official action anyway, not without a complaint from those buskers and pavement artists! And I hardly think I'll get one from them!'

'What do we do with the money, then?' asked Mrs Stokes.

'I'll leave Rosemary to decide,' I said. 'She might give some to a charity, but I'm sure if those artists and buskers knew the struggle she was having, they wouldn't mind it going into Martin's Post Office Savings Account. He can always pay some back next time he's in London.'

I left, not wishing to know more about Martin's money-making but hoped he would learn that, even in London, cash was not there for the taking. It had to be earned.

* * *

On another occasion, anxiety was caused after Miss Alice Calvert retired as Headmistress of Ashfordly Primary School. Because she had served there during her entire teaching career, a matter of some forty years, her retirement created a lot of interest in the town and surrounding area, and resulted in wide local press coverage. There were presentations to her, one from her pupils past and present, and another from the governors and parents. Then, on the last day of her career, there was a social evening in the school with speeches and yet more gifts for Miss Calvert from her small staff and numerous associates, both within the teaching profession and from the townspeople.

She announced that next year she would be taking a long holiday to tour Europe by car, and she hoped to take an extended break to visit her sister and her family in Australia. She hoped to enrol at night-school to study pottery and promised that her retirement would enable her to undertake all those things she'd been unable to do while working.

Alice Calvert was of very distinctive appearance. Now sixty years old, she was a very tall and heavily built lady with a habit of wearing long, colourful and flowing dresses which concealed any hint of her feminine shape. Some of the crueller senior boys would call her Bell-Tent Alice, and few people really knew whether she was slim on top with big hips, or big on top with narrow hips. Almost invariably, she wore flat-heeled shoes or sandals and lots of bangles.

Her face, however, was beautiful. Embraced by a mop of pure white hair, it was round and cheerful with rosy cheeks and a constant smile. Miss Calvert radiated happiness and love and I, for one, often wondered why she had never married. She loved children and was completely happy in her work. Retirement, and the subsequent parting from the children, would not be an easy adjustment to make. But Alice Calvert could cope and would make the necessary adaptations without grumbling or self-pity.

She lived in Aidensfield, where she had a neat little bungalow not far from the church. I would see her pottering around the place at weekends, for she kept an immaculate garden full of flowers and shrubs, somehow guiding her massive bulk between the plants without causing damage. The bungalow was called Honeymead and during her long school holidays, she would ask me to keep an eye on the house whenever she was away. She was always careful to lock it against intruders. I was pleased that, during her frequent absences, she did notify me and so allow me to keep a careful watch on her property. I knew that during her longer absences overseas or indeed any other travelling she undertook in Britain, she would keep me informed when the bungalow was empty. I knew she would worry about the effect of her recent publicity, and whether this would attract undesirables who would snoop around her premises. In an attempt to offset this concern, I assured her that my colleagues and I would pay regular visits when on duty.

Knowing this background, it was with more than a little concern that at four o'clock on the morning following her farewell party, I received an urgent telephone call from her. It took a long time to arouse me but by the time I reached my cold office downstairs, I was fully awake.

'Mr Rhea,' she hissed into the phone. 'There's a man outside . . . he's been trying to break into my bungalow . . . What shall I do?'

'Is he still there?' I asked, speaking in a hoarse whisper.

'Yes and it's funny, I think he's gone to sleep outside, on the patio . . .'

'Asleep? Right, don't make a sound. I'm coming straight away. Look out for me . . .'

Pausing only to call Divisional Headquarters with an urgent request for the Police Dog Section and any other handy mobiles to be available at the bungalow in case the villain ran away or there was trouble, I dressed and hurried out. I did not take the mini-van, because a stealthy approach seemed vitally important. Instead, I used a pedal cycle I'd just acquired and, after riding without lights for half a mile in the semi-darkness of that summer morning, I arrived at

Honeymead within minutes. Parking my bike several doors away. I radioed Divisional Headquarters to announce my arrival at Honeymead and to inform them I was about to search for, and hopefully arrest, the reported intruder.

Calls of this kind were made as a form of security so that if I failed to respond to radio calls in the ensuing drama, assistance would be sent. I knew the dogs and maybe other crews were already *en route*, and that gave me some comfort. I could wait for them, but I would hate to lose this prisoner; he might be frightened off at the approach of their vehicles, and so I made my move. My heart was pounding and I made sure I had my handcuffs and truncheon, my only defence against attack.

As I crept up to her back door in the near-darkness, I thought it odd that her burglar had gone to sleep, but I knew that sillier things had happened. Burglars often went to sleep inside a deserted house or even cooked meals there. Maybe this was just a drunk who'd read about her in the papers? The bungalow was in complete darkness, but in the approaching light of morning, she had seen my arrival. She unlocked her back door and opened it silently to admit me.

'Thank goodness you've come, Mr Rhea!'

I did not make the mistake of switching on my torch but could see she was enveloped in a huge flowing dressing-gown and had a heavy poker in her hand. If he'd got in here, he would have had a shock and a few bruises into the bargain.

'Where is he? Is he still here?' I whispered.

'On the patio, fast asleep. Maybe he's drunk.'

'Can I get there by going through the house?'

'No, he's lying against the French windows. You'll have to go round the side and through the garden.'

'Right,' I whispered and began my move. I knew the way, I'd been around her bungalow many previous times.

'What shall I do?' she asked.

'Stay here. Keep an eye on me from inside; it's not too dark. If I get attacked or anything, dial 999 and tell the police what's going on.'

'Be careful!' she whispered. And so I left. I crept around the side of her house, trying not to make a sound, and then, as I reached the front, I could see the dark shape of the sleeping intruder. It was a bulky man and he was huddled on the patio, lying fast asleep against her French windows. In the dim light, I could see he was very casually dressed in jeans and a sweater, and that he carried a back-pack comprising a sleeping-bag and rucksack, and this was forming his pillow. His hair was tousled and I could just discern a thick brown beard . . .

Wondering how long it would take for my assistance to arrive, I halted to take a deep breath. Miss Calvert was nearby with her poker but in cases like this, there was no knowing how a suspect would react; he might have a gun or a knife, he might be armed with a knuckleduster or a club. I began to think it would be wiser to await the dogs, but I could not flinch from my task.

I approached the sleeping form.

'Hey!' I moved his foot with my boot. 'You, hey, wake up . . . it's the police . . .'

I stood back in case of a violent reaction.

'Hmm?' he stirred but did not arouse. I kicked his boot again, shouting at him and keeping my distance.

'Police . . . wake up . . .' and now I shone my torch full in his eyes. 'Hey, come on, who are you? Stand up . . .'

In the reflected light of my torch, I could see Miss Calvert just inside her French windows, wringing her hands and wondering what she should be doing. I just hoped she did not go away — that poker might be my salvation! But the fellow was now rising to his feet, sleepily and without any sign of antagonism. He made no effort to run off, but stood there, blinking at me and apparently quite docile.

'Who are you?' I demanded loudly, hoping to penetrate his weariness. 'This is the police . . .'

'Huh?' He blinked against the light of my torch and covered his eyes. 'Who?'

'Police,' I said. 'Who are you? What are you doing here?'

'Oh God,' he muttered and his deep voice emerged with a strong Australian accent. 'Streuth, I'm shattered. I really am . . . is this Miss Calvert's house? Alice Calvert's house?'

'Yes, it is,' I said. 'So who are you?'

'G'day. I'm her nephew . . . from Adelaide . . . Derek's the name . . . I knocked but she was asleep . . . I didn't like to rouse her so I kipped here . . . she always left a key under the stone when I was little so I could get in, but it's not there, Officer. Sorry, have I upset things?'

'You've been travelling long?'

'Couple of weeks or so,' he said. 'Flew a bit, caught ferries and hitched most of the way; I aimed to get here as a surprise, for her retirement party, do you know . . .'

'Wait there,' I said, and I knocked on her window. 'It's all right, Miss Calvert. You can put the light on and open this door.'

Even with my approval, she was nervous, but she obeyed. When the door was fully open, Derek said, 'Aunt Alice!' and threw his huge arms around her.

'Derek! It is you, isn't it? Derek!'

'Yes, it's me . . .'

I maintained a discreet distance during their dramatic reunion and then she invited me inside to have a cup of tea with her nephew. I learned it was seventeen years since she'd last seen him; he was then twelve and was now twenty-nine and approaching thirty. This had been his retirement surprise . . .

'And you're coming back to Australia,' he said eventually, delving into his baggage. 'I've a return ticket for you, starting five weeks from now. For a whole month . . . you're coming to stay with us . . .'

I felt I ought to leave this scene of domestic happiness, but at that moment, the bungalow was suddenly surrounded by cars, flashing blue lights and lots of police officers . . .

'Oh crumbs!' I said. 'I forgot to cancel the cavalry!'

'Bring them in for a drink,' said Alice Calvert happily. 'It's a good job he wasn't a burglar!'

'It is,' I laughed. 'They'd have frightened him off!'

Half a dozen policemen and two dogs came into the house and filled the place with blue uniforms as I explained what had happened. They were delighted with the truth.

'Look,' said Alice, addressing us all in her school-ma'am voice, 'I know you're not supposed to drink on duty, but I do have a bottle of wine . . . perhaps a glass each, just to celebrate? My nephew has come rather a long way, half-way round the world, and he did miss my party . . .'

And so, in the early hours of that morning, seven policemen and two police dogs, aided by glasses of wine, slices of her farewell cake and cups of coffee, helped Miss Calvert to celebrate her nephew's arrival. It was a lovely night's work!

As we prepared to leave, I said to my colleagues, 'Miss Calvert's going away soon, lads, can I ask you all to keep an eye on her bungalow when I give you the word, just in case some burglar shows an unhealthy interest in it?'

'Sure,' they said. 'So long as we can have another party when she gets back!'

'That's a promise,' she beamed, hugging her nephew.

My reinforcements left in a procession of cars, doubtless rousing and puzzling the entire village, and I returned to my parked bike. Derek followed me out.

'Thanks, Mr Rhea,' he said. 'Thanks for looking after Aunt Alice. It could have been nasty, eh? A real intruder?'

'It's all part of the job,' I said, shaking his hand.

THE END

ALSO BY NICHOLAS RHEA

CONSTABLE NICK MYSTERIES
Book 1: CONSTABLE ON THE HILL
Book 2: CONSTABLE ON THE PROWL
Book 3: CONSTABLE AROUND THE VILLAGE
Book 4: CONSTABLE ACROSS THE MOORS
Book 5: CONSTABLE IN THE DALE
Book 6: CONSTABLE BY THE SEA
Book 7: CONSTABLE ALONG THE LANE
Book 8: CONSTABLE THROUGH THE MEADOW
Book 9: CONSTABLE IN DISGUISE
Book 10: CONSTABLE AMONG THE HEATHER
Book 11: CONSTABLE BY THE STREAM
Book 12: CONSTABLE AROUND THE GREEN
Book 13: CONSTABLE BENEATH THE TREES
Book 14: CONSTABLE IN CONTROL
Book 15: CONSTABLE IN THE SHRUBBERY
Book 16: CONSTABLE VERSUS GREENGRASS
Book 17: CONSTABLE ABOUT THE PARISH
Book 18: CONSTABLE AT THE GATE
Book 19: CONSTABLE AT THE DAM
Book 20: CONSTABLE OVER THE STILE
Book 21: CONSTABLE UNDER THE GOOSEBERRY BUSH
Book 22: CONSTABLE IN THE FARMYARD
Book 23: CONSTABLE AROUND THE HOUSES
Book 24: CONSTABLE ALONG THE HIGHWAY
Book 25: CONSTABLE OVER THE BRIDGE
Book 26: CONSTABLE GOES TO MARKET
Book 27: CONSTABLE ALONG THE RIVERBANK
Book 28: CONSTABLE IN THE WILDERNESS
Book 29: CONSTABLE AROUND THE PARK
Book 30: CONSTABLE ALONG THE TRAIL
Book 31: CONSTABLE IN THE COUNTRY
Book 32: CONSTABLE ON THE COAST
Book 33: CONSTABLE ON VIEW

Book 34: CONSTABLE BEATS THE BOUNDS
Book 35: CONSTABLE AT THE FAIR
Book 36: CONSTABLE OVER THE HILL
Book 37: CONSTABLE ON TRIAL

Don't miss a book in the series — join our mailing list:

www.joffebooks.com

FREE KINDLE BOOKS

Do you love mysteries, historical fiction and romance? Join 1,000s of readers enjoying great books through our mailing list. You'll get new releases and great deals every week from one of the UK's leading independent publishers.

Join today, and you'll get your first bargain book this month!

Follow us on Facebook, Twitter and Instagram
@joffebooks

DO YOU LOVE **FREE AND BARGAIN** BOOKS?

Thank you for reading this book. If you enjoyed it please leave feedback on Amazon or Goodreads, and if there is anything we missed or you have a question about, then please get in touch. The author and publishing team appreciate your feedback and time reading this book.

We're very grateful to eagle-eyed readers who take the time to contact us. Please send any errors you find to corrections@joffebooks.com

Printed in Great Britain
by Amazon